Chasing Winter

A Novel of Suspense

By

Melinda Crocker

Enjoy your time with Winter!

Cover art: www.jamesfaecke.com

DEDICATION

For Chris Eanes: editor, mentor, coach and who is the very best of
me - You know the rest.

James Faecke, your artwork takes my breath away.

KC, for all your help, edits and support…

And Mike, my forever penny man.

"And, after all,
What is a lie?
'Tis but the truth
In masquerade."
**Lord Byron

Chapter 1

A bead of sweat inched a trail down the back of Winter's neck. She resisted the urge to wipe it away. That would be admitting that fear was forcing her body to burn from the inside out and trying to cool itself. Instead, she sat a little straighter on the hard bench and gripped the smooth wood of the seat with both hands. The clock mounted high on the wall of the courthouse hallway made a metallic sound as the seconds hand twitched around the numeric face. It was as if it mocked her. "Shut up," she mumbled as she glared at the bold, black numbers.

"I beg your pardon?" said the woman sitting to her left.

"Oh, not you, sorry," Winter said. The woman frowned and slid to the end of the bench. Her bulk under the free-flowing nylon dress moved in several directions as she made her escape.

Winter drew a deep breath and then let it out as she mentally counted with each inhale and exhale. One, two, three, four. Her eyes remained glued on the clock. Five, six, seven, eight. If she could use the breathing meditation technique it might calm her. It might even stop the constant flow of sweat. She could pretend that the courtroom door did not exist and her worst nightmare wasn't waiting behind it. But as a new bead of moisture made its way down her back, the tickling sensation destroyed her concentration. She leaned back against the bench and wiggled her back until her blouse absorbed the moisture.

Her seat companion struggled up and shuffled down the hallway. "I wouldn't want to be around me right now either," Winter said under her breath. The corners of her mouth twitched as she watched the woman find another bench and flop down.

"Winter Alexander?" Winter jumped and turned. A man in a dark blue uniform held a clipboard as his eyes flicked around the hallway. As his eyes settled on her she gripped the bench tighter and squeezed her eyes shut. One, two, three, four. "Winter Alexander?" the voice barked. *What was it about people holding clipboards that made them so official and loud. Anyone could carry around a clipboard,* Winter thought.

Five, six, seven, eight. "Here," Winter whispered. She sucked in one last breath, and then opened her eyes and stood. "I'm here," she said in a louder voice. He turned to her and nodded, so she stepped forward. "It's Winter Pappas now," she said as she rose to her full 5'10" height and made eye contact with the court deputy. "Mr. Alexander and I are divorced," she said.

He was a massive man, whose soft smile belied his size and rippling muscles. In response to her name change, he raised an eyebrow and said, "Sorry, but the paper says, Mrs. Winter Alexander." He gazed down at her and held up his clipboard for her to see, then opened the double wooden doors and nodded toward the crowded courtroom. "Mrs. Alexander," he repeated as he gestured for her to enter.

One of those people, she thought. If it was written on the clipboard, it was a fact.

Winter sighed and paused before entering the courtroom. She turned to him and murmured, "Pappas not Alexander," then she marched past him and moved through the open door. Maybe the divorce papers hadn't reached the courts, but she would be damned if she was going to answer to that name one more time. Clipboard paper or no clipboard paper. Once inside she stopped so abruptly the clipboard guard almost ran into her.

A mass of faces turned in her direction. Every seat was filled. Winter swallowed and took a step, but paused again as rustling and low murmurs spread through the room. She felt her throat constrict, but on the other side of the room, she spotted Ray Dennison, the prosecutor, and he gave her an encouraging smile. Winter pulled her chin high and kept walking. She concentrated only on her destination: the raised podium with a single chair encircled by a wood railing that stood on the other side of the room. How could that railing protect her from the evil she knew was seated at the defense table? He would be surrounded and protected by his group of high priced legal mouthpieces. *Don't look.* Instead of looking at the defense table, her eyes climbed from the witness chair to the judge. They locked eyes. Was that doubt or pity she read in the dark pools hiding behind his thick wireless glasses. It didn't matter. Winter knew the truth and the truth was her only weapon.

Somehow, she found herself sitting in the chair on the podium. The walk through the room, and the words she had just sworn, were a complete blank. She blinked and realized that she might be in shock. They had rehearsed this moment for hours, but no amount of imagining, or practicing, could prepare her for sitting in this spot. Right here, right now. She swallowed hard and shifted her bottom away from the edge of the chair. The judge told the prosecutor to proceed and Winter glanced up at him. He sat wrapped in his black robe like a king on his throne. His eyes were no longer on her but directed at the courtroom. *No help from there.*

Another bead of sweat, this one felt more like a river, trailed down her back, and she felt a sudden surge of dampness cool the area encircling her underarms. *Why had she chosen a white cotton blouse?* Black, navy, even a stodgy brown would have helped disguise her shaming fear. Winter crossed her arms over her chest, then uncrossed them and held them tightly at her sides. Maybe the jury wouldn't notice. She swallowed again as the prosecutor stood and acknowledged her with a slight nod and smile. Her eyes unwilling drifted past him to the defense table and she felt her body stiffen. She jerked her eyes back to Ray, but it was too late.

Winter had glimpsed the monster and his image was burned into her brain. Carson sat with his movie star looks and that well-practiced, sad little smile on his perfectly balanced face. He wore the smile he used when he wanted sympathy. It always worked, especially with women. A glance at the jury told her the defense had chosen well. The majority were women of various ages, and they couldn't keep their eyes off her ex-husband. It didn't hurt that his thick brown hair contained just the right amount of hair product to make it appear casually mussed and he had those sorrowful eyes turned in her direction as if to ask, "*why?*" The jury would lap him up like a cat with a milk bowl. No wet armpits for him. *Poor thing* - the jilted husband: rich, handsome, and sad. Winter knew she must appear stiff, cold, and nervous by comparison. She could visualize tomorrow's tabloids, *A woman with something to hide.*

They were right. She had been an expert at keeping secrets, but what they didn't realize, was that she was no longer willing to do so, and whatever the cost, she would tell the truth. She knew all of Carson's secrets and that made her a liability. Carson demanded loyalty more than anything else, and to betray him was a death sentence.

It was Winter who knew his casually tussled hair was created and styled until it was perfection. It was not to be touched once it was in place. She had made that mistake only one time. She always was a quick learner. A grip so tight around her wrist that the bruises lasted for a week was lesson one. After that *he* had learned, also. Future bruises where left only where curious eyes could not see them.

Winter had committed the ultimate betrayal. It was so much worse than touching his coifed hair. She was about to swear in an open courtroom that Carson had killed someone. It wasn't the jail time threatening Carson that would seal her fate, it was the humiliation he would feel when everyone knew he wasn't the golden boy the media portrayed, but a wife beating monster who killed when someone got in his way. That is, *if* they believed her. She tried to swallow, but her mouth was too dry.

Ray moved between her and the monster, instantly breaking the invisible connection with her ex-husband. The *great* Carson David Alexander, III, a trust fund child and entrepreneur extraordinaire. The world loved him and his beautiful face. She had seen that gorgeous face turn into stone when a storm was brewing. Winter learned the early warning signs when those exquisite hands could change from gentle instruments of seduction, to dispensers of pain. She shivered with a memory and Ray took a step closer as he drew her eyes toward him. She nodded at him, but when she felt her chin begin to tremble, she raised her head and scooted against the back of the chair seeking support.

She was here and would do this, although her instinct was to bolt from the courtroom and never look back. Fear had already kept her in an unbearable life for much too long. The final lynchpin came as she watched Carson's hands become conveyers of death. She still had a tough time believing he had gone that far, but the horror had served its purpose. It gave her the courage to finally escape. Now it was time to tell the world who Carson David Alexander, III, really was. She looked at Ray and nodded. *No tremble this time.* She could and would do this. Ray smiled at her, and to her surprise, she smiled back. She was ready.

"May I approach the witness, Your Honor?" Ray asked.

"Yes," the Judge replied.

Ray took two steps forward when his face suddenly changed. Pain contorted his features and he clutched at his chest. His lips formed an O as he stood rigid for a moment, then fell forward. He was like a tree that had been chopped at its base until it toppled over hitting the forest floor.

Everyone gasped in unison as the guard and Ray's second chair rushed toward the body collapsed on the floor. The judge pounded his gavel next to her ear and called for order over the roar of voices. Winter rose from her seat and gripped the railing. She tore her eyes from the lifeless figure on the floor and eased them once again to the source of her nightmares.

Carson sat silently with his hands in a relaxed position on the table in front of him. He was staring at her and his generous lips rose in a smile that didn't quite reach his eyes. Then he winked at her. Her head swiveled around, but no one else saw it. All eyes were on the unmoving prosecutor lying on the floor. A chill started in the pit of her stomach. She knew, and he wanted her to know. "Our secret," she could almost feel his warm breath in a whisper against her ear as she had so many times before. She shivered and brushed her hand across her ear, although nothing was there.

The crowded courtroom faded away. It felt as if they were alone. *Just the two of them. Intimate and perverted.* Her legs trembled and she sat down hard on the witness chair. She felt the caress of his eyes on her skin as he lifted one hand and blew her a kiss. *Carson had just killed Ray Dennison,* she thought. She didn't know how, but he had. She knew it in her heart, even if no evidence existed to back it up.

She would be next. Carson's smile spoke volumes. He leaned back in his seat and covered his mouth with one hand, but then dropped it and his face had changed from seductive humor to a deep frown. Concern was written in his brown eyes as they swept toward the jury.

"No…" Winter whispered as the blood drained from her face.

Chapter 2

Winter sat on her bed and picked at a piece of lint on her jeans as she stared at her cell phone. "Hello?" The voice sounded breathless as it blasted through the speaker phone.

"It's me," Winter said.

"Oh," the voice dripped with disappointment.

Winter's head dropped as she said, "I just wanted to let you know I'll be out of touch until the trial starts again, and Becky, it may be a while. Ray's death is causing delays on both sides." She felt a stinging behind her eyes, so she shifted them to the windows. One entire wall consisted of floor to ceiling windows with a penthouse view of San Francisco's skyline. Breathtaking on a bright day, but most days were like being shrouded in a gray cloud. For once, instead of fog, the sun was streaming in and painted the stark room with light, but it did nothing to lift her spirits.

"Oh?" Curiosity rode on the breathy word, but before Winter could respond, Becky spat out, "Uh, where are you going to stay? I mean, if you aren't staying in that gorgeous penthouse apartment, are you at least staying somewhere fun in the city? Ummmm, can I help you get set up? I'd ask you here, but uh, my guest room is really overrun right now with the silent auction stuff." A giggle and intake of breath floated through the speaker before Becky said, "You know me and volunteering, and the Make a Wish benefit is this weekend." The last words tumbled out in a rush.

Winter chewed at her lip, then said, "No, I have it all set. To be safe,

I'm going out of the country and you won't be able to reach me." She noticed the lint on her jeans had become a white thread poking out of the denim fabric. She moved her hands to her lap and gazed at the windows again.

"Out of the country? Isn't that a little extreme?" Becky snorted, then said in a lilting voice, "Oh, well, if you're sure, but, remember I'm here for you." The phone went silent, but Winter tensed and waited. She knew more was coming and she prepared herself for the explosion. Becky's voice burst out of the speaker as she said, "Winter, really, don't be such a drama queen. I know your split was ugly, but you are *both* playing dirty. You *must* know that Carson wouldn't hurt you. It's just all that old family money. He has to do what his lawyers tell him to protect it. I can understand with the prenup you trying to get a better settlement, but, *honestly*, accusing him of such vicious crimes, aren't you taking it a little too far?"

And there it is. Winter's hand shot out and she swiped the screen to take her mobile phone off speaker. She shut her eyes for a moment. *Breathe in and breathe out.* She grabbed the phone and gripped it in both hands. Becky's outbursts were legendary and could be disarming, but even for her, this was outrageous. Her best friend since childhood could at least pretend to have some support for her. Few people believed Winter's handsome and charming ex-husband could be who she said he was, but *Becky*? She felt a squeeze around her heart, but then something shifted and she went cold inside. She pulled the phone to her ear and could hear Becky as she asked, "Are you still there?"

Winter's eyes narrowed and she said, "I'm here." A flash of memory of the Martha Washington middle school lunchroom: she had been the tall, gawky artsy chick, with wild, untamed black hair and Becky the petite, bubbly blonde who developed way too early. A strange bond, but it worked. No more sitting alone in the cafeteria for an adolescent Winter and she had protected Becky from the hoard of hormonal boys sniffing around. She gritted her teeth and said, "you can't be serious, Becky." Carson could charm almost anyone, *but Becky?* Becky was *her* friend. The little flirtations passing between her husband and friend at dinner parties had not gone unnoticed, but this was so much worse.

"Now, Win, don't be that way. You know I love you, it's just, well, uh, it's too hard to swallow all this shit. That's just not the Carson I know." Winter winced, not only at the words, but she hated the nickname, '*Win*,' and Becky knew it. 'Winter' was bad enough without shortening it to the objective of a race or game.

Winter felt a flash of anger boil from the bottom of her stomach and rise to chip away at the ice core in her chest. She said through clinched teeth, "Whatever, Becky." Her eyes turned to the backpack on her bed. It was filled with the few items she was taking with her. She stood and touched it, then swung around and paced to the windows. The street below was the usual scene. Traffic was backed up in front of her building and horns were blaring. The jam must have cleared, because the cars burst forward to become a steady stream again. Some invisible blockage miles away causing havoc. She placed one hand on the window and sighed. *City life*.

Winter turned and moved back to the bed and sat heavily. "That's the thing, Becky, you may think you know Carson, but no one *living,* other than me, really knows him. Well, maybe some of his men know what he is capable of. They are never very far from his side, so they must have witnessed his cruelty, but that doesn't count because they are deeply in his pockets, and unscrupulous. I somehow expected a little more from you."

"Winter," her friend gasped.

Winter sighed. She could picture Becky's eyes going wide. The woman was completely naïve and wasn't exactly a member of Mensa. Winter fell back onto the bed and sighed deeply. "Becky, I don't want to fight. I care about you. I do." Her temples begin to throb and she felt a tightness around her eyes. She turned her head and glanced at the backpack and said, "Becky, I'm going to have to go now, but please be careful if you see Carson, or his men for that matter. I really mean it. You have no idea what he is like under all that handsome charm." Becky was a sucker for good looking men and had been burned before, but never by someone as deadly as

Carson. She had experience with guys who wanted to get into her pants, or pocket book, but not someone as evil and calculating as Winter's ex-husband.

"How can I have contact with him? He is on house arrest at his hotel until the trial, *right*?" A tinkle of a nervous laugh rang out over the phone. "Now, where are you really going? Is it somewhere warm and tropical, or are you heading for a nice mountain retreat?"

Winter's frown deepened and she sat up. Was this 'playful' Becky, or her friend's lame attempt to secure information. What were those nerves she could hear in her friend's voice all about? Winter said, "You know I can't say, Becky. It's for your own good, as well as mine. I am going to hang up now but, please, please listen to me, be safe, and don't fall for any of his bull. Love you."

Winter disconnected before her friend could say anything more about her being dramatic. She sat motionless on the bed staring out of the windows at the clouds, not white puffy clouds, but gray misty looking clouds. Typical San Francisco weather was returning. That was probably good. The fog matched her mood more than the sunshine.

Becky was one of the few friends Carson allowed her to keep in her smothering marriage. *Allowed to keep?* She shook her head. What a terrible thought—how had she gotten here? She considered herself a strong, independent woman when she met *him*. Carson had systematically charmed, and then bullied her, until he had pushed away her family, girlfriends, and male friends. Especially her male friends. Even gay male friends were not allowed. Carson probably only let her stay in contact with Becky because she was not only gullible, but she was also gorgeous. There was something happening there, but her head hurt too much to try and figure it out right now. Besides, if there was something more, did she really want to know? Their high school days were over. She could no longer protect Becky, she could barely protect herself.

All she wanted to do was to curl up on the bed and have a good cry, but Winter had cried enough. She stood and strolled over to the dresser. A tall, expensive Edwardian piece picked by Carson, just like every other piece of furniture in the penthouse. Photos were lined up in perfect order by the date they had been taken. Not a speck of dust on the pictures, or the polished surface of the dresser.

The pictures were of happy people doing pleasant things. She grasped her wedding photo and glared at it. Carson looked so elegant in his black tuxedo and she was grinning like a fool. She slammed the frame face down and heard the glass shatter on the dresser surface. She had not only looked like a fool, she had been a fool. She had believed in fairytales and Prince Charming. *Well, no more.* She eyed the other photos one by one. They now all appeared staged. Fabulous vacation trips, charity events, and premiers. The perfect life for the perfect couple. The smile on her face appeared more frozen with each year. The media had eaten it up and paparazzi followed them everywhere. *"Lies, all lies,"* Winter whispered as she flicked another picture over with her finger. It didn't break, but the 'plunk' as it hit the smooth wood surface of the dresser was satisfying. She smiled and then used her arm to sweep the whole collection off the dresser and onto the floor. The photos landed on top of each other and the glass shattered on most of them. She walked over the broken frames and glass and laughed at the crunching sound they made beneath her tennis shoes on the unforgiving wood floor. She stared at the mess she made and said, "Oh, man, I really am losing it, but that sure felt good."

Winter turned around and examined the opulent bedroom. If she closed her eyes she could recite where each frame, lamp, or book went. No knickknacks or clutter other than the trophy photos of their lives. Nothing was ever *allowed* out of place. No open drawers. Not a piece of clothing left out. She couldn't stand to be in the room for one more minute. She could feel it sucking the life out of her. She gulped at the air. It was getting harder to breath.

"Enough," she said aloud. Winter crossed the room in brisk strides, zipped her backpack closed, then turned and headed for the door. She hesitated before leaving the bedroom, then said, "Why not?" She stalked back to the king size bed and climbed on it on all fours. She grabbed the pillows and threw them across the room, then turned onto her back and kicked and rumpled the bedspread as her laughter echoed in the room. She climbed off the bed, smoothed her blouse and hair, and went back to the door where her backpack was waiting for her. Winter picked it up and left the bedroom, but this time, she left the room with a grin plastered across her face. That felt good-- wickedly good.

The elevator doors opened and Winter got into an empty box. As it descended, more people joined her, and her grin and feelings of freedom evaporated. Each time was the same scenario. A smile, then a spark of recognition, and finally, a quick turn of the head with downcast eyes. Winter would never cry in public and this time would be no exception. She gritted her teeth and stared at the numbers at the top of the elevator as they descended toward the lobby. *Don't look at the faces.* 23, 22, 21. *Why did she let Carson talk her into living in a penthouse on the top floor?* 20, 19, 18. It was not her style. *Never had been, never will be.* 17, 16, 15. A small brownstone with a lovely garden and floors that creaked were more her style. Instead of that, she got a sterile tribute to riches. 14, 13, 12. She sighed and the lady beside her gave her a sideway glance, then averted her eyes. Winter tightened her lips and squared her shoulders. There would be plenty of time for her to have a pity party once she was safely out of the country. She squeezed the backpack she was holding in her arms and inched toward the back of the elevator as she tried to make herself smaller. A slight bump and shimmy and they were on the lobby floor. The doors slid open and Winter bolted into the lobby with everyone else, but then headed straight for the front entrance. The building's doorman opened the glass door for her and she sucked in a quick breath before she said to him, "Hello, Bobby."

He nodded and said, "Good morning, Mrs. Alexander."

She moved toward the curb and asked, "Can you get me a cab?"

"Sure Mrs. Alexander, where are you heading?" he asked as he glanced at her backpack.

Winter smiled, not bothering to correct her name. "Somewhere nice,

Bobby. Somewhere very nice," she said.

He raised his eyebrows, but held a hand up and a cab scooted to a stop by the curb. Bobby reached out and took her backpack as he held the cab door open for her. Winter slipped him a bill as she got into it and murmured, "Goodbye, Bobby. You've been great." As he handed her backpack to her and closed the cab door she saw curiosity brimming in his eyes, but like most good doormen, he said nothing as he smiled and waved her off. The cab pulled into traffic and Winter leaned her head against the window as she looked up at the glass and chrome front of the building. She let her eyes crawl up the vast wall of dark blue glass and murmured, "Because nice is anywhere but here."

"What, Miss?" the cabbie asked.

"Nothing. Airport, please." She slumped against the vinyl seat as she clasped her backpack in her lap. Her mouth was dry and her hands felt shaky, but she stared straight ahead instead of back at the building. She had a destination and tickets, but it didn't matter. Wherever she ended up it would be better than where she had just been.

***

Bobby the doorman watched the cab pull away from the curb. As soon as traffic swallowed it, he pulled out his cell phone and made the call. "Good morning, sir, it's Bobby. Yes, sir, she just left." He nodded his head at the phone and continued with, "I think the airport, but I'm not really sure, she wouldn't say." Another pause as he listened, and then he said, "Yes, sir, but I put the pin on the bottom of her backpack because she didn't have a suitcase." He grinned and nodded at the phone as he said, "Oh, yes, sir, that's exactly what I said, a backpack!" Another nod before he said, "Thanks, Mr. Alexander, you're the best!" He disconnected the phone and slipped it into his pocket.

He moved to his station by the entrance of the building, but he couldn't stop grinning as he whistled a tune that was playing in his head. A pigeon landed on the railing by the sidewalk and cocked its head at Bobby. "Nice lady, my little feathered friend, but we guys gotta stick together or these bitches will take us for everything," he said. The bird bobbed his head and Bobby laughed. He leaned toward the bird and said, "Mr. A can be very generous. It doesn't hurt to help him out a little. No harm no foul, I always say!" The pigeon ruffled its wings, then took flight, and sailed across the intersection to the traffic light high above the street. "Hey, I said 'foul' not 'fowl,' and no pun was intended," Bobby chuckled at his joke. He watched the bird for a moment until he heard the door to the building open and he rushed forward to help the next tenant.

***

"What an ass kisser," Carson said as he pocketed his phone. He needed people like Bobby, but it didn't mean he trusted them. Some flattery and a little money was all it took to buy their services. He had several spies on his payroll at his building. Well, his former building, if he was going to be precise. He glared around the hotel suite. Lofty ceilings, plush carpet, magnificent view of the skyline, and 24-hour room service, but it wasn't home. His home was more than his castle, it was the show piece he had painstakingly put together one item at a time. It had taken him years to get it right, and now it was gone. He moved over to the bar and poured himself a drink.

It didn't matter if she was going to the airport, or not, his spies had already given him her destination. The tracking device simply assured him he could locate her once they were in the same area. Besides, he loved watching that little red dot on his phone's location app. It was almost as satisfying as having eyes on her when she didn't know he was watching. *Almost.*

He swirled the amber liquid in his glass and gazed at the rich color as he thought of Winter. *A backpack? God, what had he ever seen in her?* She was beautiful, but there were so many beautiful, available women. He had to admit, when he first saw her all those years ago at her art opening, she had taken his breath away, and that rarely happened. Watching her still made his blood pump faster.

Carson moved to the window and eased into a comfortable leather chair. He set his glass on a coaster on an end table and placed his phone beside it. A glance at the table and he straightened the phone, glass, and lamp to line up better, then turned to enjoy the city view. It wasn't as impressive as from his penthouse apartment, but he still could feel the pulse of city life.

Winter's art was garbage. Despite what the critics said, he found it trivial, light, and fluffy. That's one of the reasons he encouraged her to give it up, *but, Winter*? He knew he had to have her as soon as he saw her. She was raw and needed refinement, just like a diamond in the rough, but he was up for the challenge. Now all his arduous work was wasted. *A backpack?* Carson thought as he snorted and crossed his legs.

The day was turning foggy again. Gray sky replaced the clear blue vista. *What did I do with that piece I bought at her opening to impress her?* Carson wondered. It was a big monstrosity of soft blues—an ocean setting if he remembered it correctly. *Oh, yeah,* Carson thought as he remembered. He gave it to his simpering personal assistant at the time. Young, blonde, bouncy, and everything she said sounded like a question. He took another sip of his drink. She had been ecstatic. She showed her appreciation immediately - right across his desk. He smiled at the memory, set down his drink, and his phone chirped. He grabbed the phone and swiped at the green acceptance button. After he listened for a moment he nodded and said, "Yes, send him up, but have him use the service elevator."

Carson raised his glass once again and took a long sip. The expensive brew sparked his taste buds as it passed over his tongue, then burned a trail as it slid down his throat and warmed him all the way to his stomach. *Nice.*

It would probably be a while before he tasted something this good again. Why would his wife choose such a primitive place to lay low? Some god forsaken island in South America? Hadn't he taught her to appreciate the finer things? All his efforts were lost on the ungrateful bitch. She was heading back to becoming the unsophisticated, bohemian artist she was when he found her. What a waste of raw beauty. Ah, well, she wasn't so young anymore and the spark *was* fading. She had grown much more docile in recent years. He still craved her, but not in the same way. Docile Winter wasn't as much fun as fiery Winter. He smiled as he remembered her face when Dennison collapsed. It made him crave her again and he knew this craving would have a delicious end.

The bell of his hotel suite rang. Carson rose and crossed the room, but as he looked through the peephole in the door he muttered, "Damn," and took a moment before he opened the door and said, "come in," as he gestured toward the suite's living room. He chose his visitor from his studio head shots, but it was startling to see this man in person. Carson checked the hallway before he shut and locked the door, then followed him into the suite.

Once they were in the living room, the actor turned to him and said, "Hello, Mr. Alexander. I'm Johnny May, but please call me Johnny." He pumped Carson's hand in a firm, dry handshake. "I am very sorry for being a little late. LAX was ridiculous, and then my plane landed late. I don't want you to think I am not taking this interview seriously, I am, and I thank you so much for giving me this fantastic opportunity." The grin almost blinded Carson. *How much whitening can a set of teeth handle? Another ass kisser.*

When the man kept pumping his hand, Carson pulled it away and said, "sit," as he placed his hand on a desk chair he had pulled into the middle of the spacious room.

 The actor perched on the very edge of the chair and swept the suite with his eyes, and then he locked in on Carson. He said, "Wow. My agent told me more depended on my physical appearance than acting ability on this one, and if that's true, I'm perfect for the part!" He shifted on the chair. "Do you want me to recite some lines?"

"*What?* No, just sit quietly for a moment," Carson said as he walked in a circle around him. He stopped directly in front of his doppelganger. "They went over the parameters of the deal and you signed the non-disclosure statement. Do you still agree to the terms of the contract?"

"Oh, yes, absolutely." The man clasped his hands in his lap and gazed over Carson's shoulder. Carson's eyebrows furrowed, then smoothed. *The idiot is looking for a camera.*

It was unnerving. Even the haircut was the same. Except for the stupid grin plastered on this man's face and the ridiculously white teeth, it was like looking in a mirror. Carson shivered and crossed his arms over his chest and asked, "You understand the job?"

"Oh, yes, sir!" the actor responded with a rapid bobbing of his head.

Carson remained standing in front of him and said, "Well? Let me hear it."

"Oh, uh, okay, sure." Johnny sat straighter and tilted his head to one side. An anchorman's baritone purred out the instructions. "I will stay here all week. I'll order room service and tip generously when I sign for it, all on your room account, of course. I'll wear your clothes. You are providing everything I will need, so I didn't even bring a toothbrush." He held his hands out and grinned.

The serious anchorman is replaced by the village idiot. Carson assumed he was demonstrating he had no tooth brush. *Good God, this is hard.* "Go on," Carson said.

"I'll make a stroll through the lobby at least once a day, but not make close contact with anyone. I will make sure I'm seen on those outings and that the security cameras pick me up." He paused and licked his lips as he eyed Carson's glass which was still sitting on the end table, but then took a breath and continued with, "I will only answer to Carson, or Mr. Alexander, when addressed, but then I will shake my head and say, not now, and go immediately to the elevators." He shook his head with his words and held up one hand as if warding off the paparazzi. When he finished speaking he grinned at Carson. He was like a child who had just performed for their parent.

Carson had to turn away a moment to keep from punching the simpleton. He needed this man, not for his intellect, but for his looks. He turned back to the actor and said, "Okay, good. You won't be able to reach me after this interview, but Jeff will remain with you always, and he can handle anything that comes up. You met Jeff on the first interview in LA, right?" The man's head bobbed even faster than the first time. *What a boob,* Carson thought. "You must follow Jeff's instructions to the letter. He is your boss, now. Any questions before I go?"

The man leaned forward and licked his lips again. He said, "Right, right, no problem, but what about the part?"

"What part?" Carson asked.

The actor frowned. "The movie? Do I get the lead for the movie, or are there others trying out for it?"

Carson smiled and nodded his head. He said, "Oh, yes, of course, *THE* movie. Yes, you have the part. If you don't screw this up, it's yours." He smiled and wagged his finger at the man and said, "Consider this your screen test. If anyone discovers you are not me, well, then you don't get the part."

The man grinned and the bobble head started again. Carson cringed and rubbed his face, then his shoulders relaxed. The idiot would have Jeff, and Jeff was Carson's best man, so he would keep this fool on track. But if they had to get rid of the actor, and they most likely would, Carson was not going to be able to do it. As annoying as this guy was it would feel like he was killing himself. Another thing to consider was that the doppelganger might also come in handy if Carson's plans didn't go well. The actor would be the ideal body if he had to fake his own death. Carson chuckled. *A week with this ass and Jeff will probably do him for free. Problem solved.*

"Again, thank you so much, Mr. Alexander for this opportunity. I will not let you down. I promise!" He leaned forward as he asked, "Uh, is the scrip finished? Could I see it?"

.

"No, they can't finish it until the trial ends." Carson didn't add, *you moron*, although he thought it.

"Oh, of course!" Johnny shook his head and laughed. "Let me just say that I hope it goes in your favor and I can join you at the premier!" The man winked and plastered a grin across his face. "What a fantastic photo op that will be!"

Yep, *ass kisser*. Flattery, dangling the movie part, and a few bucks would get exactly what he needed from this clown. "Thanks, but let's just get through this week and then it will be smooth sailing," Carson said as he moved toward the closed door to one of the bedrooms. He tapped his knuckles on it and barked, "Jeff, get out here and show Johnny around the suite. I need to get going."

The door opened and it was filled with a 6'4 mass of muscle in a polyester track suit. "Yes, sir," Jeff said as he glided into the room and took the seated man by the arm. "Come with me, Johnny. Let's get your clothes changed and set up a schedule," he said. Carson smiled and his shoulders relaxed. *Jeff has it under control.*

The actor stood, but had to crank his neck to look up at Jeff. "Uh, okay. I forgot how big you are," he said, but then added, "but, sir, the name is Carson—Carson Alexander!" He turned and winked at Carson.

Jeff looked in Carson's eyes and said, "I've got this. I won't be expecting to hear from you unless you need me."

Carson moved forward and patted the giant of a man on the back. It was as if he was patting a rock covered with nylon. Jeff loved his gym time and steroids. Simply having him by his side in meetings eliminated a lot of problems before they started. "Excellent. I'll see you in a week," Carson said as he headed for the door without a glance at his double. *This is going to work*, Carson thought. He could almost taste his victory. He was taking his life back.

Chapter 3

Carson left the hotel suite and turned toward the service elevators. There was no security camera on his section of the hallway, but he pulled a dark hoodie over his head and slumped his shoulders as he walked. You could never be too careful. The suite was costing him a bundle, but appearances must be kept, and luxury didn't come cheap. Hopefully, he would be back in his penthouse apartment where he belonged before too long.

As he left the hallway, he kept his head down and his hands stuffed deep into his faded jeans pockets. The cameras in the main hall and elevator would record what looked like a camera-shy delivery guy. *Great getup Jeff came up with*, Carson thought. No visible skin, no rings or tattoos, nothing to identify who this man really was. Security would think he was a delivery guy, possibly with a record— nothing more. They may even be tracking him right now to make sure he wasn't breaking into one of the high-priced rooms. He resisted the urge to shoot the finger at the camera. He needed the record to show no one else was leaving his floor. Carson Alexander, III was in his hotel suite for the night. He felt ridiculous in the clothing, but it was also fun. Another game, and Carson loved games. He always won. People were so easy to deceive. Just play on their need to have everything in neat little boxes. Rich, golden boys were trusted and crappy dressed delivery boys in dark hoodies needed watching.

At the elevator, he used his elbow to press the down button and once inside, he did the same thing for the garage level. He was grateful the utility elevator was lined with padding and had no mirrors to reveal his face or even his race. *Anonymous hoodie guy.*

Once he was on the garage level, he exited the elevator and headed for a motorcycle waiting for him at the designated spot. Two empty pizza boxes were strapped to the back of the bike with a helmet sitting on top. He shoved the helmet over his hoodie, straddled the bike, and turned it on. After revving the engine, he turned it toward the busy street entrance where he quickly blended into heavy traffic. His spirits rose as he wove through the crowded streets until he was free of the city and headed to his destination; a small private airport outside the city and away from prying eyes.

Carson slowed the motorcycle and came to a stop in front of the only gate for the airport. He gave a nod to the uniformed man sitting in the guard house and held up the brightly colored pass he had been given for entry. A courteous wave in place of a challenge and then the heavy gate swung open. Carson loved the way money smoothed out everything. He gunned the bike and roared down the road until he saw the large metal building housing Vagabond Charter Service.

Carson chose the private airport and charter service because of its reputation for discretion, and its extensive list of satisfied clients; including several difficult celebrities hounded by the paparazzi. Their fierce need for privacy was even greater than his, so he trusted their high standards. The many charity events he attended provided a wealth of information and connections with services that catered to the rich. The drunken actor who told him about the charter service admitted he liked to travel with his brood of tiny chihuahuas. He refused to have them quarantined when entering other countries and he was camera shy. It might hurt his image as a Hollywood tough guy to see how he fawned over his beloved pets, or his fake dogs, as Carson liked to call them.

Hiring the charter service had cost him even more than the hotel suite, but it was worth it. He gunned the bike and leaned into the last curve as the building came into sight. The cost of this project would cut deeply into his already depleted emergency funds. Winter was costing him. Very soon she would regret it and she was never going to get her hands on his hidden assets. She professed no desire to have anything from the end of their marriage, but he knew better. She swore she didn't want anything, not even the penthouse, but that wasn't in a woman's nature. *Their grubby hands are always out to take, take, take.*

He slowed the motorcycle and then braked to a stop in front of a huge metal building. The price of disloyalty was high in Carson's world. Winter would soon find out it didn't pay to disrespect him. He removed his helmet and set it on the back of the bike. His lips tightened and his eyes narrowed. *What was she thinking when she went to Dennison?* She had to know how this was going to play out. He shook his head. *She has brought this on herself.*

A man dressed in a spotless blue jump suit with a large stitched emblem for Vagabond Charter Service stood very erect by the charter service door. Military posture and short gray haircut screamed reliability and safety. He stepped forward and said, "Good, morning. Mr. Tudor?"

Carson glanced at the man's nametag placed just below the company emblem. "Yes, that's me, Frank," he said as his frown was replaced with a grin. His fake passport was in his jacket pocket, but he wouldn't need it, at least not until the ten-minute check on the other end of this flight. That was when customs would come on the plane and take a cursory look at their passports. Another reason he was paying dearly for this flight.

The name on his new passport was Henry Tudor—but, perhaps the name would be better recognized as Henry, VIII. It was going to be fun to see if anyone made the connection to the ancient royal. Carson wished he had lived then. It would be lovely to send unwanted wives to the guillotine. He suppressed a chuckle each time he heard someone call him by his fake name. This was his personal nod to the royal who took no crap from anyone, even the Pope, and sent anyone who opposed him into banishment or execution. In the end, his name choice had died from his own gluttony and self-indulgence, but what absolute control he had until the end. He identified with the younger, handsome Henry, who was irresistible to women.

"Your wife is already on the plane sir. Please, follow me," he said as he gestured toward the office door.

"Okay. Frank, could you have someone take care of my bike?" Carson replied.

The attendant gave an almost imperceptible glance toward the empty pizza boxes on the back of the motorcycle. "Of, course, sir. We will put it in storage until your return," he said as he opened the office door for Carson. Whoever said, "money can't buy happiness," was probably poor, and justifying their existence, because it was Carson's experience that money went a long way in making everything so much easier. If that wasn't happiness, what was?

It was not a typical aviation office in a metal hanger. Instead, Carson was greeted with blue gray plaster walls, rich wood floors covered with Persian carpets, and two black leather sofas sitting in front of an enormous flat screen television that had some sort of travel documentary dancing across its flawless surface. There were no windows, but huge green plants, soft lighting, and soothing artwork made up for the lack of light. No service desk, either, but a mahogany bar covered the back wall by the only other door in the room. A gorgeous woman with extremely long, tan legs protruding from a suggestion of a skirt was standing behind the bar. She nodded at them as they passed straight through the room to the other door. Dark hair and almond shaped eyes over a rosebud mouth. *Pity.* Her exotic beauty would have been an interesting visual over a nice scotch.

They entered a cavernous hanger with only one small jet residing in the middle of the concrete floor. Carson followed blue jump suit to the jet's stairway. Once there, his guide stood at the bottom and said, "Have a nice flight, Mr. Tudor."

"Thanks, Frank," Carson said, then handed him a fifty-dollar bill. Blue jumpsuit tucked it into a pocket with a nod and tight smile. Carson climbed the stairs and at the top, he had to duck to enter the plane.

Once inside, a stunning, black, middle aged woman greeted him. "Welcome aboard, sir," she said as she led him to his seat.

They approached two fawn colored plush leather swivel chairs with a small table tucked beside each of them. They were the only seats on the jet. Carson wondered if the interior seating could be changed with each grouping of high paying passengers. He looked at the woman seated in the chair closest to the window. She was holding a crystal glass half full of a pale bubbly liquid. Champaign was his guess, and her eyes were already getting that buzzed blur. It was not even noon. "Hello, Becky," Carson said.

"Hi Carson," Becky said. She placed one finger on her lips and added, "Whoops," as she giggled. "I mean, Henry." She grinned at him. "See, I remembered!"

Yep. She was already tipsy.

"Can I get you anything?" the flight attendant asked him as if Becky did not exist.

"Scotch, please," he said as he plopped down in the leather chair. "I might as well try to catch up with my lovely wife," he said and smiled at the attendant.

"Right away, sir," she said as she moved toward the front of the plane.

Carson turned to his companion and squeezed her free hand, then whispered in her ear, "You must remember, Becky, on this trip 'Carson' doesn't exist."

"Ouch. You're hurting my hand," she said and jerked it away.

He let her hand go but whispered, "Sorry, sweetie, but this is important. You don't want me to go back to jail, now do you?"

She frowned and said, "No."

"Well, let's play our little game, okay?" he said as he raised one eyebrow.

Becky's bottom lip trembled as she replied, "Okay. Sorry."

"No, problem," he said and patted the top of her hand. He handed her two little pills and said, "Take these for your motion sickness." Becky glanced at the pills, nodded, then downed them with the rest of her champagne. Carson took the glass from her and stroked her arm. "Why don't you take a little nap? It will make the flight go much faster."

She yawned and smiled. "I am kind of sleepy. I was too excited to sleep much last night." She stretched and scooted down into the chair. "I know you said to pack my bikini, but where are we going? Hawaii?" she murmured.

He smiled back at her and whispered, "Let's keep that a surprise for now, but I know you will love it."

"You're the best." Another yawn. "I can't believe Winter let you go," she said, then added, "I feel funny and my eyes don't want to stay open." Becky reached up and tugged at the lids of her eyes, then giggled.

Carson ran a hand over his face and then said, "Becky, remember, no proper names," he whispered as he turned toward the attendant. Her back was still to them as she prepared his drink. *Becky is such a ditz,* he thought. He had kept her first name the same so she would remember to answer to it, but she was never going to quit calling him Carson, or bringing up Winter. Something was going to have to be done about her, and he was going to need to tip the attendant generously, but not enough to make them too memorable.

"Okay, okay, but she can't hear me. She's way over there," Becky said with a slur as she pointed toward the front of the plane with an unsteady finger. I think I'll take that nap now." She leaned back and he adjusted her seat into a reclining position. The flight attendant returned with his drink and he smiled and put a finger to his lips as he nodded in Becky's direction. The woman returned the smile and nodded as she placed the scotch next to him on his table. Did he see relief in the pretty dark eyes? Becky could be a handful and enjoyed playing her part as 'queen of the manor,' but those little pills he gave her should keep her out for most of the flight.

After the attendant left he took a sip of his drink and set it on the table. The plane began its trip down the runway. The takeoff was as smooth as the leather he sat on. With Becky taken care of, at least for now, his thoughts turned to the task at hand. *Winter.*

Carson's jaw tightened and he gripped his glass of scotch. The situation with Winter was personal. He felt the need to take care of her with his own hands. It didn't matter how difficult or expensive his travel plans needed to be, Winter belonged only to him. Carson closed his eyes and gazed inward, as images of her floated through his mind and played out like a movie. Winter coming toward him in her wedding dress, with her thick black hair twisted up on top of her head, and her flawless, slightly olive skin glistening against the white satin and lace floating around her. *Their wedding day.* He shifted in his seat and felt a bead of sweat form on his forehead. Eyes still closed, the image faded and another became clear; Winter in her running outfit with her pony tail swaying as she worked her athletic body, pumping those ridiculously long legs and tight glutes. His hand gripped the arms of his chair as her smiling face dissolved into a grimace straining to hide pain and fear. *The pain and fear only he could inflict.* He groaned and shifted in his seat again as his hands clinched in anticipation.

A soft snore pulled Carson back to the present. He glanced at the sleeping woman in the seat beside him and his stomach tightened. She was sprawled on the chair and her mouth hung slightly open as she snored. *Simple and transparent.* Becky reminded him of a blob of clay, especially in her current relaxed position. She was spoiled and whiney, but he could plant whatever idea he wanted in her mind and it would sprout and blossom until she owned it. Becky was empty, uncomplicated, and completely malleable. Physically soft, she was petit and curvy. She couldn't be more different than Winter. It was fun playing with Becky's head and her body. Sometimes he did it just because he could.

Carson glanced up the aisle. No sign of the flight attendant but she would be checking on them soon. His eyes returned to his sleeping 'wife.' Her usefulness was quickly ending and he could see how she might become a liability. His eyes traveled up her bare legs to the crumpled short skirt and silky material stretched across her generous breasts, but he resisted the urge to replace his gaze with his hands. *Pity*. As much fun as he was having with her, she would need to be dealt with and sooner than later.

***

Winter's eyes were squeezed shut as her hands clutched the metal armrests until they ached. *Why did I get on this thing?* she thought. She should have followed her first instinct. When she stood on the tarmac before she boarded the small commuter plane she knew the metal bird should have been retired years ago, and her mind had screamed *no way*. Now here she was. Seated in the dilapidated tube of death. The constant roar of the engines made her heart pound and beads of sweat pop out on her forehead and scalp.

The landing was as bad as the flight. The first bump was brief as the plane's tires flirted with the runway, but the second bump knocked Winter's stomach to her throat. She bent her head forward and closed her eyes even tighter. A high-pitched scream from the breaks assaulted her eardrums as they protested the short runway. Winter bounced forward and her eyes flew open as the plane came to a hard stop. She sat upright and wiped at the dingy round window, but all she could see beyond it was jungle. The plane turned and eased forward as a flat roofed concrete building next to the lookout tower came into view. "International airport, my ass," she mumbled as she relaxed her grip and flexed her fingers. Her hands went from stark white to a more normal beige as the circulation returned.

She didn't fear flying, to the contrary, she enjoyed it, that is, until this flight. Winter might not want to step on a plane after this. However, her previous flying experiences were always on bigger commercial passenger planes instead of ancient puddle jumpers like this one. She shrugged and then stretched her legs and back as much as was possible in the confined space. The faded blue back to the seat in front of her bumped against her knees as she tried to move her legs around. She had a strange urge to climb over it and bound to the front of the plane.

Double seats lined her side of the plane, with single seats on the other side, and an impossibly small aisle between them. Winter was in a window seat and the woman next to her, not only blocked her escape to the aisle, but during most of the flight, her brightly flowered dress flowed over the arm rest, invading Winter's already small space. The single seat across from them was occupied by a thin, petite woman. Her legs were short enough that she could cross them and swing her leg without it touching the back of the seat in front of her. *Typical.*

Winter turned back to the window and took in the jungle setting surrounding the airstrip. She spotted banana, mango, and cinnamon trees, along with colorful wild exotic flowers. She wanted to be somewhere off the grid, so if this was an indicator, she was getting her wish. "Be careful what you wish for," she mumbled aloud as she looked at the meager airport terminal. It appeared more like an open box store than an airport. The woman in the flowered dress turned to look at her, shook her head, and then turned back toward the aisle. Winter snorted, but resisted the urge to make a snarky comment, after all, she had been mumbling to herself like a crazy woman.

Once the announcement was made that they could disembark, the woman next to her heaved herself up and began trudging down the aisle. Winter shouldered her backpack and followed the other occupants to the front of the plane. As she reached the open door the heat hit her. It was like a wall of warm moisture. She tried to take a deep breath, but it was like breathing through a wet sponge. What had she been thinking when she booked a week at a yoga retreat, deep in the rain forest, during the heat of the summer? How could she practice deep breathing and relaxation when she couldn't draw a breath?

She followed the other passengers as they descended the metal staircase from the plane to the tarmac. It was a sea of flowered shirts and dresses. She must not have gotten the memo. Her jeans, sneakers and T-shirt seemed incredibly out of place, and felt too hot. So much for blending in with the crowd.

At the bottom of the stairs she paused and took in her surroundings. Okay, heat and humble airport building aside, it was beautiful; lush vegetation, green mountains in the distance, and flowers, so many exotic flowers. The scent of the gorgeous blooms hit her along with the moist heat. Maybe this was going to be better then she first thought. She heard a throat clear behind her and she realized she was holding up the plane's exodus. "Sorry," she mumbled, then passed the large woman in the flowered dress, and continued moving until she caught up with the couple in front of her. From the back, they were almost identical sizes, and they were wearing matching shirts: bright red and covered with drinks in coconut cups with little umbrellas in them. Winter rolled her eyes but managed to contain the groan she felt bubbling up in her throat.

After making her way through customs, the chaotic airport, and a mass of drivers searching for fares, she stood on the front veranda of the airport building as she fanned herself with her passport. *What now?* she wondered. Winter had the address of the retreat, but what transportation should she take? Taxi stands and moped rentals were located at the end of the walkway, but before she could make her way there, a small van pulled up in front of the building with the logo "Serenity Yoga Retreat" emblazoned on its side. A young man in cargo shorts and a loose tank top jumped out and yelled, "Serenity Retreat?"

"Here," a female voice heavy with an Oklahoma, or maybe Texas accent, called back to him.

Winter's eyes turned toward the voice. It belonged to a slender, middle aged woman. A bright orange ankle length dress billowed around her and she had a huge straw hat jammed on her long red hair. She was struggling with two large rolling suitcases and a giant straw beach bag embroidered with 'Oklahoma is OK.'

Nailed it. Winter prided herself on having a knack for determining regional dialects.

The young man rushed forward, took the woman's suitcases, and stowed them in the back of the van, before he helped her into one of the van's back seats. Winter tucked her passport into her backpack and moved forward as she said, "Uh, here. Me too." He glanced at her solitary backpack and smiled as he reached for it, but Winter said, "I've got it."

He shrugged and waved his hand toward the other seat as he said, "Okay, Miss. I'm Jose, and will be your driver today." She climbed into the van and took the seat across from Oklahoma.

"Hi, I'm Riley Wilson," the woman said as Winter took her seat. Oklahoma extended a hand.

Winter smiled and shook her hand. "Winter," she said and then turned toward her window. Winter heard the woman sigh deeply, but she kept her eyes glued toward the view of the town as the van pulled out and began their trek to 'Serenity.'

A paved road lead them into the village. Colorful shops and hotels competed for space along the two-lane road and the town bustled with taxis, mopeds, and foot traffic. Bars, restaurants, and souvenir shops dominated the buildings - mostly souvenir shops, and each displayed almost identical wares in the windows: beach towels, boogie boards, bikinis, and t-shirts. The van came to a stop at a red light and Winter watched as three or four stray dogs congregated in an alley by the back door of a restaurant. The door swung open and the dogs stood at attention as a man with a soiled apron threw them scraps. The van took off again as the dogs chowed down.

"Can you turn the air up a little, honey?" Oklahoma asked the driver as she fanned herself.

"So, sorry, Miss, but it's not working today," Jose replied.

Winter glanced at the window and realized it was crank not power, so she edged it down as she wondered if the air conditioner worked on any day. She leaned toward the window, but only heat floated in, along with some interesting smells that she wasn't sure she wanted to identify.

As they left the main section of the village, the van picked up speed and a breeze flowed through the open window. Houses became further apart, then vanished altogether, as the landscape turned into tree covered hills on one side and the ocean on the other. Winter felt her shoulders relax as she gazed at the turquoise blue water on her side of the van. A scent of salt slipped in on the damp air and tickled her nostrils.

After a short distance, the van began to slow, and then they turned away from the sea. The road changed from asphalt to hard-packed dirt and Jose swerved the van continuously to avoid numerous holes. "So, sorry, guys. We got lots of holes from the rain," he said.

Winter bumped her head against the window on one of the more energetic swerves, rubbed it and mumbled, "From the rain or a tsunami?"

They traveled on the road for some time, but then the landscape abruptly changed from open fields to a densely-forested area. The air cooled and a sweet scent of damp moss flowed through the window. Winter couldn't see much more than the tunnel of green they were traveling through, but she felt Jose slow the van as they turned onto an even more narrow road, and then began a steep climb up a mountain. The road went down to one lane before it all but disappeared as it was engulfed by the jungle. Winter removed her sunglasses as the sunlight became only patches of light.

"Uh, Jose, honey, what happens if someone is coming down the mountain as we are going up?" Oklahoma asked their driver.

"No problem. We pull over, they pass," he said.

Thick vegetation surrounding both sides of the van and Winter mumbled, "Pull over? Where?" This was not the quaint portrait the internet pictures had painted. This was remote and primitive.

"Woo wee," Oklahoma almost shouted as they hit a big pothole. Winter jumped and turned toward her and the redhead said, "Sorry, sweetie, but I'll be damned. This is just like I imagined it." She wore a big grin and her green eyes sparked. She had removed the outrageous hat and her red hair fell in waves around her face with tiny wisps curling against her damp forehead. The corners of Winter's mouth twitched as she watched the woman. It was like watching a puppy discover water with unbridled enthusiasm.

"Not me. I have to say, none of this is what I was anticipating, but then again, I'm not sure exactly what I was expecting," Winter responded.

"Honey, I could say the same thing about my entire life," Oklahoma responded.

Listening to the woman's drawl made Winter's mouth go from a twitch at the corners to a real smile. It felt good to smile. *Note to self, everyone has a story and I may not be the only one trying to escape something or someone,* Winter thought. Maybe solitude and a pity party wasn't what she needed after all, maybe she needed to meet people outside the tiny circle Carson had cultivated and have some laughs. *This woman is about as far from that circle as I can get,* she couldn't help but think.

Winter turned back to the window. The thick jungle continued as they kept climbing. Deep rich greens with explosions of color surrounded her. "Yeah, I hear you on that," she said over her shoulder as she watched the tangled maze of greenery. Winter turned back to the woman and murmured, "Life is what happens while you're planning, just like the bumper sticker says." Oklahoma gave her a funny look. Winter wasn't sure what she saw in her eyes, was it curiosity or recognition? She swiveled back to the window and studied the jungle as it inched by.

The van finally turned again and edged into a level clearing before it rolled to a stop. "We are here, guys," the young man said as he jumped from the vehicle and slid open the door. After helping them out of the van, he scooted around to the back and grabbed Riley's luggage. As he pulled the bags across the dirt lot he said, "Follow me, guys."

Winter looked at Riley and held her hand up as she gestured for her to go first. The redhead shrugged and moved forward as she stayed close behind Jose and her bags. Winter followed until they reached a wide gate framed in bamboo with a sign that read: "Serenity Yoga Retreat" hanging above it, but once they moved through the gate, Winter stopped at the cobblestone walkway to take in the lush garden in the front of the building. Green moss carpeted the area around the cobblestones and inched through the cracks between the stones. More exotic flowers in vibrant colors: red, yellow, orange, and blue. Tall wild grasses and a large koi pond on her right, and to the left, there was more of the wild vegetation with several concrete benches. Winter decided the name 'Serenity' was aptly chosen.

"This is gorgeous, Jose," Riley said.

"Yes, ma'am," the young man said as he used the pause to adjust his grip on the handle of the largest suitcase. "We think so," he said and nodded, then he moved forward toward their destination; a long, low wooden building with a thatch roof. The structure had a row of floor to ceiling windows flanking both sides of the bright turquoise wooden front door. The paint was peeling a little on the door and the matching shutters flanking the windows, but it only added to the charm of the building.

"How long has this building been here, Jose?" Winter asked.

"Since long before I was born, Miss. I have been told it was one of the first houses on the island," he said.

Once Jose reached the turquoise door he set Riley's bags to one side as he pulled it open and gestured toward the entrance. Riley moved past him and into the building, but Winter remained where she was as she examined the building's windows. They were old fashioned lead lined windows with hand cranks at the bottom. Several were open to the garden and she could see dining tables through them on one side, but the other side was curtained off. *What a lovely spot,* Winter thought.

"Ma'am?" Jose's words pulled Winter out of her contemplation.

"Oh, sorry," Winter said. She moved ahead and followed Riley into the building. She noticed her feet felt lighter and she realized she was looking forward to exploring the grounds. The retreat was quaint and secluded. It was the contrast she needed to the world she had recently left.

Once they were inside, Jose pointed at a small corner counter to the left of the front door where a young girl, who couldn't be out of high school yet, smiled and said, "Namaste. Welcome to the Serenity Yoga Retreat."

Riley approached the counter and said, "Well, hi Y'all. Namaste to you, too. I'm Riley Wilson and I'm ready to be renewed." She leaned against the waist high counter and said, "Honey, you are gorgeous. If that is what this place does for you, I'm signing up for another booking!"

The girl grinned and a deep red blush stained her light brown cheeks as she said, "Welcome, Mrs. Wilson, we've been expecting you." She turned toward Winter and said, "and you too, Ms. Pappas."

Riley's eyes widened and she raised an eyebrow at Winter, who ignored her as she nodded at the girl and said, "Thank you. If I could get my room key, I could really use a shower." Winter recognized the look on Oklahoma's face this time. *She knew.* Winter examined her feet and refused to look at the woman. Her tennis shoes looked so out of place. She should have gotten a pedicure before leaving San Francisco - everyone else was clad in sandals. Then she smiled at the absurdity of the thought. She sighed, even in this remote part of the world, she was sure to be recognized, along with all the dirty laundry she continued to drag around behind her. After all, the redhead was from the states. Even if Oklahoma was far from San Francisco, Winter's story was all over the national news and splashed across the paparazzi rags.

"Of, course." The girl handed two keys to Jose and said, "Mrs. Wilson is in Serenity A and Ms. Pappas in Serenity B."

Jose pocketed the keys and gripped the bags as he turned toward the women and said, "If you please, follow me, guys." He turned and headed down a hallway beside the open dining area. Riley and Winter followed.

"Dinner at 6:00, ladies," the girl called to the exiting procession.

Chapter 4

Winter shut the door and leaned against it as she looked around the small casita. The four-poster double bed drew her, so she set her backpack on the floor and moved toward it. It was engulfed in a thick cloud of mosquito netting, but there was a slit down the side of the netting by the headboard, so she pulled it aside and tied it to the post. A snowy white bedspread covered the bed's surface and all four corners were tucked into the frame with military precision. She leaned over and pushed. *Not too soft, but not a board, either*. She turned, sat, and then bounced up and down. Falling back on the bed she spread her arms wide and rolled her neck. The rock lodged between her shoulder blades eased slightly, but it was still there. Imbedded. Perhaps forever. "Maybe I'll name it Carson," she said as her smile returned in full force.

She gazed at the white canopy above her head and wondered if they had massages at this retreat. When she was still single, she had a wonderful massage therapist, Diane. That woman's hands could release stress knots no matter how tight they were. But Carson 'discouraged' outside massages. "No hands but mine will ever touch your silky skin again." She grimaced and blushed with the memory. "Cheesy and total crap. What an idiot I was to fall for all that BS," Winter said aloud to the empty room.

She sat up and pulled the band off her ponytail as she shook her hair free, then finger-combed the tangled curls, and rubbed her scalp with both hands. Her hair was probably sticking out like a wild tumbleweed, but damn it felt good. Kicking off her sneakers, she tugged her socks off and stood. The tile floor felt cool beneath her bare feet. She wiggled her toes and stared down at them. The nails had no polish, but her feet looked okay, and it felt wonderful. She had not been allowed to walk through their penthouse apartment either in her shoes or with bare feet. It had to be socks only - to keep her 'body oils' and shoe grime off the expensive rugs on the hard wood floors.

The sparsely furnished casita held a small writing desk strategically placed under the front window, an ancient but freshly painted white wicker rocker, and a pedestal sink that stood in the back corner of the room with a small mirror hanging above it. There was a door next to the sink. Ignoring the mirror, Winter padded across the room barefooted and opened the door. A basic cube shower and toilet. The tiny bathroom was covered in blue and white mosaic tiles that glistened; not a speck of dirt or grime on the shiny tile surfaces. "Works for me," Winter said as she shut the door.

In the middle of the cabin ceiling she noticed an overhead fan, so she flipped a switch by the bed and it started its slow circle. As she stood by the bed she could feel the breeze coming from the fan as it made a pleasant whirring noise. A desire gripped her to take a nap, but she resisted it and picked up her backpack as she looked for a place to unpack it.

No closet or chest of drawers in the room, so the desk looked like the only option to stow her belongings. It had several deep drawers so that it could serve double duty. "Good thing I packed light," she said, then wondered how Oklahoma was making out with her gigantic suitcases. Winter moved her backpack to the desk chair and began digging through it. The small cosmetics case and a book came out first and she placed them on the desk. The few items of clothing she had went into the drawers, but she left some snacks, a bottle of water, and a flashlight in the backpack, and placed it next to the bed. *Done.*

Winter turned and looked around the room and said, "This is exactly what I need. I can breathe here." She suddenly wished she had an easel and her paints. She couldn't remember how long it had been since she wished to paint. She turned back to the desk and traded her jeans for a pair of shorts, then pulled out some sandals to slide onto her feet. The yogis would simply have to put up with her naked toes.

Sliding glass doors opposite the front entrance were shrouded with a blackout curtain. Winter moved over to the doors and pulled the curtain aside. Sunshine filtered by trees streamed into the room. A tiny deck greeted her and beyond it was only jungle and a thick curtain of green. Bamboo, banana trees, and giant fronds made up the natural privacy screen. She could be standing out there with no clothes on and no one would see her. Winter snorted. Not that she would test her theory, but it was like something out of an exotic jungle movie. Her own private tree house. She half expected Tarzan to appear at her door. That thought coaxed another smile and a small chuckle.

A hard push and the heavy glass door slid open with a loud squeak. Winter stepped out onto the wooden deck and breathed deeply in the humid air. Pungent tropical smells floated around her. A hanging basket chair, two rough wooden chairs, and a bistro table fit nicely in the small area. She chose the hanging chair, and after first checking it for any small creatures nestled in the cushion, she eased into the basket and tested it with her weight. It held, so she began a gentle rocking with only the tip of her sandals touching on the wood deck.

The air was thick with moisture and she felt a layer bead up on her skin. As she pushed a stray strand of hair away from her face she allowed the heat to wash over her and relax her body even more. It felt like sitting in a steam bath, but she was surprised at finding it a pleasant sensation. Winter had never enjoyed the steam bath in the penthouse suite apartment. She had found it claustrophobic. This was soothing. She tucked one leg up under herself as she leaned back in the basket chair and used the other leg to keep the rocking motion going.

Exotic scents teased her from the jungle. She rested her head against the back of the chair and closed her eyes as she tried to identify the smells. *A musty, citric smell, with a hint of jasmine?* A screech made her jump and her eyes jerked open. A monkey sat on the railing staring at her. "Well, hello there," she said. He was brown and tan, and the top of his head looked like a bad toupee. He screeched even louder and jumped from the rail onto a banana tree. "Don't like me in your territory? Well, tough stuff," she called to him. The monkey bared his teeth and screeched again, then disappeared into the jungle. "Get used to it, Mr. Monkey. I'm here all week," she said, and then yawned and closed her eyes again. "I've seen much worse than your ugly mug so I'm not budging," she murmured as she rocked. The monkey must have left, or given up on scaring her, because the jungle sounds were reduced to a few insects and singing birds. Winter slipped into a deep sleep - the first real sleep she had in days.

***

Carson nodded at the flight attendant and touched Becky on the arm. "Wake up. We've landed," he said.

Becky jumped and gripped the arms of the chair as she stuttered, "What's happening?" Her head swiveled from Carson to the woman standing beside him. She sat straighter and said, "Oh, yeah. Okay, I'm good," she said as her eyes struggled to focus. "Uh, honey, could you fetch my bags?"

"Becky, I've got your bags," Carson said as he gripped her makeup bag and purse in each hand and pushed them toward her. He shifted his weight and said, "The customs officials are waiting for us."

"Okay, okay, hold your horses, sweetie," Becky said as she patted her hair. She opened her makeup bag and applied her lipstick.

"Becky?" Carson said through clinched lips.

"I'm ready," she said as she snapped the cosmetics case closed. Becky peered out of the plane's window, then swiveled toward Carson and tugged her short skirt down over her round hips. "Where are we?" she asked, then grinned and said, "Hawaii?" The grin disappeared as she said, "Wait, customs? You said customs, didn't you? We don't need customs for Hawaii—*Do we?*"

Carson turned to the flight attendant and said, "This trip is a surprise for my wife. Could you please tell them we are ready?"

The woman nodded at him and signaled for the two uniformed customs officials to join them. A large man and short rotund woman dressed in navy blue slacks and blue, short sleeve shirts moved forward. The woman held a clipboard and both wore large, toothy grins as the man said, "Welcome to Honduras. May I see your passports, please?"

"Honduras?" Becky's voice rose shrilly and she said, "Where the hell is Honduras?" Both officials raised their eyebrows but kept the grin plastered across their faces.

Carson glared at Becky and shook his head. He handed the male officer their two passports and some forms he had filled out while Becky slept. The man studied the passports and papers, and then he handed them to his co-worker. She began reading from them and writing on her form. "This trip is a surprise for my wife," Carson repeated to the officials. They each nodded, but the female didn't look up from her clipboard. Becky's eyes narrowed to slits and her mouth hung slightly open as she studied the group. Carson sensed trouble and turned to her and squeezed her arm as he said, "Honey, I'll tell you all about our adventure shortly, but right now let's let these folks do their job."

"Okay," She said as she jerked her arm away and turned to look out the window. Her lower lip stuck out in a pout. The first-time Carson saw that expression he thought it was sexy. Now she simply looked petulant.

"Okay, sir. Everything looks like it is in order and thank you for filling out the paperwork ahead of time. Now, if you will please sign these forms you can be on your way to enjoy our country." He reached over and placed a stamp on each passport and returned them to Carson. He nodded to his co-worker and she handed the clipboard to Carson, also.

"Here and here, sir, and your wife needs to sign the form right below that one." She pointed to four x's on the document as she spoke. Carson signed the document and then handed it to Becky. She scribbled her signatures but didn't look at any of them as she shoved the clipboard back to Carson. Carson took it and handed it back to the female customs agent with a shrug as he said, "Thank you." The two officers nodded, smiled, and left the plane.

Carson stood and held out a hand to Becky. She accepted his help, picked up her purse and bag, and then walked ahead of him toward the front of the plane. Carson followed, but before exiting he slipped the flight attendant two crisp one hundred-dollar bills. "For your service," he said.

"Thank you, sir." She pocketed the bills. With her looks, and the clientele the plane service received, his gratuity was in line, or even paltry.

At the bottom of the stairs an attendant was waiting for them. This one was dressed in a crisp white uniform with navy blue trim. "Good afternoon, Mr. and Mrs. Tudor. The vehicle you requested is parked by the flight building. Here are your keys and your luggage is in the car," he said as he handed Carson the keys and gestured toward a metal building. "If you will follow me, please," he said as he started toward the building. They followed him into the office and through the lobby. As they exited the building a dark green Humvee was parked in front and the engine was already running. "We've got the air conditioning going for you and the GPS is set to your hotel," he said as he handed them each a cold bottle of water. "This is for your drive."

"Thank you," Carson said and handed the man a fifty-dollar bill. This kind of service was expensive, but Carson loved the special treatment. He watched as the man pocketed the bill, then helped Becky around the vehicle and into the passenger side, then he returned to open the door for Carson.

"Thank you, sir. Have a wonderful vacation."

***

"I still don't understand why you chose South America for our get-away, but this is a nice hotel," Becky said. She stood by the window. The pool below was a huge S shape and was surrounded by palm trees and tiki bars.

Carson sighed. Somewhere on the ride over the pouty lip had been replaced with bubbly, non-stop speech and questions. He wasn't sure which was worse. "*Nice?* You could say that since it's a five-star resort and we are in the penthouse suite," Carson mumbled.

Becky turned toward him and kicked off her heels and asked, "Why did you tell them we are only going to be here one night?" Her eyes narrowed and she continued with, "This doesn't have something to do with Winter, does it?"

"Why on earth would you ask that?" Carson asked as his face darkened. "You know I want nothing to do with *her*. You *do* remember the accusations she is making against me - and her love of my money!" He turned his back to Becky and allowed his shoulders to slump.

Becky crossed the room and touched him on the arm as she said, "I'm sorry, baby. I know how much she hurt you."

"You have no idea how much that kind of betrayal hurts. I thought you understood," he said as he dropped his head.

"I'm sorry, really I am. I don't know what gets into me. Sometimes I just get jealous is all. Hearing you say we are only staying one night, and choosing South America and all, uuuummmm, it just was a little odd, that's all," she said.

"The one night is another part of the surprise. We are heading to Isla Grande tomorrow!" He looked up and grinned.

"Isla Grande?" Becky frowned and asked, "Where is that?"

"It's an island just off the northern coast of Honduras. It's not far, just a ferry ride away," he said as he moved to the table by the window where an iced bottle of champagne and two glasses sat. He poured some of the bubbly, amber liquid into the glasses. *Nice touch*, he thought. He had ordered it while Becky was in the ladies' room when they were still in the lobby. "I understand that it's a beautiful island and still fairly untouched: white sandy beaches, wild jungles, and friendly people."

"An island?" Becky asked as she clapped her hands and said, "What fun!"

"It will be fun." Carson set the bottle of champagne down, then moved over and took her in his arms. He kissed her neck and then whispered, "How about a little fun right now and then we can go down for a delicious dinner, Mrs. Tudor."

Becky shivered and giggled. "Oh, Carson," she said as she turned and led the way to the king size bed. "I still can't get used to that name, Tudor, but, I could get used to the 'Mrs.' part," she said, then winked at him and wiggled her generous hips. "You really know how to treat a girl. Follow me, and I'll show you my gratitude."

Chapter 5

Winter jerked her head up and jumped from the wicker swing chair. She stood rigid with her knees bent and her calves tight as she swiveled her head back and forth. She was poised to bolt from the patio deck, but thick jungle assaulted her on all sides cutting off her escape. "Wha? Where?" she mumbled. A loud knocking drew her attention to the front of the bungalow. Awareness washed over her. "Yoga retreat," she mumbled, then rubbed her eyes and whispered, "and you're safe." Her legs relaxed as well as her stance. The knocking became more insistent, so she headed toward the sound and pulled the door of the bungalow open. Oklahoma was standing in the entryway with a big grin plastered across her face. Winter said in a tight voice, "Yes?"

The woman was dressed in another flowing sundress. This one was black with bright yellow flowers plastered all over it, but the same huge straw hat was perched on her dark red tresses. "Wine time! Aren't you coming to dinner, hon?" she asked, then she frowned and took a step back as she said, "Whoa. Are you okay, sweetie? You are sweating like crazy. Are ya sick?"

Winter squinted at her and asked, "What time is it?"

"6:10. Dinner started ten minutes ago and I was worried about you," Oklahoma said as her eyes broke contact and drifted up to Winter's hair. The redheads smile faded into a straight line but the crinkles around her eyes increased. *She's trying not to burst out laughing*, Winter thought.

Winter reached up and tried to smooth her hair, but it was in an impossibly tangled mass. She dropped her hands and shrugged as she said, "I'm fine, but I must have fallen asleep. Thanks for the heads up. I'll be over in a few minutes." She stretched and yawned. "Just let me throw some water on my face."

"Okay, honey, I'll get them to hold you a plate." Oklahoma turned to leave, but then turned back and said, "Y'all might want to put on something a little fresher, too. It'll make ya feel better." She grinned broadly and waved her hand as she turned and swished off toward the main structure.

Winter took a quick shower, tamed her wet hair into a ponytail, and then threw on some clean shorts and a t-shirt before she headed to the dining hall. Once inside the main building she looked around the tables. About a dozen guests, mostly women, sat in small clumps around the room. A hush settled over the room as Winter searched for the redhead. *There.* Oklahoma, minus the giant hat, was sitting alone at a table for six on the opposite side of the dining hall. She waved and pointed at an empty chair and a plate filled with food, a goblet of ice water, and a glass of white wine. Winter sighed and crossed the room. Conversations started up again as she slid onto the empty chair. "I took the liberty of getting you some wine. My treat, sweetie," Oklahoma said.

"Thanks." Winter stared at the food. *Okay, it looks wonderful*, she thought as she realized she was famished. *Salad and fruit. Perfect choice in this heat.* She dug in and ate silently as she listened to the woman talk. *And talk. And talk.* Oklahoma was an open book and her life sounded almost as messy as Winter's. It was like listening to a soap opera. As the wine disappeared from Winter's glass, not only did the redhead's voice become more soothing, the story became more compelling.

"So, that's me in a nutshell. I'm a walking cliché. I was married to the same boring guy for 41 years. High school sweethearts. Kicked his sorry ass out when I caught him in the back seat of his car with the waitress from the local watering hole." Her green eyes flashed with anger as she said, "Like I wouldn't catch the jerk. Small town, and all that. Only one Honky-Tonk for drinking and cheating. My

Elbert never was the sharpest tool in the shed. All those nights he came home smelling like stale beer and cigarettes. Asshole wanted to be caught." She snorted and leaned forward as she said, "I think he was proud of being able to nail the flippin young twit and wanted to share it with me-- his best friend." She snorted and drained her glass before signaling to the waitress. "We've been best friends for so long that I think the crazy old coot was busting to brag to me. We're both 59 years old and he's nailing a twenty something blonde," she said as she sniffed and dabbed at her eyes with her napkin. "Trouble is that I still love that sorry old son of a gun."

"Hmmmmm," Winter replied as she thought, *does this woman ever take a breath?* But her cheeks reddened as she realized she was enjoying hearing about someone else's dirty laundry for a change. The waitress appeared and cleared their dishes. Winter smiled at the young woman and said, "You work the front desk and the dining room?"

The girl grinned and said, "My mom owns the place and Jose is my brother. We are a family owned and operated business." Pride sparked in her dark eyes and rang clear in her words.

"Good for you," Winter said and then nodded at their empty wine glasses. "How about bringing us a bottle of red and this time it's my treat."

Oklahoma nodded and winked at Winter and said, "Thanks, darlin, I think that might be just what the doctor ordered for both of us."

Winter noticed her companion had barely touched her food. A bubble of sympathy rose in her chest. *Not good*, she thought. She did not want to make personal connections. *Most inconvenient. Not here and not now.* The retreat was for hiding and healing and maybe some uncomplicated laughs. It was not intended for getting involved in someone else's life or making friends.

The redhead gazed at her empty wine glass for a moment. Silence hung thick in the air. She looked up and studied Winter as her eyes narrowed and then she said, "Okay, give. What brings you to this place? I was trying to get somewhere as far away from Oklahoma and my own personal Country and Western song as I could," she said, then she turned to look out of the window at the lush vegetation, "and I think I did," she murmured.

The young waitress brought the new bottle of wine and they smiled at her but remained silent until she left. The redhead picked up the new bottle and poured them both a full glass, and then took a long sip. "This is good," she said as she smacked her lips. "But, tell me about you, what's your story?"

Winter looked at her and said in a low voice, "I think you know who I am. I saw it in your eyes when we checked in."

"Fair enough. I *do* happen to read the tabloids and watch the news," she said, then leaned forward and whispered, "but honey, not too many folks from the states *don't* know who you are, and that said, I still don't know the real *you,* and what you're doing here." She leaned back in her chair and said, "After all, the news doesn't always tell the full story, does it?"

A quick look around the room. Most of the occupants kept glancing their way as they carried on their own low conversations. Winter felt her face burn and poured her glass full as well as she said, "Okay, that's true. But, the question is, where do you stand? Most people have assumed I'm a gold digger who made up a lot of my testimony simply to get more out of the settlement. Even my best friend thinks that." Winter said as she thought, *I must quit thinking of this woman as 'Oklahoma.' What was her name? Oh, yeah, Riley something...*

Riley leaned forward and said, "Then she's not much of a best friend." Her green eyes flashed and narrowed. "Besides, I'm not most people. I'm pretty observant, even when I don't want to see something, like with my jackass of a husband cheating." She touched Winter's wrist, but Winter eased it away and clasped her wine glass in both hands. The glass shook a little, so Winter set it on the table and circled the base with her hands. Riley raised an eyebrow and said in a voice that someone would use with a small child, "Like that, honey," as she nodded toward Winter's hands.

Winter felt her cheeks burn even hotter and she raised her glass and took a gulp of wine as Riley continued, "I saw the beaten down look in your eyes and the way you answered your door. All puffed up and defensive. Angry, even. I've seen that same demeanor in abused and cornered strays I take in at the ranch. All God's creatures can only take so much before it shows."

Winter remained quiet, but turned to the window as she fought the stinging behind her eyes. She bit her lip. Riley's words flowed across the table and washed over her. Winter wished she would stop talking before the stupid flood gates opened, but the woman kept going and said almost in a whisper, "I also know what it's like to be fooled and betrayed by the man you love." Winter didn't trust herself to speak, so she took another sip of wine. Riley sat up straight and said, "Not only that, you picked a primitive, restful place instead of a five-star hotel where you could be pampered. I don't know of any gold diggers who would do that. But, enough about that, we won't speak of it again unless you want to say something."

"Thanks," Winter whispered as her voice cracked. She downed the rest of her wine in one swallow. She looked back at Riley and said, "I can't believe they serve wine here, but I am sure glad they do. It's getting to look more like *Serenity* by the minute." Her lips tugged up in a hint of a smile.

"That's my girl!" Riley said with a grin. Then she said, "Haven't you heard? Wine is the new health kick." She took a sip and smacked her lips again before she added, "It's something I always knew. For a backwoods girl, I was ahead of my time!" She gave Winter an elaborate wink.

They both laughed and heads swiveled in their direction. It felt good to laugh. *Really good.* Winter held her glass up and they clinked a silent toast.

Riley said, "Look, most of these ladies are leaving in the morning, and I checked, they only have four booked in our group tomorrow, so relax. I've got your back, sweetie, besides, the few women that are left won't dare say anything to your face. They are much too polite for confrontation." She leaned forward and whispered, "They are more geared for back-stabbing with those sharp little tongues of theirs."

Winter chuckled and felt the muscles in her shoulders soften. The best part of being here was even with some people knowing her sordid story, at least Carson was a world away under house arrest and she wouldn't have to see his face until the next trial. She felt a chill and glanced at the overhead fans, then shrugged. Maybe Carson would drop dead of a heart attack by then, or one of his underworld enemies would silence *him* for a change. *Anything could happen.* She lifted her newly filled wineglass and touched it to Riley's as she said, "Here's to that and thank you, Riley. I've got your back as well!"

Chapter 6

"Aiden!"

The shout hit his eardrum like a slap. Aiden Saunders raised his head a few inches but his cheek stuck to the bar. "What?" he mumbled as he tried to identify the source of irritation. He kept his eyes tightly shut as his mind tried to slip back into the sweet oblivion he felt before the interruption.

"Aiden…up! It's past closin, and you need to git gone," the voice said.

Right. Okay, he thought. He knew where he was and he knew that voice. Not home, but he was at his home away from home. Aiden's cheek broke free from the sticky bar and he sat erect. He felt himself sway from side to side on the rickety bar stool. A chuckle erupted as he opened his eyes. He had a vision of being a boat tied to the dock listing from side to side. "Whoa, these waters are rough," he said with a laugh.

"You're not making sense, mister. And you're not funny *at all*," she said.

His cheek felt strange where it had connected to the bar, so he scratched it and a couple of peanut shells fell off. He grimaced and said, "Not so loud. Come on, momma." His green eyes went from half lidded to wide open as he tried to focus on the woman behind the bar. Her hands were spread out on her wide hips and her eyes narrowed to slits as she pulled a bar towel from her shoulder and flicked it at him.

"Don call me momma. I ain't nobody's momma," she said as she placed both hands on the bar, leaned toward him and spat out, "especially not yours! Gad, mon, you are disgusting." She leaned even closer until her face was inches from him and sniffed, then wrinkled her nose and said, "You smell like something dat crawled out of tha swamps." She pulled back and shook her head as her beaded dreadlocks rattled. She made a "tich, tich, tich" sound as she frowned. A pause, and then she cocked her head to one side and said, "Can you drive? Should I call Walter?"

"I'm fine, sweetheart, and I don't need a cabbie," he said.

Her eyes narrowed and she leaned on the bar as she said, "I'm not your sweetheart either, you *know* my name." Her eyes sparked, but then they softened and she said, "You sure you can make it home? You don look so fine to me." She clucked her tongue and said, "What a waste of such a perfect specimen of a man. You a 6-foot bag of lean muscle and you throw away what the good Lord done give you!"

"Love you too, Yolanda," he said as he got up, then stood swaying for a moment before he grabbed the edge of the bar. "See, I do know your name," he said and blew her a kiss. The woman frowned and crossed her arms over her ample chest. It was as if she was corralling two giant pillows, it was an impossible task. She stood in the middle of the bar area directly below a sign, "Peg Leg Pete and Bluebeard Welcome You!" The sign covered the length of the long bar and had a pirate with a wooden leg on one end and a pirate with a thick black beard and eyepatch on the other side. Once the two pirates were in focus, Aiden turned and headed for the front door.

He loved *Big Momma*. He shouldn't call her that to her face, though, she hated the nickname, but it was so much more fitting than her real name. She made him feel like he was in Jamaica instead of Isla Grande, Honduras. It made him want to order little umbrella drinks in coconuts and go barefoot in the sand. When she wasn't scolding, or shouting at him, her voice was as soothing as a warm bath, but she was usually pretty pissed at him, so not too many warm bath moments.

Aiden waved one hand at the door as he exited the bar and shuffled down the wooden steps to his open-air jeep. The sky was still dark, but there were streaks of pink on the horizon. He paused and took a deep breath. The air tasted of salt and the street was quiet and deserted. Even here, in the busiest area of the island, there was no one around. Still dark but no longer night. *Peaceful.*

The West End of the island was the perfect party spot. There was plenty of bars and restaurants that stayed open until the wee hours. It was also very walkable, but Aiden always ended up back at Peg Leg Pete's, so that's where he would start his night and leave his jeep.

Aiden stood on the bottom step and took another deep breath as the salty air stung his nostrils. He closed his eyes. Not a sound coming from the other establishments on both sides of the road. *Time to head home.* He spread his arms wide and then touched his nose with the index finger of his right hand, then left, and decided he was sober enough to drive. He opened his eyes. With the empty streets, who would he hurt but himself, anyway? He could care less if he did damage to himself --he might even welcome it. So, he shrugged and left the steps for his jeep. He chuckled again. The jeep was easy to spot, it was the only vehicle left in the parking lot.

Climbing into the driver's seat, Aiden fished the keys out of a pocket in his cargo shorts and started the jeep. Pulling the rearview mirror down to reflect his mocha colored face, he rubbed his hand over the dark stubble covering his cheeks. He turned the mirror back to its original position, bent to take a whiff of his armpits, winced, and said, "Big Momma may have a point." He turned and looked over his shoulder as he backed out of the gravel lot and then turned and headed slowly down the road that lead out of town. No point in alerting the local police. *If any of them are still awake,* he thought as it occurred to him that he wanted to sleep it off in his own bed instead of a cot in a jail cell.

"What happened to San Diego's most eligible bachelor?" Aiden said aloud. He laughed and said, "Cancer. That's what happened. Stupid.

Friggin. Cancer."

At the edge of town, he reached under his seat and pulled out a bottle
of rum which he squeezed between his thighs as he sat up and yelled,
"Cancer is the great equalizer of man!" He snorted and sped up as a
light went on in one of the houses. No use waking the world up. He
kinda liked the feeling that he was the only one left on the planet.

As soon as he was free of the village all he could see was open
fields. No more houses to worry about. Aiden took a long swig from
the bottle of rum and then held it up toward the dark sky and sang,
"Welcome darkness my old friend." He increased his speed even
more and then leaned back against the hard seat, enjoying the
sensation of the wind whipping against his face as empty fields
became jungle and the trees whizzed by. "I've come to talk to you
again," he sang as more of the Simon and Garfunkel tune that rattled
through his foggy brain. *The Sounds of Silence. Beautiful song,* he
thought.

The road changed from asphalt to hard packed dirt but Aiden kept
his speed high. A tire hit a rut and the jeep jerked to the right and
swerved. "Whoa," Aiden shouted as rum splashed from his bottle
and spilled on his cargo shorts. "Shit!" he said. He slowed the jeep to
a stop, took another swig, then started back down the road at a
slower pace. "Can't waste it. Waste not, want not," he said, then
laughed aloud as he continued his journey home.

Chapter 7

"Wake up sleepy head," Carson said as he pulled the curtains open. The sun was just starting to peek over the horizon as red streaks slashed its path across the morning sky. Carson admired the view a moment, then turned toward the bed and said, "Time to wake up."

"Mmmmmm." The sound came from a jumbled pile of blankets.

"Come on, Becky," Carson said as he moved to the bed and sat by the blanketed lump. "I have a surprise for you."

"Not now, Carson. It's too early. Didn't I get enough of your 'surprises' last night?" The whining voice was muffled by blankets.

He laughed and patted what he thought might be her round bottom poking through the blanket as he said, "Not that kind of surprise, silly. I have a different surprise for you-- something really special."

The upper half of her face appeared from under the blanket. Tousled blond hair all but covered her half-lidded eyes. She gazed at the window and groaned. "What time is it? It's the middle of the night!" She tugged at the blanket, but then paused and asked, "What kind of surprise?" She looked at his hands, then up at his face as she raised an eyebrow and said, "There's a nice jewelry store in the lobby, but I don't see anything in your hands. Did you buy me something?"

"No jewelry—this is even better. You have to get dressed if you want to get it, though. I have to take you to it," he said.

"Dressed? But, Carson, it's so early and I haven't even had coffee, yet." The voice had turned back into a whine and the lips began to pout.

Carson reached over her to the bedside table, picked up a cup, and handed it to her and said, "See, here's your coffee. I got it just like you like it, with two Splenda's and cream. Now go get dressed and I'll take you to your surprise."

Becky took a big slurp of the coffee, then wiggled up on the bed and leaned against the headboard as she said, "What about breakfast?"

Pouty lips again. She is getting too old for that routine to still work. Carson leaned forward and eased the blankets off her as he said, "That's waiting for us with the surprise." He lifted her legs and placed them over the side of the bed as he said, "Come on, Becky, you have to get dressed so we aren't late."

"All right," she said and she got up. "This better be good, Carson. Getting me out at this ungodly hour, I'm just saying, this better be *really* good." She stomped into the bathroom and shoved the door closed.

"Oh, it's good all right, but you aren't going to like it very much," he mumbled to the closed bathroom door. Carson collected the rest of her clothes and tucked them into the suitcases. He called downstairs and asked for the bellhop to collect their bags and put them in the Humvee. He had paid the hotel bill the night before. He hadn't gotten much sleep, but he had everything ready. He smiled as he thought about all his preparations. Sometimes the groundwork was more enjoyable than the event, but he suspected that was not going to be the case in this instance. He would think of this as a test run for his 'surprise' for Winter.

As soon as Becky came out of the bathroom she noticed the packed bags. "Are we leaving, already? I know you said one night, but I like this hotel," she said.

"You ask too many questions. You will spoil the surprise!" He kissed her on her forehead and turned her around with a little push and said, "Now go get your cosmetics. The bellhop is on his way."

"Okay, okay. I'm coming. Geeze, what's the hurry, anyway?" she said as she went back into the bathroom and packed her things.

Carson met the bellhop at the door, handed off their luggage, along with the key to the Humvee and a generous tip. "Leave the keys in the ignition. We'll be down shortly." As he shut the door behind the bellhop, he turned and called to Becky, "Ready?"

"Almost," she said.

He glanced at his watch, frowned, then pulled out a twenty-dollar bill and left it on the dresser for the maid. He saw her in the hallway earlier and enjoyed watching her bend over her cart. When she had looked up, instead of a glare, he got a generous smile. Maybe he would stop by this hotel on his way back to the states. She might be worth an extra night's stay.

Becky bounced out of the bathroom and said, "All right, I'm ready!" He smiled and took her cosmetics bag as he steered her to the door.

The elevator ride to the lobby was blanketed by silence, except for Becky's constant yawning. Carson took them straight to the parking garage bypassing the lobby. Once they were in the garage, he guided Becky to their truck and helped her into the passenger side of the Humvee, then he got behind the wheel and backed out of the space. He left the parking garage and headed for the highway. He picked up speed immediately and whistled a tune as they sped along the road.

"You sure are cheerful for this time of the morning," Becky said as she shifted her weight and adjusted the seat belt, and after another big yawn she said, "and in a hurry."

"I *am* happy. I love mornings, not that you would know that, and I think it is going to be a glorious day," he said, and then glanced at her as he continued with, "I am also excited about your surprise and don't want us to be late."

"What do you have planned?" Becky asked as she gazed out of the window. His eyes traveled from the generous lips to her soft round breasts. He checked and thought, *Nope. No arousal. I am so over her.*

"If I told you, it wouldn't be a surprise, now would it?" He grinned. He was really enjoying this.

"I suppose not," she said. Becky scooted to the edge of her seat as they turned off the highway.

They entered a narrow road that ran through some rundown warehouses. The few residential houses that were visible in the early morning hour were small and they had a lot of junk piled up in the ill-kept yards. No one was in the yards, or on the rickety porches at this early hour, but a couple of mangy looking dogs were tethered at a few of the houses, and they barked when the Humvee drove by. *Slum burglar alarms,* he thought.

The area changed even more as they got closer to the waterfront. Tangled bushes and thick trees replaced the warehouses and very few houses could be spotted through the growth. Carson put on his turn signal and headed down a road that had a 'Park Entrance' sign posted at the corner. As they drove along what appeared to be a service road, the buildings completely disappeared and it became even more heavily forested. "Do you know where you are going?" Becky asked as she leaned forward even more and peered through the windshield. "How could this be a park? It looks pretty wild and remote." She turned toward him and her voice was low as she asked, "What kind of surprise is this? You know I don't like backwoods stuff and those houses back there were pretty sketchy."

"Oh, I know where we are going. I checked this out while you were sleeping last night. This is the perfect place for your surprise," he said. He stared straight ahead and concentrated on the road. A sudden stop and then Carson backed the car up. The car idled for a moment as he examined the woods. "There it is," he said as he turned down a road that was not much more than a trail. It was almost invisible between the moss covered trees.

The new road was deeply rutted and the Humvee rocked back and forth as limbs slapped against the sides of the truck. Becky gripped the door handle, swallowed hard, and said, "You found this last night? In the dark? I don't believe you." Her voice became shrill and tight as she said, "Oh, I'm sorry, but Carson, honey, where are we going?"

He turned to look at her briefly. She was clutching at the door handle and her face had gone white. He looked back at the road and a smile itched at the corners of his mouth as he said, "Almost there." He found himself feeling slightly aroused. *Bad timing.*

"I don't like this, Carson. I want to go back to the hotel," Becky said, and then in a very tiny voice she asked, "*Please?*" She scooted against the passenger door and her eyes seemed riveted to the front window. "Please, Carson," she whispered. He had to strain to hear her. He grinned. *This is exquisite.*

Carson remained silent as he felt a surge of pleasure rise in his chest. He wished he had thought of using his cell phone to record her pleas. To hear her begging repeatedly would be delicious, but he was very good at remembering details. He shivered with pleasure. Becky's fear was almost palatable. *Winter never displayed this much fear.*

The trees opened abruptly to a clearing. Carson pulled the truck to a stop and parked. The land in front of the Humvee sloped until it reached the water's edge. But it wasn't the ocean in front of them. It was a swamp. Black oily water, moss hanging from the trees, and tall wild grass growing on both sides of the clearing. Carson grinned. *Perfect setting.*

Becky's head swerved from side to side taking it all in, then she sighed, moved her hands into her lap, and gazed at them as if transfixed. Carson got out of the truck and moved around to the passenger side and opened her door. Becky kept her head down and whispered, "No. I don't want to get out of the car. I want to go back to the hotel."

He smiled and held his hand up to her as he said, "It's time for your surprise." When she didn't move, he grasped her hand and squeezed it as he said, "Come on, don't be a baby."

Becky squared her shoulders and let him help her from the truck. Together they walked to the water's edge hand in hand. Carson bent and kissed her deeply on the lips and then pulled back and looked at her. *She is so petite.* He hadn't noticed just how much taller he was than her until now. She was trembling beneath his touch. "Silly, girl," he said, then ran a finger down her check. "You are so beautiful." He cupped her chin and said, "This has been so fun, but time's up." A single tear ran down her cheek.

Carson turned her around until she was facing the other way, then he leaned in against her back. He eased his arms around her and ran his hands over her silk blouse until he inched them up and around her neck. He was completely aroused now, but no time, and besides, he had made sure she bathed thoroughly after last night. *I don't want to leave any of my little soldiers behind*, he thought. *Not that they would be discovered in this primitive country.*

He began to squeeze her tiny neck as she pulled away from him and tried to run, then he increased the pressure as she struggled against him until she finally hung limp. He let her slide to the ground and then he put his foot in the middle of her back and shoved. Becky rolled into the water and made a small splash when she hit the surface. "Surprise," Carson said as she floated face down away from the bank and into the middle of the stagnant pond. She hadn't fought very hard. *Her struggling felt like the flutter of a butterfly's wings. Not unexpected. She isn't a fighter like Winter,* he thought.

He noticed a crocodile on the opposite bank lift its head and watch as Becky's body bobbed a little when it reached the middle of the pond and stopped drifting. Her red silk blouse was bright against the dark, stagnate surface. *It looks like a puddle of blood,* he thought. When the crocodile started sliding into the water, Carson turned and headed for the Humvee. He laughed as he thought, *So, Becky, I told you there would be breakfast served with your surprise.*

Carson backed around until he could head nose first down the narrow road. As he drove down the trail he chuckled and thought, *I wonder if all that silk will give Mr. Croc a stomach ache?*

Once he reached the 'sketchy' neighborhood, he pulled into one of the abandoned warehouses. He jumped out of the Humvee and opened the trunk. He stared at Becky's luggage. He was tempted to keep one of her silk blouses. Becky had a penchant for expensive silk even if it was completely impractical in a tropical climate. Of course, to be fair, she didn't know they were heading for a tropical climate when she packed. The silk would feel wonderful against his bare skin when thinking of her 'surprise,' but he sighed, and logic took over, so he removed her passport and wallet, but left the rest. Pulling the luggage from the truck, he wiped the outside clean and tossed the bags to the side of the road. He might as well put a sign on them saying, 'take me.' He had reduced his own belongings to a duffle bag which would be easier to handle and help him to blend in.

He pulled out onto the main road and headed for the ferry that would take him to Isla Grande. He whistled as he drove. *If by some remote chance Becky's body is found and identified, whoever is in possession of her luggage will be blamed. After all, I was never here.* He laughed. Carson Alexander, III was safely ensconced in his hotel in San Francisco at the time of the murder.

When he was a couple of blocks from the ferry building he stopped and parked. The streets were thick with souvenir shops, but there wasn't a lot of street traffic this early in the morning. *Perfect.* Carson grabbed his duffle bag, stuffed Becky's wallet, and passport into it, and hopped out of the truck. He locked the Humvee, pocketed the keys, and started walking.

The closer he got to the ferry the more shops dotted the street. They were just opening their doors to get ready for the tourists boarding the morning ferry. Carson ducked into one of the shops and moved through the racks of clothing. He grabbed a t-shirt with an *Isla Grande, Honduras* logo, a pair of cargo shorts, and a baseball cap with 'beachcomber' embroidered across the brim. After he paid for his purchases he asked the clerk if there was somewhere he could change. The young man glanced curiously at the nice polo shirt and shorts he was wearing, but pointed to a dressing room behind the counter. As he moved behind him, Carson could see the clerk shake his head. He had to admit, he agreed with the kid, but dressing down was necessary.

Carson changed into the tourist gear and tucked his resort clothing into his duffle bag. As he left the store he pulled the baseball cap out of his back pocket and pulled it snuggly on his head as he headed for the dock. Not too many people were waiting for the ferry this early, so he boarded quickly. He chose a seat in the back of the boat and stretched out his long legs. He grinned. This day was shaping up nicely.

The boat left the dock and picked up speed as the sun climbed higher in the sky. The sea air felt cool and his lips stung with salt. A feeling rumbled in his stomach. *Hunger?* A little, maybe, but he knew he hungered for more than his breakfast. Becky's 'surprise' had made him even more anxious to find Winter. He closed his eyes and brought the sound of Becky's pleas into his mind. He moaned, then caught himself and opened his eyes. A family had settled close to him, but they got up and moved. Just as well, but he better be more careful. No sense bringing attention to himself. Just another tourist taking in the beauty of the island. He raised his arms and linked his hands behind his head as he enjoyed the vast view of the ocean. *Lovely.*

Chapter 8

Winter bounded down the bungalow steps and turned toward the path for the yoga pagoda. "Why didn't you remember to set your alarm, you idiot?" she grumbled aloud as she quickened her step. *Oh, yeah,* she thought as her pounding head reminded her of the tumble into bed after finishing off a second bottle of wine with Riley.

The jungle path to the pagoda was advertised as 'a serene walk' to 'begin your transformation to a tranquil state.' "Tranquil state, my ass," Winter mumbled as she tripped on the root of a tree, caught herself, and kept moving. Sweat was already forming on her back and underarms. She was taking the path in a sprint instead of the leisurely walk the twists and turns demanded, and while wearing flip flops.

She and Riley had decided to check the path out the night before, although in the dark, and with only their cell phone flashlight apps, they had moved much more slowly. Once they reached the pagoda, they danced in the dark to the Pharrell Williams song, "Happy," blasting from Winter's iPhone, then collapsed into a fit of giggles. It made Winter feel like a schoolgirl. After the dance, they sat cross legged on the floor and finished off the rest of the 2nd bottle of wine. Talk about a tranquil state, they had certainly reached it.

Winter had not had that much wine since before she met Carson. With him, she kept herself in control and on guard. It was glorious to let go and then sleep again unafraid. She needed this. Her survival depended on it. She had to climb out of the dark hole Carson dug for her.

As she broke free of the jungle, Winter stopped short. It looked very different in the early morning light. The pagoda's silhouette appeared to hover in space as the sun peeked over the surface of the vast ocean beyond it. The sky was clear and the ocean was a shade of turquoise Winter had only seen in her imagination. Cliffs abruptly dropped down to the sea, and wild waves crashed against jagged rocks at the bottom of the cliffs as they sent white spray flying into the air. Her artist eye was mesmerized as she thought, *It is truly breathtaking.*

The pagoda itself was a piece of native art; a raised open-air room, with a thatched roof that was held up by roughhewn posts the size of small trees. It was perched on the very edge of a cliff. It was much like the rooftop infinity pool at Winter's apartment building, only this view was of limitless water, instead of a congested city landscape.

They could barely see the ocean in the dim light the night before and it was dumb luck they hadn't fallen over the edge of the cliff. The drop to the sea was dramatic, and since no one heard their music and giggles, they wouldn't have heard their cries for help. Winter strolled toward the structure. The pagoda must be why the tiny resort got such a high rating. *I could stay here forever*, Winter thought.

The group was small, even smaller than they had thought it would be. There was only the yogi and two other ladies besides Riley. They already had their mats spread in their chosen spots and were seated cross legged on them. All except Riley were sitting motionless and quiet, but she was waving frantically at Winter from the back row. Did she think Winter couldn't see her in a group of four? She was wearing bright orange and yellow leotards and a matching yoga tank top, so she was hard to miss. She patted the empty mat to her left and mouthed, "Got you a mat."

Winter smiled and nodded at the yogi as she climbed the steps to the open-air room. The woman smiled back, but the other two other ladies stared at her with flat expressions. They were two of the whispers from dinner. All were dressed in appropriate yoga pants and tops. Winter glanced at her own black compression shorts and dark green T-shirt and wanted to shrink, but then she took a breath and stood her full 5'9" height. She kicked off her flip flops, strolled into the pagoda, and when she reached the mat beside her new-found friend, she stretched and dropped on it without a glance at the women. *No more hiding.* At least not from judging looks. Riley whispered, "It's a lot different sober, *right?*" A wink followed the statement. Winter struggled to keep the belly laugh she felt bubbling up to only a smile. Oklahoma sure liked to wink and Winter was beginning to appreciate her humor.

Winter's mouth was dry and her head ached, but it was a small price to pay for the release their evening had brought. She looked at the ocean and appreciated its beauty, but she admitted, at least to herself, that she would kill for a cup of strong coffee right now instead of a yoga practice.

Winter turned her attention to the instructor and noticed a subdued smile and a twinkle in the woman's eye. Winter smiled back at her and felt more at ease. The yogi was fit with muscles and skin that defied her age. Behind her wind chimes moved in the morning breeze with a muted tune. Soothing meditation music floated from an iPad hooked to small battery powered speakers on one side of the yogi, and smoke wafted from a small round pot burning incense on the other side. *Ancient art meets modern technology.*

Winter closed her eyes and breathed in the smell of incense mixed with salt air as she tried to center herself on her mat. The ugly trial, the District Attorney's death, her best friend's indifference, and her ex-husband's snarling face melted away, as a feeling of contentment, if not peace, washed over her. Maybe there was hope. If so, this was the place to find it, *and* herself, again. Winter was ready to be Winter once more: not Carson's wife, not the material witness—just *Winter*, whoever that was now. She would never be the youthful, naïve person she was before she met Carson, but that was okay. She could not let him own real estate in her head, she would not let that happen. It was up to her, and her alone, who she became. She needed to take responsibility for who she was right now, today, before she could be at peace with herself.

She listened to the soothing music, felt the sea breeze wash over her skin, and felt lighter. A tiny shimmy radiated up from the platform, so Winter opened her eyes and looked around. Was that in her head, or real? Riley looked at Winter and mouthed, "What was that?"

It was real. The floor shook hard enough to make the wind chimes jingle and then it was still again. Winter lived in California for enough years that she knew exactly what the second jolt was. She jumped from her mat and shouted, "Earthquake!" Riley, being from Oklahoma, must have had the same realization, because the look on her face spoke volumes. They both bolted from the pagoda.

As they made it down the steps the earth began to shake and roll in earnest. This was not like the quakes Winter had experienced previously. They lasted only a few minutes then tapered off, or stopped abruptly, but this one felt like it was increasing in intensity instead of ending. Her stomach lurched as she turned back toward the pagoda. The yogi and the two women were still on their mats. "Get out of there, now!" Winter screamed. But then the entire thatched roof fell and swallowed them whole.

Riley grabbed her hand as they were both knocked backwards to the ground. Winter tried to rise, but she had no sense of balance, so she fell back onto the ground. Her vision blurred as the tremors shook her like a rag doll. Then everything stopped moving. For the first time since her arrival she was encased in utter silence. No jungle noises: no monkeys screeching, no birds cawing, nothing. *Total silence.*

Winter eased onto her hands and knees, then pushed herself up to stand on trembling legs. She turned to help Riley, but the redhead had already bounded up and said, "Oh, my sweet Lord." The woman's eyes were wide open and her face a stark white against her dark red tresses. Winter turned and followed her gaze to the pagoda. Only one of the timbers still stood, but as she watched, it swayed, and then fell with a loud whoosh and flattened what was left of the roof.

Winter started to move toward the pagoda, but another tremor held her in place. This time a crack in the ground in front of them formed, and then widened within seconds. Riley grabbed her hand again and they shuffled backwards toward the jungle. The cliff shifted, then gave way as a deafening rumble announced the separation of earth.

When the tremors stopped again, sound erupted from the jungle. Loud screeching and squealing of protest from its inhabitants echoed in her ears. Winter stared out at the sea. An uninterrupted view. *No, that was wrong.* No cliff, no pagoda, no people. A gaping hole. She couldn't even move forward to see if there were any survivors. It was all gone. *Gone? How could that be?* The sounds from the jungle retreated as a loud ringing possessed her ears. She tried to process what just happened, but her brain felt like it was wrapped in cotton.

Something was tugging at her arm, so she turned. Riley was pulling at her elbow and Winter tried to focus on her words, "Let's go Winter, we can't do anything for them now. We. Need. To. GO. *NOW!*"

"*What?*" Winter asked. Her eyes turned back to the blank space and the open expanse of turquoise sea. "What about them?" she mumbled as Riley continued pulling at her arm and pointing toward the jungle path.

"They're gone. We can't do anything right now to help them," Riley said as she tugged.

"Yeah, okay, right," Winter said. She turned and looked once more at the spot where the pagoda had sat. Even if the women had survived, she couldn't get to them. She could not even get close enough to the edge to see the bottom of the cliff. There was a ragged hole where the pagoda had stood. As she watched, another portion of the exposed dirt slid away as the hole widened. If she tried to climb down, her weight would make more of it give way and she would end up on top of them. The best thing she could do was to go for help and hope for the best. *Riley was right.* She turned and followed the fast-moving streak of orange and yellow. One more glance over her shoulder. *Still gone.* Winter followed Riley into the jungle.

***

The back of the ferry boat where Carson sat emptied as soon as they approached the island. Apparently, everyone wanted in the front of the boat to watch it dock. *What a bunch of empty headed morons.* It was surprising the whole boat didn't capsize with the weight of idiots. Carson shook his head and pulled out his mobile phone. *Tying ropes to a dock, just fascinating*, he thought as he opened the tracking app on his phone. The red dot blinked. He smiled at the beacon. "Hello, Winter," he mumbled. "Haven't found that pin on your backpack yet, I see?"

The dot had gotten him through the long, boring day before. While Becky had whined, the little red dot had moved from the island airport to the spot on the map right where he expected it, and it had stayed there throughout the night. Watching that dot brought him such joy. Becky had kept at him about being on his phone, but that had made it only more delicious. *No problem with that now*, he thought as he tucked the phone into his pocket. He had tossed the last tie with Becky, her passport and wallet, off the ferry half way through the ride. *Gone, gone, gone.* He tightened and flexed his long fingers as he felt the boat slow and start its turn to line up with the dock. There was no longer anything or anyone standing between him and his wife. "To have and to hold until death do us part," he whispered as he pictured her face at their reunion.

The Serenity Yoga Retreat. He snorted. As soon as he learned of her destination, he vetted the place on the web. It was an artsy, hippie-type dump, located deep in the jungle instead of a nice five-star resort in town. They probably all walked around in breathable cotton or spandex and repeated peace crap to each other all day. *Namaste. What a load of crap.* All the time he had spent educating her on the finer things was completely wasted. She was slipping back into her lower-class habits after only a brief time without him. *What a waste.* Next, she would be sleeping with women. Now that he wouldn't mind seeing, but only if he could join in. He patted the bulge of his phone in the pocket of his cargo shorts. Hideous fashion, but he had to admit, so many pockets did prove useful. Phone in one, knife in one, small gun in another. He might have to reconsider his disdain for the style.

The ferry boat pulled up to the dock and Carson waited patiently as they tied it off and the hoard of tourists exited. *Just like the Walking Dead and a zombie apocalypse.* He piled in with the rest of the tourists and managed to get into the center of the group as they followed the board walk into the village. He was just another day tripper off to see the sights. He had even begun to grow a beard, although he detested beards, and he didn't know how long he could put up with it. You could not eat and keep them clean. It was simply impossible. Beards were truly disgusting, but he needed to lower the possibility he would be recognized and become part of the general rabble.

The village was just beginning to wake up and other than their group of tourists from the ferry, there was very little activity. A food truck vender on the far side of the main road propped up an awning on his truck and the smell of something frying wafted out and floated over their group. Carson stopped walking. The smell of grease and bacon was intoxicating. He shivered. Maybe he was becoming who his disguise portrayed. "Cesar's Taco and Burrito Wagon," the sign boasted and just below the bold writing in smaller hand painted print, "breakfast burritos served until 10:30AM." He imagined all the possible germs floating around in the greasy kitchen, but then he shrugged and started across the street toward the truck. *When in Rome*, he thought. He reached the middle of the road and the earth trembled. Carson froze. The earth began to shake so hard it felt as if he was on a roller coaster.

Some of the people from the ferry ran into a dilapidated building behind the Taco truck, but before Carson could move, he lost his footing and fell to his knees in the middle of the road. The awning on the truck slammed down with a loud bang and flames began eating the bright red and white striped awning cloth. The Taco sign banner across the front of the truck collapsed in a heap on the street. The porch to the building behind the food truck fell with a loud whoosh and a cloud of dust rose, then pushed forward as it blocked his field of vision. Carson fell the rest of the way to the ground and curled into a fetal ball as he wrapped his arms across his face and head.

When the earth stopped moving Carson uncurled and rose to a sitting position. The dust had settled, but he was seized by a coughing fit, so he pulled out a bandana from his pocket and wiped his face and eyes. He tied the cloth around the lower half of his face and surveyed the street. *Total chaos.* Moans and screams surrounding him as people called for help. Then it started again. Carson ducked his head and covered it with his arms as he felt the earth shake and roll. When it finally stopped moving he raised his head and looked around.

Buildings were now piles of rubble, or at the very least had broken windows. Tourist supplies spilled from the doors of the shops and spread over on the sidewalks and street. Carson watched a half mannequin dressed in a bright pink bikini roll to a stop in front of him. The taco truck was engulfed in flames as the owner stood back and watched it burn. He had both hands on his head as he yelled, "My truck, my truck," over and over.

Carson pushed himself up and stood. His coughing stopped, but he wiped tears of irritation from his eyes. *What the hell?* He thought as he took it all in. *An earthquake?* He shook his head and turned slowly in a circle as he thought, *Yep. The mother of all earthquakes and I'm stuck here in this third world piss hole? Fantastic. Just fantastic. Thanks for this, too, Winter.*

The hotel behind him lay in shambles, as well as most of the buildings surrounding it. Carson eyed the burning food truck and thought about the gas tanks under the stove, so he shouldered his duffle bag and walked silently in the opposite direction toward the collapsed hotel. He stopped when he was far enough away and jerked his phone from his pocket. The red dot still pulsed across the map but within seconds it went blank. *No bars.* "Shit," he mumbled. The infrastructure had also collapsed. No doubt it would stay that way in this primitive country.

A young man standing in front of a pile of rocks and debris where the hotel once stood was looking at his phone, but then he glanced up at him and yelled, "We've lost cell service," in a German accent. The twenty-something young man was covered in white dust and a look of shock, or bewilderment, froze his features like Botox. He walked toward Carson as he pleaded, "Can you help? My brother is hurt and trapped."

Carson stared at him and said nothing. He was about to walk away when he noticed the kid was wearing a well-equipped backpack. An extra-large water bottle was tucked firmly into a side pocket and camping gear was strapped on the back of the fat pack that probably contained rations. Carson nodded and said, "Sure, lead the way." The young man started off for the side of the collapsed hotel and Carson followed.

When they reached the side of the downed hotel a man Carson assumed was his brother lay trapped under a pile of debris. *He is toast,* Carson thought. Barely breathing with blood trickling from his nose and mouth, the man's eyes said he was already dead. His brother knelt beside him and the injured man tried to speak, but it came out as a garbled whisper with tiny blood bubbles popping out around his lips.

Carson glanced around. The street, which was more of an alley than a main road, was empty. *Nice of him to choose such an isolated area to get squashed.* Big brother struggled to remove his heavy pack as he spoke over his shoulder, "I think together we can lift this beam." There was a huge piece timber from the roof across the man's chest and the lower half of his body was covered in broken cinder blocks.

Carson set down his duffle bag and bent to lift a heavy rock off the man's torso, but instead of tossing it aside, he slammed it into the kneeling brother's head. The young man fell across his injured brother who emitted a low moan. Carson glanced around again. *Still alone.* He bent and grabbed the well-equipped backpack and then stood as he tugged it on. Another glance at the debris covered man. He had stopped breathing and his brother was still out cold. The gash in his short cropped blond hair oozed red. Carson tied his duffle bag around his waist and began to jog in the direction of the red dot. The brothers were forgotten before he reached the main road.

Chapter 9

"Ouch," Winter said as she pushed the tree branch out of the way. It struck her shoulder as she kept her eyes on the path, but when she looked up to watch for limbs, a vine slapped at her bare legs. "Damn," she muttered. She forced herself into a fast-paced walk instead of trying to run. Breathing was difficult and she found it hard not to pant. She finally understood what her Southwestern friends meant when they said, "But, it's a dry heat," when arguing that their desert climate was easier to tolerate.

The dirt path beneath her feet was quiet, too quiet. The electric shock she felt while sitting in the pagoda remained only a memory, but every strange sound or sensation made her look at her feet. Winter kept expecting the earth to shake and the ground to open again at any moment. The sight of the disappearing pagoda kept playing over and over in her head. It was like a YouTube clip with a horrible image flashing on her screen that she couldn't seem to pull her eyes from. She couldn't believe it had really happened and kept hoping to wake up from this nightmare.

Winter wasn't sure why she was in such a hurry, but the need to escape was strong, as it bubbled up from somewhere deep in her soul. It felt like a giant hand on her back giving her a shove. Riley was still in front, but she kept losing sight of her. The older woman moved fast despite her flip-flops. Neither of them had spoken since they left the clearing. They both seemed to be running away from what they had experienced. To talk and breathe as they scurried through the jungle was impossible and Winter had no intention of stopping until they reached the resort, so discussions of the event could wait.

Winter caught up to Riley in time to watch her jump over a downed tree, so Winter followed her lead and scrambled over. It was the second tree to block the path but luckily the trees were small and easy to maneuver over or around. So far there wasn't a lot of damage in the rain forest.

Maybe the pagoda had been built on an unstable cliff, so it was easier for the ground to give way and send it tumbling into the sea. Even as the thought played through Winter's head she realized it didn't make sense. The structure had looked old, so it had been there long enough to withstand many earthquakes. This quake had to be an incredibly large one to tear the structure from the cliff like it did.

Winter broke free of the forest and almost ran into Riley's back. She eased around her, but then froze. Riley stood very still with her lips moving, but she wasn't saying anything, so Winter followed her gaze and felt her chest tightened. The entire resort was in ruins.

The cabanas behind the main structure were flattened to rubble and half of the main building was on the ground. The other half of the building had smoke billowing out of the windows and flames were starting to lick at the thatched roof. Winter headed in the direction of the burning building but Riley grabbed her arm as she shouted, "Wait, Winter! What are you doing?"

"I've got to see if anyone is in there. They may need help," Winter said.

"But it's empty. There was no one in the building. Jenny, the girl from the front desk and her brother, Jose, drove the rest of the guests to the airport just before I went down for our session. No one is in there, darlin," Riley said.

The building that had held the dining hall was now fully engulfed in flames. She looked back at Riley and asked, "You're sure?" Then she turned back toward the building just as the thatched roof fell and the flames soared higher. "No kitchen staff still in there?" she whispered.

"No one. Remember, it is a family run business. The mother, Phyllis is the yogi and the cook. You know I'm a busy body and I have to keep track of everybody," Riley replied.

Winters lips twitched and she said, "True enough." Her shoulders slumped and she said to Riley, "Okay, thanks for keeping me from running into a burning building."

Riley said, "No problem. Question is, what do we do now?"

They turned toward the flattened cabanas and Winter said, "Let's see if we can grab at least a couple of things from that mess. Some bottled water and flashlights would be good, our cell phones won't hold a charge forever. Oh, and tennis shoes if you have them instead of these flip-flops, and something more practical for our bodies," Winter said over her shoulder. She walked toward what was once her room, but stopped and turned toward Riley as she said, "We don't know what is waiting for us out there, or how long we will be on the road."

"Okay, good. You're right. From what happened here, we could be dealing with the entire village in chaos. Hell, the whole island might be in ruins," Riley said. She shook her head and placed her hands on her hips as she examined her legs and feet. "You're right about practical clothing. I better see if I can find some jeans to put on instead of these yoga pants."

Winter looked at the redhead and asked, "You actually own a pair of jeans?"

Riley frowned and said, "You like to call me Oklahoma for a reason, sweetie, it's my home!" She snorted and then said, "Every respectable Oklahoma woman owns a pair of jeans, actually, several. There's dress jeans, casual jeans, and working jeans in my wardrobe." She faced Winter and put her hands on her slender hips as she said, "All these island outfits I wear just make me happy and

the pictures of me in them on Facebook will make *asshole* eat his heart out." She tilted her head to one side, winked, and then turned and sprinted off toward her flattened cabana.

Winter watched her go and chuckled. The woman was at least ten or fifteen years older than Winter, but you wouldn't know it by the way she moved. Winter felt herself blush as she remembered calling her "Oklahoma" repeatedly the night before, but she groaned as she remembered doing a tipsy rendition of the song "Oklahoma" at the pagoda. She mumbled, "Riley, her name is Riley."

***

Winter shouldered her backpack. It was dusty and had a small rip on one side, but it held all the supplies she managed to scrounge from the wreckage of her room. She shifted the weight of the pack and adjusted the straps. It was heavy but it held the flashlight and snacks she left in it the night before, a couple of T-shirts and sweat shirts, two bottles of water, and a handful of trail bars. She glanced around the chaotic debris. It was a good haul and she was lucky to have found everything.

The trail bars were a real find and one of the first things she looked for in the mess. *My contraband.* She smuggled them from the dining area the night before even though food in the room was frowned on at the health-conscious spa. This was one time not always following the rules paid off. When she dug each one from under pieces of the grass roof, it was all Winter could do not to gobble them down. Instead, she had zipped them into the backpack as she said, "No!" aloud to her rumbling stomach. A lifelong stress eater, she felt lucky to have a fast metabolism, or her marriage would have placed her in the Guinness book of records for size. The flip side was that she was always hungry.

Winter stepped over broken timbers and clumps of thatched roof as she headed out of the rubble of her room. Close to the front of the cabana, she spotted a slash of blue material poking out from under the flattened desk. She bent to tug at it. *Bingo.* She pulled out her prize and held it up. Her one pair of jeans and they had no signs of damage. This was almost as good as the tennis shoes she had salvaged and were now protecting her feet.

In the rubble under the jeans she spotted some loose sheets of paper and a pen with the resort emblem on it. Winter's eyes lit up and she snatched them, then looked around for a level place to write. Nothing looked good, so she squatted and used her backpack as a desk, scribbled out a few words, and then stuffed it all into her pack. She was just pulling the jeans on over her compression shorts when Riley appeared. Winter looked up at her and asked, "Who are you and what did you do with Riley?" *She nailed it! Riley instead of Oklahoma.*

Gone was the resort queen and the replacement looked like she was ready to ride the range: boots, jeans, and a long sleeve work shirt over a t-shirt that was tucked into a belt with a big silver buckle. Her long red hair was in a sensible ponytail and a red bandana was wrapped around her throat.

"I replaced her because she was no longer needed. This lady is ready to get down to business," Riley said with her petite and delicately pointed chin held high. With a grin, she grasped her belt buckle and turned it toward Winter as she said, "Five-time champ in barrel racing and owner of a working ranch. Woman, I'll have you know I've been through floods, tornados, droughts, and dug enough horse shit to fill a landfill. I can handle whatever this paradise place can dish out." She turned and marched down the path as she said, "Y'all coming?" over her shoulder.

Winter said, "Well, all right, then." She zipped and snapped her jeans, brushed off the pieces of thatched roof still clinging to her legs, and trotted down the lane after her.

When they reached the front of the resort, Winter said, "Wait." She pulled out the paper from her backpack, climbed up on the fence, and stuck it on a nail holding the "Serenity" sign in place. She hopped down and they both looked up at her handiwork. It was a note in big block letters directing searchers to the cliff where the pagoda went over. "Just in case someone makes it here before we find help," she said.

"Or in case something happens to us on the way to town," Riley said. Winter turned to look at her, but Riley shrugged and said, "Just saying. You never know." Winter nodded and they both headed across the empty parking area and down the narrow road toward the highway in silence.

Once they were on the main road they turned toward the village. The road was in decent shape considering the size of the earthquake. A few trees were down, but as Winter walked around a deep rut, she said, "At least we don't have to deal with a lot of broken asphalt."

Riley nodded, but when then she slipped on some loose soil, she said, "Crap. I almost lost it on that one." She moved to the middle of the road and added, "Maybe loose asphalt wouldn't be so bad, at least we could see it coming. This stuff slips right out from under you and these holes are hard to spot."

"Yeah, and at this rate we might not make it to the village before dark," Winter said. She looked at the sky before she added, "Even if the road was in the same shape as when we drove out here yesterday walking it will take hours."

Riley took off her long sleeve shirt and tied it around her waist. She kept moving, but slowed her pace as she said, "Was that only yesterday? Seems like we have been here a long time." Winter nodded but didn't respond as she fell into step behind her. Riley continued with, "These jeans are hot, but practical, especially if we have to go off-road into the jungle. Glad you suggested the change."

"You would have done it anyway. I think I was simply trying to find something, anything, to talk about besides the destruction of the resort and the pagoda," Winter said, then sighed. "It felt like we were in a war zone."

"It did, and I have to admit, it kinda freaked me out, too. At least a little," Riley replied.

"You couldn't tell. You seemed like you were in complete control," Winter said as she moved up beside her.

"Thanks, you too. We'll get through this," Riley said and reached over to pat Winter's arm.

"You bet we will," Winter said as she smiled and nodded.

They rounded a bend in the road and both of them stopped. An open-air jeep sat a few feet away on the side of the road. The sole occupant was draped over the steering wheel and wasn't moving. Winter and Riley looked at each other, then sprinted toward the jeep.

Winter reached it first and approached the driver. He was a tall, muscular, light skinned black man in his mid-30's or 40's. His eyes were closed but there was no visible blood or signs of injuries. She eased her fingers around his wrist to check for a pulse, but dropped it and jumped back when he jerked it away from her. He raised his head, opened his eyes, and then asked, "Who are you?"

Her hand went to her throat as she said, "My name is Winter. Are you hurt?" she asked. She revised her age estimation. He was probably at least in his mid-40's and he looked scruffy and unkempt, then the smell hit her and she backed up a little more. *Alcohol and body odor-- not a great mix.*

"*What*? What are you talking about?" he asked in a slurred voice. He squinted his green eyes at her and added, "What kind of name is *Winter*?"

She frowned, turned toward Riley and said in a voice dripping with disgust, "He's just drunk."

Riley laughed and said, "You're kidding?"

"No, he must have slept through it," Winter said.

"I'm right here, ladies," he said as he stared at them. "Slept through what? *Who are you*?" he asked again as his eyes narrowed. He added, "What are you doing walking out here on the main road?"

Winter and Riley both laughed and Riley said, "Unbelievable."

He sat up and pulled a flask from between his legs and said, "There it is." He took a long pull and then turned and stared at some fallen trees by the road. "What happened to the trees?" he asked.

"While you were getting your beauty sleep a gigantic earthquake all but destroyed this place," Winter said. *Beauty sleep might be appropriate in his case,* she thought. Beneath that scruffy look the man was gorgeous. Her eyes narrowed. Gorgeous meant trouble in her world. "Look, we've got to get to town. Move over and I'll drive us," she said.

"This is my jeep. You're not driving my jeep," he said as he put the cap on his flask and tucked it under the front seat.

Riley climbed into the back seat and said, "Look, mister. I can appreciate a good time as well as the next person and I enjoy a bit of the drink, but not behind the wheel. You are in no shape to drive and Winter is right, we've got to get into town, so just move on over and let her get us there."

Winter crossed her arms over her chest and glared at him and he stared back at her. He opened his mouth, but instead of arguing he sighed deeply, shrugged and said, "Okay, but you better not wreck my jeep. This is my baby," he patted the steering wheel, then moved over to the passenger seat.

"Right, your baby, *got it*," Winter said as she climbed into the driver's seat. She jammed the jeep into reverse and the gears protested with a loud screech.

The man frowned and said, "Hey!"

She mumbled, "Sorry," but her grin betrayed her true feelings as she twisted the steering wheel around until she was facing the opposite direction and gunned the jeep. They bounced along the rutted road as

Winter swerved back and forth across the highway as she attempted to avoid downed limbs, holes, and debris.

"Watch out!" He shouted at Winter as they rounded a curve. She pulled the steering wheel hard to the left then straightened it out to avoid a large tree limb.

She turned toward her passenger and said, "Don't do that," through gritted teeth. "If you shout at me you will make me hit something." She braked and eased the jeep around the downed tree. "I saw it in plenty of time but your shouting almost made me go off the road."

"Well, you certainly weren't driving like you saw it," he grumbled as he held onto the side door. "I'm totally sober now. You've scared me straight. Pull over and I'll take it from here."

"Not a chance," Winter said as she stared through the front window and gripped the wheel tight enough for her knuckles to whiten.

Riley leaned forward between the seats and said, "Children, play nice." She patted the man on the shoulder and said, "Look, uh...what's your name mister?"

"Aiden. Aiden Saunders," he said.

"Please ta meet ya. My name is Riley." She reached through and shook his hand. "Now, look Aiden, Winter has it under control. I know it's your jeep, but you were passed out when we found you and you took a pretty good swig from that flask of yours. I don't think it was filled with water, so let's allow her to drive us for now." She leaned back as she gripped both sides of the jeep and said, "But, Winter, he might have a point about slowing down a bit, sweetie."

"Yeah, whatever," he mumbled. Winter started picking up speed again on an even stretch of the road and before long he shouted, "Stop!"

Winter kept going, but turned toward him and said, "Like she said, we're not stopping so you can drive."

"No, I mean it, STOP!" he shouted as he pointed through the dirty windshield.

They all three looked ahead as Winter said, "Holy crap!" and jammed her foot on the break. The jeep fishtailed and she corrected. They came to an abrupt stop and Winter felt her seat belt dig into her shoulder. As the dust cleared she asked, "Everyone okay?"

"Just peachy," Aiden muttered.

"Uh, I'm good," Riley said from the backseat.

Winter frowned, undid her seat belt, and jumped out of the jeep. She walked forward a few steps in front of the jeep. *No road.* Just a giant gap where the road once was. She examined the sinkhole and swallowed hard. Deep enough to hold a jeep—*maybe two jeeps*. It was like the pagoda on the cliff all over again but this time it would have been their turn to have tumbled over the side. Well, not the same as falling down a cliff into the sea, but still, falling into a hole wasn't desirable either.

"Holy crap is right!" Riley said. Winter jumped. Riley was standing by her side and Winter watched as she nudged the edge of the hole with her boot. It gave way and dirt and rocks crumbled into the chasm, so they both moved back a step. Riley's head swiveled from side to side and she said, "We're not getting around this hole."

Winter looked at either side of the gap where the jungle met the road. *Riley is right.* The jungle was much too thick to navigate with a vehicle. She turned back toward the jeep. Aiden was now sitting in the driver's seat tapping his fingers on the steering wheel. "No way!" Winter said.

"You want to come with me, I'll let you, otherwise, enjoy your walk ladies." He began to slowly back away from the chasm.

Riley looked at Winter. "I don't want to get caught in the jungle after dark," she said, then turned and looked past the chasm, "or on the open road on foot. I say let's take our chances with this guy."

"You've got to be kidding," Winter said. She looked across the hole and the road disappeared with no sign of civilization. Thick vegetation to the left and right of the road hid whatever perils it contained. "Crap," she mumbled as she rolled her eyes and then turned and followed Riley who was heading toward the jeep. Aiden stopped the vehicle and Riley climbed into the passenger seat. Winter hesitated and asked, "Where are you going?"

"My place," he said.

"Where is your place, Aiden?" Riley asked.

"A few miles from the yoga retreat. It's on the East side of the island at the end of the public roads. I've got a boat and I think we stand a better chance of getting to town with it. Take it or leave it, but honestly, I'm tempted to leave Miss Sunshine here to fend for herself." He nodded his head toward Winter.

"Awwww, she grows on you, you'll see," Riley said as she grinned at him. "A boat sounds good, though. No big holes to fall into."

"I'm right here you know," Winter said, stealing his line. She climbed into the back seat and said, "This is a really bad idea. Really bad." Aiden and Riley both laughed and he eased the jeep around until they were headed back the way they had just come. "This day just keeps getting better and better," Winter mumbled. The chasm was hard to spot until you were right on top of it and she *had* missed seeing it. If Aiden hadn't spotted it, she probably would have plunged them over the edge. Not that she would admit it aloud. She squinted at the road in the distance beyond the hole. *Was that a motorcycle?* She sat up and strained to get a better look, but before she could call out it was gone. It must have been her imagination, or wishful thinking. They went around a curve and the jungle swallowed the road behind them. She turned back toward the front seat where Riley and Aiden were chatting. "Great…instant buds," she mumbled.

Riley turned toward her and called, "What did you say, hon?"

Winter grimaced, then smiled as she said, "Oh, nothing. I didn't say anything," but her words were ignored. Riley had already turned back toward the front of the jeep as it bounced down the road. Aiden Saunders was driving like a little old lady and not the one from Pasadena. She sighed and sank further down in the seat. This man was going to drive her crazy. She could feel it in her bones.

Chapter 10

Carson stood motionless at the opening of a narrow alleyway. Half way down the alley a body lay on top of a pile of rubble and a man knelt beside it as he tugged at the dead man's pockets. A detailed map in the kid's backpack led him to this spot. The alley was the shortest way to the street that lead out of town and Carson didn't want detours or delays. When the scavenger looked up, Carson ducked behind the corner of the building. He eased his head out as the man went back to his work. The alley had a shotgun view and he could see all the way through to the opening at the other end. It was an easy sprint to the other side. The man appeared to be working alone, but one determined guy could be a problem and there was always the chance more of his buddies were within earshot.

The sides of the buildings forming the passageway looked solid, but a lot of debris had fallen and it blocked the alley to all but foot traffic. He couldn't see any available cover, not even a trash dumpster, so he would be out in the open and exposed all the way through the alley. On the plus side, he couldn't see anyone else hiding in the alley to ambush him.

Big chunks of brick surrounded the dead man's body and his head was crushed on one side. The man was obviously dead and probably had been since the first tremor had rocked the island. Carson needed to get past them. There was no decision to make-- it simply came down to timing. This was the most direct route to the yoga retreat and that red dot was burning in Carson's brain. He *had* to get there as fast as possible. He pulled the gun from his shorts pocket and jammed it into the front of his waistband and covered it with his shirt, then he took a step forward to the center of the opening.

Carson edged into the alley as he kept his eyes on the thief. "Shit," he cursed under his breath as he stopped moving. He was so busy watching the vulture with his road kill he hadn't seen the concrete block until his foot slammed into it.

The scavenger froze in his task and looked toward him. His eyes narrowed and he growled, "What do you want?" Carson felt the man's gaze as it traveled up and down his body for a moment, but instead of waiting for an answer, the thief turned his back to him and continued with his task.

Carson raised his eyebrows but remained silent. A cell phone and wallet appeared from the pockets of the corpse. The thief checked the cell, pocketed it, and then pulled cash out of the wallet. He tossed the empty wallet on top of the body before he stood and counted the money. *Must not care about fingerprints,* Carson thought as he waited until the man finished his bill count and stuffed the money deep into his jeans pocket.

The thief turned his attention back to Carson and his hands fell to his side as they balled into tight fists. He took a step toward Carson and his voice rose as he said, "I asked you what you want?"

Carson shifted his weight, cleared his throat, and said, "I need to get down this alley. I'm heading for the highway out of town." He held up his empty hands and said, "I don't want trouble."

"You'll go back the way you came if you don't want trouble," the thief said as he puffed out his chest. He was only about 5'4 but his body was hard and wire thin, and he stood with the confidence of a man who had nothing to lose. His left hand slid toward his waist and he eased a large serrated hunting knife out of a sheath on his belt.

The size of that knife might be part of his confidence, Carson thought. The man held the knife loosely at his side and tapped it against his soiled jeans. Carson could see some crude ink tats on his neck and yellow teeth peeked between cracked, dry lips as he spoke. *Probably prison tats.* Carson grinned. *Perfect.*

Carson dropped one hand to his waist and held the other palm forward as he said, "Like I said, I don't want trouble, but you look like you might know your way around this island."

The man glared and said, "*So?*" He took another step toward Carson, but Carson held his ground. "I don't like nosy people and I sure don't like turistas."

"Point taken, I don't like them either." Carson inched his hand up until it exposed his gun and he said, "I am neither. I don't mean you harm or disrespect, and normally I could care less what you are doing with that dead guy, but it seems that I need a guide and uh, possibly some other work for a man like you."

The thief stopped approaching as his black eyes aimed toward the gun, then he snorted as he examined Carson's dusty tourist clothing. He pointed the knife at Carson and asked, "What do you mean 'a man like me'?"

"You are obviously someone who knows how to take care of yourself and use a weapon when necessary."

The man grinned exposing the sharp yellow teeth and rocked back on his heals as he said, "True, enough, but why would I want to help you? I think you must be loco or stupid."

"Again, I am neither," Carson said as he leaned forward, "and as for *why* you would no longer have to dig around dead bodies for cash. I have plenty and you would be in for a very fat payday *if* you prove to be useful."

The man tensed as he squinted at Carson and growled, "You got money? Maybe I'll just take the money." He gripped the knife a little tighter and raised it higher as he pointed it toward Carson and said, "Who's gonna stop me? You think you got the nerve to use that pea shooter?"

Carson pulled up his shirt revealing a ripped, flat stomach with an elaborate tattoo of a coiled rattlesnake. His gun was resting close to the rattle at the end of the snake's tail. He stood relaxed and grinned as he said, "Wouldn't do that if I were you, things aren't always as they appear." He casually reached his left hand into his pocket and pulled out a wad of bills and tossed them at the guy's feet before he lowered his shirt and said, "Half now, half when the job is done." His eyes narrowed as he said, "If you are thinking about taking it when I turn my back on you, which eventually will happen, think about this; how do you know the rest of the cash is on me?"

The thief hesitated a moment as his dark eyes flicked between Carson's face and where the gun rested under his shirt, then he shrugged and stuck his knife back into its sheath. He grabbed the wad of bills from the ground, did a quick count, and then stuffed them into his pocket. He stuck his hands in the top of his bulging pockets and said, "Why should I believe you have more money?"

"Because I'm a rich man who can be very generous, or very dangerous, you choose, besides, what have you got to lose?"

The man took a step back and frowned, then said, "Okay, I still think you are loco, but what is the job?"

Carson pulled out his map and stepped forward as he handed it to him. He pointed to the position where his phone app had last shown the red dot and said, "This spot. Can you get me to this spot?" He tapped his finger several times on the paper.

The man looked at the map, studied it, then nodded and said, "Yeah, sure, but it won't be easy." He folded it and handed it back to Carson. "The roads are not great out that way and with the quake, we might not be able to drive it. If you haven't noticed, things are a little crazy. This place is a shit hole most days, but now *everything* has fallen apart."

"I don't care how we get there, but I have to reach it. Even if we walk. I want to go the way anyone from there would take to approach town. That's partially why I need someone who knows the area," Carson said as he rolled up the map and slid it back into his duffel bag. "My wife was last seen there and I have to find her. I don't want to miss her if she is heading toward town," Carson said. He gazed down the alleyway before he continued with, "The other reason is there may be some folks that try to get in my way when I'm trying to find my wife and you look like you can handle yourself if it comes to tricky situations. I don't want any roadblocks and that includes people. If it comes to it, you will need to do some dirty work."

"She's at that yoga place?" The man snorted and said, "Okay, yeah, I can get you there. I can't imagine anyone from that place giving us trouble, but I can take care of whoever." He hitched up his pants and squared his shoulders as his dark eyes narrowed. He said, "But you better make it worth it. Like I said, it won't be easy getting there."

Carson moved to the man's side and slapped him on the shoulder, but the man winced and moved an armlength away. Carson ignored the slight and said, "I can be very generous to those who help me, but if you try to cross me, well, let's just say it's better to be on my good side." He grinned asked, "What do I call you?"

"Ricardo," the man said.

"Okay, Ricardo, lead the way," Carson said as he pointed down the alley. Ricardo looked at him for a moment and something flashed in his eyes. *Doubt?* Carson grinned and thought, *Good. Let him be a little unsure of the gringo.* Ricardo headed down the alley and Carson fell into step a few paces behind him.

***

Moaning and shouts of "Help me," assaulted Carson as he and Ricardo emerged from the alley. Clouds of dust had painted the area a dull gray. It reminded him of the apocalyptic appearance of a movie set.

Carson stood still for a moment. His eyes flicked around the street until they settled on the east end where the road lead out of town. He took a step in that direction but halted when he heard Ricardo say, "There." He stopped and turned toward where his new guide pointed. A moped rental stand was across the street. He had been so fixated on their destination he had missed it. There were only a couple of bikes still upright, but they looked untouched. A man in a uniform with a moped emblem on his shirt sat on the sidewalk beside the bikes holding a bloody towel to his head.

"Good catch," Carson said. He headed for the moped attendant with Ricardo one step behind him. "How much for two bikes?" Carson asked as he stood over the injured man.

"What?" the moped man said. He pulled the towel from his dust covered face. Blood oozed from a gapping head wound on the old man's forehead. A jagged trail of red cut through the dust on his face until it reached his chin, where a drop balanced, as it caught between tuffs of wiry gray hair. Carson watched as the old man looked up at him with glazed eyes, then his chin trembled and the drop fell into his lap. "What?" he asked again.

Carson glanced around. There was at least a half dozen people within hearing distance, and most of them were gazing in their direction with curiosity glistening in their eyes. He dropped some bills in moped man's lap and said in a loud voice, "Thank you! We'll take good care of your bikes," then he moved over and straddled the first one. Once bright red, the bike appeared maroon under the layer of dust coating the entire surface, but no dents or dings marred the surface. The key was dangling from the ignition, so Carson twisted it and the engine started on the first try. He eased it around and pointed it toward the road. "Come on," he said to Ricardo.

"What?" Moped man repeated as he pushed the towel back toward his head. When it contacted with the wound, he cried out and pulled the towel away again. The gash on his forehead had opened even wider and blood flowed freely down his cheek landing on the wad of green bills. The man's eyes followed the blood drip to the cash in his lap, then he lifted his head to Ricardo who was still standing in front of him. "My head hurts. Help me?" he mumbled.

Ricardo moved in closer and bent over the injured old man. He took the towel from his hand, stretched it out, folded it, and then eased it on the old man's forehead until it covered the wound, and then he tied it off at the back of his head. He patted the old guy on his shoulder and Carson frowned and said, "Anytime now, amigo."

Ricardo ignored Carson and gripped the man by the shoulder and said, "Don't worry, old man. It's going to be okay." Carson's frown turned into a slow smile as he watched him palm the bloody bills out of the old guy's lap and stuff them into his own pocket. Ricardo straightened and said in a loud voice, "We'll get you some medical help. Don't worry, we'll be back soon." He moved to the next bike, climbed on, and started the engine as he growled in a low voice, "Go."

Carson laughed and pulled away from the stand. He had chosen his guide well. The bike sputtered, then the engine caught and surged forward as he dodged debris and pedestrians littering the narrow road. Ricardo was money hungry and had no scruples. *The perfect tool, but what if the tool turns against me?* Carson thought as he twisted the accelerator and the engine whined. He leaned forward and just barely avoided hitting a dazed child standing in the middle of the road. "Move out of the road, you idiot," Carson said as he swerved the bike around him. If Ricardo became a problem, he would be an easy fix. It would be like swatting a mosquito. Winter on the other hand--Winter was a treasure that would be hard to discard. He sighed. It would be excruciation to no longer look forward to their intimate times, but as their vows stated, 'To have and to hold until death do us part.' It was time for them to part. She had chosen the path not him. He grimaced and pushed the moped to its limits as he aimed for the open highway.

The end of town was a welcome relief from the downed buildings, scattered debris, and confused pedestrians wandering around the streets. A paved road and open fields stretched out for miles in front of them, at least until it was swallowed by the distant foothills dotted with vegetation. Ricardo pulled over as they left the village and Carson followed him to the side of the road. His guide shouted over the moped's whining engine noise, "It's open road from here until we get to the jungle, then you need to watch out for downed trees and holes."

"Obviously," Carson said, then added, "these damn things go so slow, it will be easy to spot anything in the road." Taking advantage of the stop, he pulled out his phone and checked, but there was still no cell service. He missed that reassuring red dot.

"There won't be any cell service for days, maybe weeks, or longer. It takes forever when a tropical storm knocks it out. With this kind of disaster, who knows?" Ricardo shouted as he shrugged his shoulders, then he slipped the little bike out of neutral and chugged back onto the road.

"Damn third world island. Of course, this is where my wife would choose to hang out until our next court date. She just loves to push my buttons and she knew I would follow her," Carson mumbled, but his words were swallowed by the moped's high-pitched whine as he fell in behind Ricardo. He gritted his teeth and turned the throttle until the whine was deafening.

The wind slapped at Carson's face and hair, but once he shoved his sunglasses as tight as he could against his face, his eyes stopped tearing up. What an inefficient way to travel. A bicycle with a lawn mower motor strapped on it. He wished he had the motorcycle he had left in San Francisco. It felt as if he was driving without getting anywhere as the jungle seemed to remain in the distance. When they finally reached the jungle, it was an instant change. Pavement gave way to a hard dirt surface and a canopy of trees made the temperature drop. Carson leaned back and wiped his neck with his kerchief. "Ouch," he said. It was still unbearably humid, but the sun was no longer beating on his sunburned neck.

Carson removed and pocketed his sunglasses when the road became more difficult to read. After traveling for a while into the rain forest, he strained to see a break in the trees, then froze. Something was on the road in the distance. He rose higher in his seat and squinted, then his eyes widened. *An open-air jeep.* It looked like three people. Two were standing in front of the jeep and one was climbing from the passenger seat to the driver's seat. They were still too far away to distinguish features, but it appeared to be two women in front of the jeep and a man now in the driver's seat. He sped up and passed Ricardo as he concentrated on the three figures.

Carson twisted at the throttle until it whined at maximum power, but it was still not closing the gap quick enough to make out faces. He lowered his body to where it was almost flat on the moped and squinted to see better, but then the bike dropped down into a dip in the road and he could no longer see the people. When he climbed the opposite side of the dip and leveled out on a flat surface, the jeep was loaded and heading in the opposite direction. "No," Carson shouted, but they were too far away to hear him. The man was driving and his passengers were the two women. *Had they seen him? Were they running away?* Carson swerved to the side of the road to miss a large pothole and lost sight of them again. As he veered back to the middle of the road they came into sight. The jeep was moving slowly, but then it zigzagged back and forth across the road before it disappeared around a corner.

Carson headed at top speed toward them. "Wait!" he heard Ricardo shout, but the warning disappeared into the roar in Carson's head. The woman in the back of the jeep had turned her face in his direction just before the jeep disappeared. Her dark curls were tied up in a long, thick ponytail. He knew that ponytail's bounce even at this distance.

My red dot. My Winter, he thought as he squeezed the throttle.

Ricardo yelled from somewhere in the distance, "No, stop! The road."

Shut up, thought Carson, then awareness flooded through him. *Too late.* A gaping hole where the road should be. He released the throttle and squeezed the brake, but the sudden switch made the bike skid and then it banked onto its side. He felt it hit his leg as he went down, but he managed to squeeze out from under it and rolled aside as the bike slid over the edge of the sinkhole.

Carson lay on his side panting as Ricardo pulled up beside him. "I tried to warn you, señor," Ricardo said. He was grinning.

Asshole, Carson thought. "That was Winter--my wife!" Carson shouted. He sat up and pointed at the now empty road on the other side of the chasm. "She was in the jeep." He pushed himself up and brushed at his clothing. "Shit," he said. He gazed at the now empty road. "Shit, shit, shit," he repeated.

"You're bleeding," Ricardo stated.

Carson looked down at his leg. The roar in his head subsided and he felt the full burn in his leg. He pulled a cloth from his backpack and dabbed at his knee and leg where the road had left its mark with imbedded gravel and dirt.

Ricardo looked at the distant road and asked, "Your wife was in that jeep?"

"Yes, *that jeep*. How many other vehicles have you seen out here?" Carson growled and glared at Ricardo. He winced and frowned, then looked at his right palm. Deep gouges oozed blood, and dirt and gravel peppered his palm. He picked at some pieces of gravel, then wrapped the cloth loosely around the damaged hand. He pulled the cloth tighter and tied it around his wrist. The distraction of the pain almost felt good. He tugged the cloth even tighter.

Ricardo was still staring at the empty road, but then he swiveled his head from side to side as he studied the thick vegetation bordering it and the chasm. "No problem. That was Aiden's jeep. I know where he lives."

Carson's head snapped up. "Aiden?" he whispered. His eyes narrowed and shifted to the spot on the empty road where the jeep had sat. "Who is *Aiden*?" he asked as a fire rose from his belly to his throat and constricted his voice into a tight whisper.

"An expat from the US and a drunk. Some of the villagers said he was a computer wizard and rich before he landed here, but I don't believe it," Ricardo said as he pushed his moped to the side of the road and dropped it on its side. He continued with, "Nobody rich would live in a dump and spend all his time in the dive bars on the west end." He paused and studied the jungle, then turned and said, "Don't worry about the bikes, we have to go on foot now. They won't work in the jungle and we can't get mine across that hole." He pulled his knife out and chopped at the brush beside the road as he said, "I know a shortcut that will help with our time." With that he disappeared into the wall of greenery.

Carson stared at the spot where Ricardo entered the jungle for a moment. "Aiden," he whispered, then looked back at the empty road and spat out some road dust. He shrugged, then he eased into the thick vegetation behind Ricardo. He shoved branches away from his upper body and felt thick grass reeds grab at his legs as he moved deeper into the jungle.

When he spotted Ricardo, his guide called over his shoulder, "Watch out for snakes. They will be jumpy after the quake."

Carson glanced around. "Right," he said, but the warning was lost on him. Snakes didn't matter. The pain in his leg and hand didn't matter. He had seen Winter and that was all that mattered. His hands balled into fists and he winced at the injured palm, but then he squeezed it tighter until dots of blood eased through the tightly wound cloth.

Winter was with a man...A man.

Chapter 11

The jeep slowed, then almost stopped as it made a hard turn onto an even rougher road. Winter lurched forward with the turn, but then pushed herself back in her seat as Aiden eased down the narrow lane. The jeep jerked from side to side, and up and down. The multiple holes were unavoidable, so she gripped the seat belt strap and asked, "Is this even a road?" Silence was her only answer from the front seat. *Can they hear me, or are they ignoring me?* Winter wondered. Between the loud engine noise and the screeching protests coming from the jungle, she wasn't sure.

Winter leaned forward until she could see between the seats and through the front windshield. The new road wasn't much more than two hard packed ruts with vegetation growing in the middle and crowding in on either side. She ducked as a low hanging frond swung toward her face and as she raised up again, she jumped when a vine grabbed at her elbow. This was even more primitive then the road leading to the yoga retreat. "Where are we?" Winter asked as she gripped the side of the jeep after a hard lurch forward. Again, no reply, so she raised her voice to a shout as she asked, "Are we almost there?" She realized she sounded louder than she intended, but maybe they would hear her this time, even if it made her sound like a petulant child.

"We're close. Really close," Aiden said as his reflection grinned at her in the rear-view mirror. "Getting restless?" he asked.

"I'm ready to get out of this bouncing jeep and I could use a bathroom," she said. Before she lost their attention, she added, "Where would the main road have taken us if we'd stayed on it?"

Wouldn't our chances be better somewhere less remote?"

"The main road only runs about a half a mile past my turn-off. There are no roads any farther on the east side of the island and access is primarily by boat," he replied, then turned his eyes back to the front of the jeep as limbs slapped at the windshield. "This is my private road, or as I like to call it, the path to home sweet home."

"Fabulous," Winter said as she ducked and swiped at one of the limbs. As soon as she lowered her arm, another limb hit her in the face. She grimaced, undid her seat belt, and scooted to the middle of the seat. She shouted as she leaned forward, "So, not a fan of civilization, much?"

Aiden grinned broader and shrugged. "Civilization is highly overrated and I am currently at war with it," he said. She turned her head to the side so he couldn't see her mouth as it curved upward. No sense encouraging him. He seemed almost amused by her snarky remarks.

Riley laughed and turned toward the backseat. Winter could see her profile as she yelled, "I kinda have to agree with Aiden on that one. My place in Oklahoma is a little slice of heaven and you can't see one sign of the civilized world from my cozy front porch rocker."

Aiden glanced at her and said, "Sounds awesome, Riley. I have to admit I haven't been able to let go of all my connections to the outside world, but you'll see for yourself, that is, if my place is still standing."

"Now you've got me curious," Riley responded.

"Probably talking about his porn collection," Winter muttered.

"What was that, Winter?" Riley shouted.

"Nothing. Don't pay any attention to the back seat. I'm just *hangry* and I need a toilet. I always get grumpy when I'm hungry. Keep your eyes up front to what is trying to pass for a road," she yelled.

She pushed another branch away, but it hit her arm instead of her face and she said, "Ouch!" She slumped lower in the backseat and gripped the cushions as she glared at the limbs and vines surrounding the jeep. She was beginning to feel like the jungle was alive and attacking her.

They rounded a sharp corner in the road and Aiden slowed and then braked until the jeep stopped. "Are we here?" Winter sat up higher and asked. She leaned forward so she could see through the windshield. The reason for the stop stretched across their path. *A massive downed tree.*

"No, but there's a tree in the road," Aiden said.

"Tree? It looks more like a wall," she grumbled, then whispered, "What the hell have we gotten ourselves into?" They all climbed out of the jeep and stood silently in front of the fallen tree. It was huge. "No way we're moving that beast," Winter said.

Aiden turned to look at her and said, "You're right about that. It's going to take a larger rig than mine to pull that monster out of the way." He walked back to the jeep, grabbed his knapsack, then returned to the downed tree, straddled it, eased over and landed on the other side. "Looks like we are walking from here, ladies," he said with a grin, then turned and started off down the road, but he stopped, turned and said, "but if you need the toilet, better duck behind the jeep. I'll be on the other side of this barrier."

Riley and Winter looked at each other, shrugged, then returned to the jeep to get their backpacks and follow Aiden's lead. Winter looked past the tree. The rutted dirt road seemed to go on forever until it disappeared into jungle. She looked at Riley and said, "You go ahead. I'll be right behind you." Riley nodded and scrambled up and over the tree and then hurried to Aiden's side. As she watched them move away from her, Winter ran behind the jeep, took care of nature's call, then scooted back to the big tree. She sighed and said, "Crap," then pulled herself onto the top of the massive tree, swung her legs over, and then scooted to the ground on the other side. As soon as she landed, she glanced around at the forest on either side of her, then sprinted down the road. When she neared Aiden and Riley, she slowed and began to trudge along behind them.

If she weren't so pissed off at Aiden she would have enjoyed the walk. The dense rain forest was a little intimidating, but quite beautiful. Wild ferns, exotic flowers, and unusual trees bordered both sides of the road. The air was filled with a heavy scent of flowers and damp earth. Birds' protests, along with the occasional screech of a monkey, sounded all around them, but not as loud as when they were churning along in the jeep. The loud engine noise must have driven the jungle inhabitants' crazy. The walk was strange but somehow peaceful.

It was cooler walking through the jungle and the overhead canopy of trees kept the sun off them, but it was still hot and sticky. Winter stopped to wipe her face and neck, but as soon as she stopped, the buzzing of mosquitos made her brush at the air. "Ouch," she said as she slapped her neck when one whirring soldier found its target.

She started walking again and noticed Aiden and Riley had moved farther away from her. "Hey, don't worry about me," she mumbled as her brows reached for each other and her lips fell into a straight line. Their heads were bobbing as they chatted together. It was as if they were on a fun hike on a gorgeous, carefree, South American day. *What is wrong with them?* She thought.

Winter stopped again and put her hands on her hips as she thought, *What is wrong with me?" Why am I so pissed at Aiden, anyway? Is it only because he is a man? Has Carson done that to me?* She shook her head and started walking again. "I hope I'm not that bitter," Winter whispered. She smiled as she thought that the reason for her anger could be more obvious. It could be because they stumbled on Aiden when he was dead drunk behind the wheel of a car and unaware of what was happening all around him.

She shook her head and kept walking, but her chin went down and she stared at the dirt rut beneath her feet. She was trying to stay within the narrow rut, but long reed grass from the center of the road kept grabbing her legs and leaving barbs and stickers on the bottom of her jeans. She kicked at a particularly thick growth of weeds and then moved on. Winter sighed as she thought that she might be angry because everything in her world seemed turned upside down. "Stop!" she said to end the tumbling thoughts, but she must have said it aloud, and as a shout, because both Aiden and Riley stopped and turned toward her.

"Uh, wait up," Winter blushed and called as she closed the distance between them. Aiden pulled a bottle of water from his pack and took a sip. Winter thought of a sarcastic comment, but this time she didn't say anything. She wondered again why she felt so snarky toward this man. She would need to think about that some more, but right now her emotions had her wanting to throttle him, so she would try to reign in her sharp tongue. It would be good if she could do a better job of keeping her thoughts on the inside, at least until she could work through some of the garbage Carson had left her with.

"If you have water drink it now. You don't want to get dehydrated," Aiden said. "If you don't have any left, I have some extra."

Winter bit her tongue to keep from asking if it was water he was drinking, not booze. *Play nice*, she thought, and instead of speaking she pulled her water from her backpack and drank deeply. Riley followed suit after she took her pack off and sat in the middle of the road on a patch of flattened grass.

After a moment, Aiden said, "That's probably enough for now. I guess we better conserve our water just in case my place is demolished and we can't refill our bottles."

Winter stared at him for a moment. He had no accent that she could detect, except maybe a little southern California beachy-surfer-dude that crept into his speech now and then, but he was an American, of that, she was sure. He was exceptionally built, strong and lean, like an athlete, not like an ex-con, or like her ex or his body guards, who spent endless hours in the gym. He was built more like a runner who worked out occasionally. It contradicted the idea that he was an unkempt drunk. He had no visible tattoos, bright white teeth that flashed between generous lips, and light green eyes that crinkled at the edge when he smiled. He had mocha colored skin that peeked out of a scruffy beard, and a nose that was just a little crooked, but it only enhanced his appearance somehow. His head was shaved smooth, just to keep the contradiction going with the scruffy beard. Winter frowned. The man was gorgeous and she didn't trust gorgeous, anymore. To be fair, *trust* was something that had been ripped out of her world, and she wasn't sure she could ever learn to feel it again.

Maybe that was the core of her anger. *Trust.* Carson was just as handsome and unbelievably charming when their relationship started, but that was where the paradox lay. Beauty filled with rotten evil. She was so naïve and gullible when she met Carson. *Well, never again*, Winter thought as she shivered despite the heat. She glanced at their surroundings. Even this gorgeous country wasn't what it seemed. Such raw beauty, then the earth had opened and swallowed their tranquil yoga retreat. *Had it come to this?* Could she never trust beauty again?

"Let's go, ladies. We aren't far now," Aiden's words broke through her thoughts and she tightened the lid and put her water bottle away. He reached out a hand to help Riley to her feet. Once Riley was up he turned and led the way down the road, but he paused, turned around and asked her, "Are you coming?"

Winter realized she was standing frozen in place like a mannequin as she stared off into the jungle. She turned to him, nodded, and started walking as she said, "Uh, yeah, sure, I'm coming."

Riley moved in close to her and kept pace by her side as she asked in a low voice, "You sure you're okay, kid? You seem a little spooked."

Winter smiled and nodded at her then replied in a low voice, "Yeah, I'm good. Just a little of the past creeping in. I'm still learning to deal with some stuff."

Riley kept walking but stared at her feet as she said, "Lord, do I know that game. I am trying so hard to live my life for me, but I seem to keep slipping into living it as if I'm proving myself. Elbert has too much real estate in my head and heart. I need to move him just to my heart and get him out of my head."

"Riley, you are a wise woman," Winter said, then laughed and continued with, "or, you've been listening to too many of those country songs you love so much." They both burst out laughing. Aiden was farther up the road, but he glanced back and raised his eyebrows at their laughter. He shrugged but didn't stop or ask questions, instead he turned and quickened his step. As he rounded a corner he disappeared.

"That one," Riley began, then nodded toward where Aiden disappeared and continued with, "has some of his own demons he is working through. I see a lot of pain in those gorgeous eyes of his."

Winter nodded and said, "I think you are probably right, but right now we better catch him so we don't wind up all alone in the middle of the jungle." The women glanced at each other and then quickened their steps.

Winter stopped when she almost bumped into Aiden as she came around the curve in the road. Riley moved in and stood beside her. A small cabin with an expansive porch and green hurricane shutters stood in the middle of a cleared area, and beyond it was a wide river. At the river's edge, a mid-size fishing boat rocked gently against a dock. Two curved palm trees stood next to the cabin with a hammock strung between them. It was like a picture postcard for the tropics. Winter said, "You've got to be kidding me."

"Looks like a travel postcard," Riley said.

Winter turned to her and said, "That was exactly what I was thinking."

"Still standing!" Aiden said as he grinned broadly.

It was not only still standing, but didn't appear to have any damage. As they entered the yard to the cabin, a bundle of tan scruffy fur came bounding off the porch and threw itself at Aiden. The 30-pound mutt moved amazingly fast for having only three legs. He bounced against Aiden's leg with his one remaining front paw as he barked a hoarse coughing sound. Both women laughed. His bark sounded like an old man clearing his throat.

"Hey, Pete, did you miss me boy?" Aiden gave the dog a scratch behind the ear and headed up the wooden plank steps to the wide front porch. Two large rocking chairs faced the water view. Winter could imagine herself sitting there at sunset, or in the morning over coffee. The view would be gorgeous from the vantage point. The porch roof was held up with logs that were scraped and stained a light brown. As Winter reached the top step and moved onto the porch, she turned and leaned against one of the log columns. The view was as spectacular as she had imagined. She took a deep breath and relaxed for the first time since the yoga pagoda had started shaking. "Welcome to my casa!" Aiden said from behind her. She turned and he was standing by the open front door and Riley was already stepping inside.

Once inside, the interior of the cabin was a different story. Winter said, "I take it the maid had the day off?"

"Damn," Aiden mumbled as he moved to the middle of the room and picked up a potted plant resting on its side. The pot was intact, so he squatted and started scooping dirt from the floor back into the pot with his hands. "Sorry," he mumbled.

"Holy crap," Riley said as she stood rooted by Winter's side. "Looks like a tornado came through here." Aiden glanced up and grinned as Riley said, "Hey, don't apologize for swear words with this Oklahoma gal. I can out curse you any day of the week."

Winter walked into the room and said, "So now it's a contest? Well, bring it on, army brat here." They all laughed and started picking up downed items spread around the room.

The lofty ceilings had dark wooden beams running at an angle across the white expanse and the great room was completely open to a kitchen, dining and living areas. The kitchen had absorbed the most damage. All the cabinets stood open, and broken dishes and food littered the wide plank wooden floors. Several jars of jam and honey lay in pieces and the contents made bright, sticky circles. Paw prints tracked through the circles and continued to other parts of the rooms like a giant abstract painting. In the living area, a couple of chairs were turned over and artwork and lamps were either crooked, or lying face down on the floor.

The dining area held a long picnic style table that was currently dominated by an enormous yellow cat. It had to be at least 20 pounds and had long fur the color of corn. It sat very still and erect in the middle of the table as it gazed at them with its one bright yellow eye, the other eye was permanently sealed shut, so it appeared to be winking at them. The cat turned its solitary eye on Aiden and let out a long, loud yowl. Aiden laughed, stood and moved toward the table as he brushed dirt off his hands and said, "What happened here, Patch? Did the earth give you a tumble?" He held a hand palm down toward the animal and she answered him with a soft sound from deep in her throat, and then stood and butted her head against his hand. She turned toward Winter and Riley, then she leaped gracefully from the table and approached Riley, sniffed at her boots, and preceded to rub against them.

"She probably smells my boys from home and needs to establish that this is her territory," Riley said, then she bent and rubbed the cat behind an ear. "I know this is your place, darlin, no one is going to challenge that!"

"Do you have cats?" Aiden asked.

"I have everything. We foster a lot of strays until they can find their forever homes and a few feral cats live in the barn. One of the many benefits of having a working ranch with lots of space," she frowned and said, "at least it was. Not sure what's gonna happen now with Elbert leaving and all." She sighed and stroked the cat's back.

Winter moved over and patted Riley on the shoulder. The cat switched to her feet, but after a cursory sniff, she showed no interest in Winter's tennis shoes and moved on. Aiden asked, "No animals at your home?"

"No." She didn't want to explain that Carson would never let something into the pristine penthouse apartment that might create even the slightest mess. For some reason, she did not want this man to know how much she had allowed Carson to dictate every detail of her life.

Aiden shrugged, picked up a broom, and began sweeping the debris in the kitchen. The cat took one look at the broom and disappeared into what Winter assumed was a bedroom. She and Riley watched Aiden work for a moment, then Riley started picking up chairs and straightening pillows. Winter turned to the fallen artwork. She picked up the first piece and hung it on the wall. She continued until all his paintings were back up and then she started straightening the ones that were crooked. "You have a lot of artwork, Aiden," she said as she straightened a large water color. The painting was the water view she admired from the front porch. She stood back and admired the use of color and light.

Aiden stopped sweeping and moved over to stand beside her. He turned to her as he raised one eyebrow and said, "You mean for a drunken bum?" She noticed one side of his mouth twitched, but it still made her cheeks burn, because that was exactly what she had been thinking.

"I didn't say that!" Winter sputtered, then she laughed and said, "I may have thought it, but I didn't say it."

Aiden rubbed the stubble on his chin as he said, "I guess I can understand the assumption with our first meeting and, well, let's just say I haven't been myself in a while. I've been taking a bit of a sabbatical from my life."

"That sounds like there is a story in there somewhere," Riley said as she carried pieces of a broken vase to Aiden. He held open a black plastic trash bag he had been using for the kitchen debris and she dropped them into it.

He moved back to the mess in the kitchen and set the bag beside it on the floor and asked, "Doesn't everyone have a story?" He used a dust pan to clear the kitchen counter and dumped the last of the broken dishes into the trash bag, then turned back toward Winter as he asked, "Do you have an interest in art? A local artist did that piece. I gave him a little help setting up some computer equipment and the painting was my payment and a thank you." He tied off the full bag and carried it to the door. The little three-legged pooch followed him and sat patiently while Aiden waited for her answer.

"I was an artist a lifetime ago." Winter looked up and frowned. "Wait, what? You're a computer consultant?" She shrugged her shoulders and said, "Sir, you are full of surprises."

Aiden laughed. "In a manner of speaking. To use your words, 'a lifetime ago' I had a software company and I was very hands on, now I supervise from afar." He nodded toward the corner of the room where a desk held a couple of monitors, a laptop and printer. He winked at Riley and then shook his head at the dog as he said, "We'll walk later, Pete." Then he slipped out of the door. The little tan dog sat and stared at the closed door as he ignored the women.

Riley looked at Winter and silently mouthed, "See? Stories." She shrugged and went back to straightening the room.

Winter said, "You know, he really does have some nice pieces. I wonder how long he has lived here?"

Riley stopped straightening and looked at the painting of the river and dock. "This is a pretty comfortable spot, but it also looks like a good place to hide from the world." She turned toward the corner of the room with the desk and computer equipment and pointed and said, "Except for that."

Winter followed her gaze and said, "Yeah, I wonder what made him hide? He is right. Everyone has stories."

"You would know something about that, and if I'm truthful, so would I." Riley touched Winter on her arm and leaned toward her and added, "Funny, we seem to be three broken souls brought together by a disaster. I just wonder if it's for a reason, and if it is, what is the reason?"

Before Winter could respond, the little dog's tail started thumping a quick rhythm on the wood floor, then he jumped up and barked that strange coughing sound. The door swung open and Aiden came in. They both froze and stared at him. "What?" he asked.

"Nothing," they said in unison then scattered in opposite directions.

"If you say so," Aiden said and shrugged, then moved into the kitchen. He filled a large water bowl on the kitchen floor with fresh water, then he added dry food to two pet food dispensers. The cat's dispenser was high on a shelf in the dining area and the dogs was kept on the kitchen floor. As soon as he shook the food into the cat's bowl, she appeared at the bedroom door and rubbed her face against the frame. After Aiden placed her dispenser back on the shelf, she trotted across the floor to the cabinet, made an easy leap to her bowl, and then daintily took a couple of bites. The little tan dog hurried over and began wolfing his down.

"Man, that cat must have excellent hearing. She doesn't look like she's missed too many meals, either." Riley chuckled. "What's their story? How did they come into your life?"

Aiden reached over to stroke the cat. His fingers paused at the end of her back where the tail connected and he scratched lightly. She arched her back and kept her tail rigidly upright, but never paused in her eating. Aiden pulled his hand away and said, "Patch just appeared out of the jungle one day. She strolled up on the front porch like she owned the place and has been here ever since." He looked at the tabby and smiled. "Always surveying your kingdom, right gorgeous?" he said and then moved over to the table and took a seat.

"She does seem to act pretty regal now that you mention it," Winter said. She grabbed an unbroken coffee mug from the cabinet, wiped it with a paper towel, and filled it with water before joining him at the table. "So, she stayed and no one claimed her?"

"That she did. I don't know how old she is but she's been with me for about a year." He nodded in the cat's direction as Riley joined them and slid in beside Winter. "The eye was an old scar by then. I don't know if she got it in the jungle hunting, from being mistreated, or if it's been that way since birth." The cat finished eating and walked across the cabinet until she was close to the refrigerator. One graceful jump and she was on the top. She sat and began washing her paws as a small pink tongue darted in and out. The three humans staring at her didn't draw a glance.

"For such a large cat she moves well," Riley mused.

"Well, her size is mostly my fault. She was skin and bones when she found me. Somehow, I can't seem to deny her all she wants to eat. She turns that one good eye on me and I melt." The dog finished his food and came over to lean against Aiden's leg, so he reached down and scratched him behind the ear and the animal's tail thumped against the wood floor.

Winter saw the dog's mouth twitch and laughed. "He looks like he is smiling! So, what's his story?"

"Well, Pete came from the village." Aiden shifted his leg and the dog slid to the floor and lay across his foot. "I was having a little issue with walking one night, uh, okay, after I left a bar, and some not nice dudes thought they had an easy mark. Before I realized what was happening, I was on the ground and one of them was kicking me. Suddenly, this little ball of three-legged energy came out of the dark and bit him on his leg. It gave me a chance to get up and fight back. Since I was a lot bigger than my tormentors they gave up and ran off. Pete was dirty, matted, and looked like he had never had a decent meal, so I invited him to join me in the jeep. He hopped up on the passenger seat and the rest is history." Aiden nudged him with his foot. The dog rose to a sitting position and barked the strange coughing sound and then panted another smile. "That's right, Pete, you saved the day!" Aiden reached into his pocket and pulled out a treat and tossed it to him. The dog caught it midair.

"Where did you come up with the names Patch and Pete?" Riley asked.

Aiden's cheeks turned pink and he said, "The bar where I met Pete, well," he reddened deeper, "the name of it is *Peg Leg Pete and Black Beard's bar*." Aiden grinned. "A banner over the bar has a picture of two pirates; Pete with his peg leg and Black Beard with a patch over one eye. What can I say?" His hands went up and he shrugged. "I'm a simple man. Granted, one-eyed Black Beard is a man, but my Patch doesn't seem to mind. Her full name is *Patch of Black Beard, Her Royal Highness* and he is, of course, *Peg Leg Pete*." Aiden gestured toward Pete and got up and asked, "Anyone hungry?"

Winter laughed and said, "Nice subject change, but you have my attention," she rubbed her stomach and said, "I'm starving, but shouldn't we start for town soon? Are we going on the boat that's tied at the dock?"

Aiden looked out of the window and said, "It's almost sundown and I don't want to navigate the river or the ocean in the dark. The river gets narrow and tricky in spots and the ocean can be wild off this side of the island." He washed his hands in the sink and said, "We're all tired and hungry. Let's get some grub and some sleep, and then we can leave early in the morning. The couch makes a queen size bed and you two can have that. As you know, the bathroom is the door to the left, and my bedroom is through there." He pointed just beyond the kitchen. "Now, I don't want you ladies getting mixed up in the night and stumbling into my room. Pete here will be on guard." He said it with a straight face, so Winter rolled her eyes and groaned. Riley grinned and winked at him.

"Okay, let me wash up and I'll help you with some food," Riley said as she headed for the bathroom door.

Winter asked, "What can I do?"

Aiden nodded at the table and said, "Why don't you see if you can find enough unbroken dishes and set the table. I'll whip some food up. I'm actually a pretty good cook."

He began pulling supplies from cabinets and before long the cabin was filled with intoxicating smells. Riley returned and helped Winter set the table and then they both sat and watched Aiden. He paused, glanced at them, then reached under one of the cabinets and pulled out a bottle of wine. After retrieving a wine opener from the drawer, he set them in front of Winter and said, "Make yourself useful."

Winter kept watching Aiden cook. He seemed to know his way around a kitchen, the man continued to be full of surprises, but Winter wasn't sure if she would ever be comfortable with surprises again. Right now, she craved a solid, transparent world. She couldn't help but wonder about this man's story. *Why is he out here in the middle of nowhere on a tropical island getting drunk every night?* she thought.

"I wonder who broke his heart?" she whispered to Riley who elbowed her and raised one eyebrow.

Aiden turned and asked, "What?"

"Nothing," Winter and Riley said in unison. Then Winter quickly said, "Please, just keep doing what you're doing because it smells wonderful!"

Aiden laughed and shook his head. "You two realize that you do that a lot? Somehow, I suspect when you both say *nothing* at the same time it means, *something*," he said and then turned back to his preparations.

Winter picked up the bottle and opener, then glanced at the label of the red wine, raised an eyebrow at Riley, then began twisting the corkscrew into the top as she asked, "Aiden, where did you get this wine? This is a very good year and vineyard. I can't imagine buying it here on the island."

Aiden glanced over his shoulder and said, "Are you a bit of a wine snob?"

Winter felt her cheeks grow warm as she said, "Not at all, but I did have a crash course in the art of choosing wine, uh, let's say it was a matter of diplomacy at the time."

Aiden turned and placed a bowl of steaming pasta in the middle of the table as he said, "I'm teasing you. I did bring a few things with me when I moved here, but only the things I couldn't part with, like my limited wine collection." He added a bowl of red sauce with chucks of mushrooms, peppers, and carrots floating in it, a loaf of freshly baked French bread, and a chunk of parmesan cheese. "I do love a good wine, but it doesn't have to be expensive to be good."

Winter stared at the bowl of angel hair pasta, it had several chunks of butter melting on top of it, and she felt her mouth water. She poured some wine in the coffee mugs since all the wine glasses were now in a crystalized heap in the garbage. "This is heavenly."

Riley picked up her coffee mug and held it high as she said, "Here's to Aiden the magician, who can make a scrumptious meal appear from nothing!" She took a sip, set it down and licked her lips. She said, "Oh, damn, that's good."

Winter picked up her plate and dug into the pasta as she said, "I'm jumping in, this looks incredible, and we've only had some trail bars to eat today." She licked her lips and reached for the red sauce. "I did warn you both that I get *hangry!*"

"Oh, you did, honey," Riley said. "But considering our day, you haven't had too much emphasis on the angry part of that statement." She cut off the end of the bread loaf and slashed some butter on it, then followed Winter and scooped a mass of angel hair pasta onto her plate, then said, "Aiden, you sure have a well-stocked kitchen."

"I like to cook and shopping isn't that simple on the island, so I hit the mainland for extra supplies about once a month," he said.

After they finished dinner, they all cleared the table, but Riley and

Winter shooed Aiden from the kitchen and did the dishes while he took Pete for a walk. "You cooked, we clean, it's only fair," Riley said.

When the last dish was put away, the women refilled their coffee mugs with wine and headed out to the porch and the rockers. Winter settled into one and Riley took the other. The night air was warm, but pleasant. Winter rocked and sipped her wine. She could smell jasmine floating around her from an enormous bush planted by the front steps. "This is perfect. I hope we have time to explore the grounds a little in the morning before we go. What a gorgeous setting."

 Riley nodded. "I certainly didn't imagine we would be here at the end of the day. Full bellies, a good wine, and relaxing in this gorgeous setting. Very different from the destruction we witnessed just hours ago," Riley said.

The sun had set, but the moon was full and danced on the waves as they lapped against the shore. Winter could see Aiden walking around his boat with the little three-legged dog hopping after him. She said, "You are right about that, Riley. In my wildest imagination, I couldn't picture this kind of peace at the end of such a chaotic day. It proves you should never feel like the darkness is going to consume you, because if you just hold on a little longer, everything changes."

Riley lifted her cup and bumped it with Winter's and said, "Amen to that, sister."

***

Winter felt movement in her bed and she froze. She turned and saw a lump in the covers lying next to her in the dim early morning light. She emitted a sigh at the jumble of red hair poking out at the top of the covers. *Oh, yeah*, she thought, *I'm at Aiden's cabin. I'm safe.* How long would she need to repeat that mantra before she believed it?

Soft snores assured her Riley was still sleeping. Winter slipped her legs out from the sheet and swung around until her feet rested on the smooth wood floor. The floor felt cool and refreshing on her bare feet, so she stood and stretched. Calf and back muscles screamed from her trek the day before. She bent and touched the floor as she tried to stretch out the tight muscles. *Geeze, that's sore,* she thought. Her head turned toward the kitchen where a pot of coffee was sending intoxicating aromas into the open room, so she padded over. The coffee was on a timer Aiden set up the night before. *Thanks, Aiden*, she thought as she sniffed the aromatic brew. The full pot and a glance at the closed bedroom door let her know she was the first to rise. A smile as she poured herself a mug and headed for the bathroom.

After she shut and latched the bathroom door, Winter turned toward the mirror. "I have to do something about that," she whispered to the woman staring back at her. She squinted at the image. Bloodshot eyes and tangled hair, and, oh my, even a smudge of red wine stain on her upper lip. She cringed and stepped out of her compression shorts, pushed them aside with her toe, and tugged the soiled T-shirt off over her head. One sniff of the T-shirt and she wrinkled her nose and said, "Gross!" and then placed it on the floor next to her shorts and panties. "I can't believe I slept in those," she said before she dropped her sports bra on top of the pile.

The shower wasn't much bigger than an old-time phone booth, but the acrylic cube looked like heaven. Winter turned the faucet all the way toward hot, but as the steam began to fill the room, she adjusted the temperature somewhere between tepid and a 3rd degree burn. She stepped under the shower head and let the water run freely over her face, hair, and body. "Oh, man, that's good," she mumbled into the downpour and then blindly found a bar of soap and a shampoo bottle. She scrubbed herself until her skin felt raw and her scalp tingled. When she emerged, and wiped the steam from the mirror, she spoke to her refection again as she said, "Almost human."

After drying off, she tugged her thick curls up into a pony tail, then pulled on her last change of clothing. She washed her soiled clothes in the sink and wrung them out. Juggling her coffee mug in one hand, and the wet clothing in the other, she left the bathroom, and eased past the sofa bed. Winter managed to get the cabin door open without waking Riley, or spilling her coffee, and once outside, she eased the door shut with her foot until she heard the latch click. She set her mug down and hung the clothing on the porch railing to dry, then turned to face the day.

The sun was just warming the horizon. A cobbled walkway stretched from the porch to the dock on the river and Winter could hear the water lapping against the dock and shoreline. A soft breeze tickled at her curls. *What a peaceful setting.* No wonder Aiden had picked this spot to live. But what brought him here? Did he harbor a secret as dark as hers? Was he her counterpart or was he another Carson? Surely the Universe wouldn't throw another Carson into her life, that just couldn't have happened. She glanced up at the sky and whispered, "Okay, I've had this life lesson, please don't give me another one just like it." She laughed and thought, *I've known this man one day and I am already making him into a life lesson. Too much thinking, Pappas!*

Winter shivered, even though the sun was climbing higher in the sky, and the morning was already warming. She turned toward the bushes at the edge of the property by the road. Something had spooked her. Was that movement she glimpsed out of the corner of her eye or was her mind playing tricks on her? She squinted and examined the leaves as she moved her eyes along the line of bush. *Nothing.* It was like one of her computer games of *hidden objects.* Searching an intricate picture for an object but nothing stands out. She concentrated on the area closest to the road. Still nothing, and no 'help' button to locate the hidden object. She shook her head. Would she ever stop looking over her shoulder and jumping at nothing? She sighed and thought, *Probably not.*

"Calm down, you idiot," she mumbled, then took a long sip of her coffee as she clutched the mug in both hands. Once more glance at the bushes. "Enough!" she said aloud, and then cringed when she realized it was almost a shout. A glance at the front door, but no one appeared, so hopefully her outburst did not wake Riley. Winter chuckled. Oklahoma certainly was a sound sleeper.

A walk. That's what she needed. It would calm her jitters and stretch her calves. Besides, she had said she wanted to explore the grounds. With her coffee mug clutched in her hand, she headed down the cobbled walkway toward the dock, but before she could reach it and check out the boat tethered there, she spotted another path leading into the jungle. The opening was well maintained and obviously man-made, but virtually invisible until you were standing in front of it. The path drew her. A glance over her shoulder across the yard toward the road. Big plus, it was in the opposite direction of the questionable bushes. Another glance over her shoulder toward the house revealed no activity. She shrugged and slipped into the jungle path.

As she walked along the trail Winter marveled at the rain forest foliage and felt her muscles begin to loosen. Vibrant colors of red, orange, yellow, green, and purple stood out in the early morning sunlight. The scent emanating from the exotic plants and flowers was intoxicating. She paused, squeezed her eyes shut and breathed deeply. Winter let the sounds of the jungle animals and the scent of wild flowers wash over her.

As her eyes opened a slight tug at the corners of her mouth turned into a wide grin. It had been a long time since she had been completely alone and in total control of her own actions. Every decision, large or small, did not have to be made in anticipation of another's emotional environment. It was both liberating and frightening at the same time. For better or for worse, Winter could choose her own destiny. There was absolutely no one she had to answer to. The thought was heady. Her mind began to buzz with limitless possibilities. She could even do what Aiden had done, move to some island where no one knew her and start over.

A sip from her mug and she started walking again. As she walked, she noticed she was ascending a gentle incline. When her thighs began to burn, she realized the incline was becoming steeper and she noticed the path had narrowed. She stumbled on a rock and her coffee sloshed over the lip of the mug. "Crap," She muttered and touched the rock with her tennis shoe, then kicked it into the bushes.

Maybe it was time to head back and see what the others were doing. They might be up and wondering where she was, besides, her tummy was grumbling for something more than coffee.

Winter turned to head back the way she had come when she heard a twig snap. Her feet froze and her head snapped up. She could no longer see the opening of the path to the yard, only jungle. "Someone there?" she called. No reply, so she shrugged and took a couple of steps. Probably a little jungle creature. Maybe a lizard or even a squirrel. *I wonder if they even have squirrels here?* she thought.

As she moved further down the incline she heard a branch break. "Aiden? Riley?" she called, then stopped again and listened. That branch was broken by something bigger than a small creature. *Maybe Riley or Aiden was joining her, but weren't close enough to hear her call?* She tilted her head to one side and gazed down the path. Her slight elevation gave her an unobstructed view as her nightmare appeared in the distance. She froze, but only a moment, then turned, dropped her coffee mug and sprinted up the hill. *Oh, God, no,* she screamed as her legs churned, but the scream was only in her head as she blindly raced up the hill.

Chapter 12

The house appeared deserted. There were no lights shining through the windows or any activity in the yard. The sun was still only a hint on the horizon, so Carson didn't think they could be seen, but when Ricardo dropped onto his stomach and slipped behind a bush, he did the same. The ground felt damp and Carson could feel rocks and sticks poking him as he inched forward, but he kept going until the house was visible again.

Their journey the night before had ended when darkness made travel impossible without the use of flashlights. A night in the rain forest had garnered him very little sleep, but Ricardo's snores had as much to do with it as the jungle noises and unforgiving ground. As soon as the dawn provided enough light to distinguish their surroundings, he kicked at Ricardo's boot to waken him. If he had known what a short trek it was from where they slept to this spot, he would have insisted they push through to get here last night. They could have taken the people in the cabin by surprise while they slept.

Ricardo seemed familiar with the property. Carson wondered how well he knew the man who was with Winter. He glanced at Ricardo and asked, "So this is where the man with the jeep lives?"

"Si. His first name is Aiden but I don't know his last name," Ricardo replied.

Carson frowned and asked, "What do you know about him?"

"Not much," Ricardo answered. Then added, "Just what I already told you."

Carson eased forward a few more inches and glared at the house as he asked, "Is Aiden a tough guy?"

"He's big, but a drunk," Ricardo growled. "Better if he is drinking, not sure if he's sober, he might be pretty tough then." He turned and spat to one side. "Not so tough for me." He sniffed and said, "I can take care of him if you want."

Carson started to reply, but then froze when Winter stepped onto the porch. *Oh, God.* Her dark hair glistened wet in the morning light. Carson licked his lips and cleared his throat. She must have just showered. Her long, tan legs stretched out of black workout shorts and a white T-shirt hung loosely over her upper body. She was draping wet clothes over the porch railing. A white bra and underwear. *Oh, God.*

Carson eased up on one knee and parted the bush he was behind to get a better view. He leaned forward as he wondered if the man, Aiden, had seen her naked? *Did they shower together?* Carson felt his hands turn into fists and he pushed himself forward a little further. She turned toward him and stared. He froze. Had she seen him? He wanted to charge from the bushes across the yard, but he knew how fast she could be. She loved to run. Winter turned her head away from him toward the water. Carson pushed himself up to a half crouch.

Ricardo touched his arm and said, "Not yet. See what she does."

Carson's jaw tightened but he nodded and eased back down on his knee. He watched as she strolled down a path toward the dock and unwanted visions danced in his head. Visions of her dark hair tumbling on white sheets with the mocha colored man embracing her. Visions of the two of them entwined in the shower. A small moan escaped his lips but he held his position.

No one else emerged from the house and Winter continued her walk alone. She paused before reaching the dock and glanced again in his direction, but then turned and disappeared into the jungle. Did she know he was here? Maybe she hadn't seen him, but sensed him. *That was even better.* His mouth slipped into a smile as he stood. She had to know he would follow. He would always follow. Was she afraid or did she want to play their game? *Maybe she was baiting him.* He chuckled. *She wants me to follow her. This is fun.*

"No movement at the house," Ricardo said as he stood.

Carson reached out and griped his arm and said, "I'm going after my wife, but see that boat tethered at the dock?"

Ricardo glared at Carson's hand on his arm and growled, "Yeah?"

Carson removed his hand but said, "Disable it. You think you can do that? Put it out of commission?"

"Yeah. No problem," Ricardo said. "I know about boats. I live on an island."

Carson stared across the clearing to the path heading into the jungle where Winter had disappeared. He bit his lower lip and took a step in that direction, but then stopped and said, "After you finish with the boat can you circle around and approach her from the other side, so she won't get away if I spook her? Do you know that path?"

"Yes. I used to come here when the family before the drunk owned it. I had a thing with the oldest daughter and used to meet her at night by the waterfall. There is a bridge by the falls and I came up the path that leads to the other side of it," Ricardo said as he pulled his waist band up. "She was a good woman, soft and round, and generous with her man." He grinned and his sharp little yellow teeth glistened.

"There's a bridge and a waterfall?" Carson asked.

"Yeah, the bridge crosses the gorge by the falls. Below the falls is a deep pool where everyone used to come to swim and mess around before the American bought the land," Ricardo said, then spit again. "I wait on other side of bridge. It's far enough from the house that they won't hear us. You can do whatever you need to do there," he said and shrugged. "The water in the pool can be unpredictable and wild, though, so be careful."

Carson smiled and nodded. "Perfect," he said, then started running in a low stance across the yard toward the path.

***

The coffee pot was down about a cup. Aiden felt the side of the glass beaker and it was still hot. He poured himself a cup and placed the steaming brew just below his nose and inhaled. His eyes opened a fraction wider as the aroma hit his sinuses. He placed the mug to his lips and tried a few sips. Even after the magic elixir warmed its way into his system, his eyes still felt grainy, and a steady drum beat pounded in his head, so he reached into the cabinet and pulled out a bottle of aspirin, and then threw a couple on the back of his tongue before he took another sip.

Leaning over the kitchen sink, Aiden cupped his palms and ran cold water into them, and then buried his face in the pool before opening his fingers and letting it drain out. As he reached for the dish towel, his elbow bumped the coffee cup, and it spilled onto the counter. "Shit," he said as he found the towel, wiped his face, then mopped up the coffee. He tossed the towel into the clothes hamper and decided he needed to start rethinking the amount of alcohol he was drinking if he was going to get up before noon. This just wasn't working. He poured himself the final cup from the pot and turned it off just as Riley emerged from the bathroom freshly showered. "Good morning," he said. "Do you want me to make more coffee?"

"Morning," She replied. "Naw, I'm good. I drink tea and usually a little later in the morning. Winter must have gotten up early and grabbed the first cup."

"Did you sleep well?" he asked. "I've spent a few nights on that couch and it was pretty comfortable."

"Like a baby," she said, then grinned and added, "course, I don't know why people always say that. Babies don't sleep much, at least not for the first year." She joined him in the kitchen and leaned against the counter.

"Do you have children, Riley?" Aiden asked.

"One—a daughter. She has always been the love of my life, and always will be. She has given me two beautiful grandchildren and that is the gift that keeps on giving."

Aiden managed a smile and said, "It must be nice to have a family like that."

Riley cocked her head to one side and said, "It is. Even with my Elbert turning into such an ass. I wouldn't change a bit of it. Without him, I wouldn't have them."

Aiden laughed and said, "Sounds like you and Winter might have a few issues with men."

"You've got that right. Winter more than me. Talk about getting the short straw, that woman drew it," Riley said.

Aiden raised an eyebrow and said, "Really? Tell me more."

Riley shook her head and said, "That's right, you've been out of touch for a while, so you aren't up on the news, but that's her story to tell, not mine. My story is simple, just listen to most country songs and you'll get it. *Cheating Heart* sums it up. *Him,* not me."

Aiden said, "Ouch." He brought his eyebrows together for a moment, then his eyes widened and he said, "Oh, now I remember where I heard the name Winter—in the news. So, she's *that* Winter?"

"Yep, but keep it to yourself, will you? She is kinda sensitive about being recognized," she replied.

"I can do that. I'm private myself. By the way, where is she? I haven't seen her this morning."

"I don't know. I was wondering that myself. For just a moment after I got up, I wondered if she was in your room, but just for a moment," she said, then winked at him.

He snorted. "Not hardly. I think she can barely tolerate me."

"Honey, that's how it all starts."

His face grew warm and he said, "I guess I better see if she's outside. Hope she didn't take the boat and leave us here."

"Naaaaa. That's not her style, but if you will check on her, I'll get the couch made and we can leave soon." She headed toward the sofa bed, but turned and said over her shoulder, "Maybe we can whip up some breakfast out of that magic kitchen of yours first, though."

Aiden laughed. "I bet we can manage that and if you want it, you'll find some tea in the cupboard." He started toward the door with Pete tight on his heels.

On the front porch Aiden paused and stretched. Pete sat by his side, but the dog growled low in his throat as he looked at the boat. "What's wrong buddy?" Aiden followed the dog's gaze across the yard, but couldn't see or hear anything. He shrugged and started down the steps toward the boat dock. Pete bounded along beside him, but stopped and sniffed at the air, then branched off and planted himself in front of the entrance to the jungle path. "What?" Aiden asked. The dog remained at the path opening and whined. A glance at the boat showed no activity, so Aiden headed toward Pete and said, "Did she take a walk in the jungle? Is that what has you upset?"

As he got to the jungle path, the dog started in ahead of him, but kept pausing in his three-legged hop to sniff the ground and growl. Aiden felt a chill at the base of his neck and glanced around, but the path was empty and quiet. He couldn't see anything, but he still couldn't shake the feeling of unease. He shrugged and thought, *I'm probably just picking up on Pete's jitters.* He looked up the path. *But what is causing this tough little guy to be so spooked?*

Just as they began to climb toward the falls, he saw something blue on the ground. Pete sniffed it and whined. Aiden bent to pick it up. It was one of his coffee mugs and the base still felt warm. Something was wrong. *Winter wouldn't have just left it here-- unless she dropped it, but why would she have done that?* He studied the trail in front of him. There were several foot prints in the damp soil. He bent and examined them as Pete sniffed. Some of them looked like they might be Winter's, but there was another much bigger set of prints. Winter's prints were deep and far apart as if she were running. His head snapped up and he shouted at the dog, "Go, Pete, go," as they both sprinted up the steep incline.

Chapter 13

Winter broke free of the jungle and swung around, but there was no one behind her on the path. *At least not yet*, she thought. Her mouth was open as she struggled to breathe and her calves and thighs were screaming. Carson had to be close, but she knew him, he would take his time. She cocked her head and listened; all she could hear was her own panting, so she bent at the waist, placed her hands on her knees, and tried to bring her breathing back to normal. When her lungs stopped heaving, she stood straight and took in her surroundings as she pulled her sweat soaked t-shirt away from her body.

She was in the middle of a clearing with jungle behind her and a wide, raging river on the other side. The river rushed over rocks and boulders and she could see a swirling whirlpool in the middle of it, and if that weren't impossible enough, it ended at a waterfall. *A waterfall? Come on!* Winter thought as she glanced over her shoulder and shivered. She would rather jump into the surging water and drown, or hazard slipping over the falls, than have Carson lunge from the jungle and grab her.

Carson was a planner who calculated his every move, Winter knew he must somehow have the odds set in his favor. It would make his *game* so much sweeter. He could travel at his own pace while she scrambled to escape. He loved the hunt as much, or probably more, than as when he cornered his prey. She squared her shoulders. *I'm tired of being prey*, she thought.

Her eyes swept the river and surrounding banks on both sides as her mind churned out possible escapes. Winter shook her head, she was a strong swimmer, but she would never make it to the other side without being dragged over the falls. She needed to see what she was dealing with past the waterfall, so she edged along the river on a path between it and the jungle until she reached the top of the cliff by the falls.

As she stood beside the cascading water her heart sank. It flowed over the steep cliff into a sheer drop to a pool at the bottom. The foaming pool looked deep and had rocks and boulders jutting out of the dark surface. From the pool, the river ran in a wide ribbon into the distance. A magnificent sight, if her heart weren't pounding in her chest so hard she feared it would burst. A glance up and she gasped. *A butterfly of hope.* There was a rope suspension bridge a few feet past the waterfall. The bridge looked old and questionable, but it stretched across the chasm to the jungle on the other side. *A chance.* Life or death. It didn't matter. She would be in control, not Carson.

She examined the cliff on her side of the falls but could see no safe way down to the pool below. Her eyes rose to study the narrow path along the jagged cliff's edge to the bridge. The path ended just past the bridge as the cliff disappeared into a rocky point. Only creatures with wings would get past that point. Her eyes flicked back to the bridge. It was her only escape. "Oh, crap," she mumbled.

The noise of the falls deafened any sound coming from behind her, so Winter turned and stared at the opening in the jungle. "How?" she mumbled aloud, then she shook her head, it didn't matter. She had made it to a remote island, through an earthquake, then found sanctuary at a complete stranger's house, and he had still found and isolated her, and that was that. All that mattered now was getting away from him, and it appeared the only way to do that was over the bridge.

Winter hated bridges. Any bridges, really, but especially rope bridges. *Who the hell thought of making rope bridges, anyway?* Who was the first person to imagine, *Oh, lets tie some rope and wood together since they rot so easily in the elements, and then let's string them over a gorge where it will be certain death if you fall. Oh, and let's make sure it will swing back and forth with any weight that is placed on it.* She grimaced with the thought, then glanced at the jungle one more time and muttered, "Crap," once again. She shrugged, held her head up and then began making her way along the path toward the bridge.

At the bridge, Winter glanced down, regretted it, then pulled her eyes up to rest on the opposite side. The wood slats of the bridge were wide and looked in decent shape, so she grasped the rope railings on either side and took the first step. As she moved forward, she could feel the slats spring down, and then up, with each footfall, and the railings moved in sync with the base, as did her stomach. "I hate this," she said through gritted teeth as she tried not to think of the swirling water and jagged rocks below her feet. It was hard to forget about them as she felt the mist from the falls dampen her exposed skin and make the hair around her face curl.

Winter made it to the center of the bridge and then paused as she released her hands from the rope railing, flexed her fingers, then returned them to the railing with a slightly looser grip. She lifted her foot, but a laugh from behind her made her stop in mid-step. She didn't have to look, she knew that laugh, but she couldn't help herself, so she dropped her foot and glared over her shoulder.

Carson stood at the edge of the falls. He grinned, waved, and then sauntered toward the bridge. It was as like they were old friends and he was greeting her as if nothing had happened between them. *He was toying with her.* His favorite pastime, and she was letting him get in her head once again. This was a road they traveled many times in their marriage and she knew how it would end. Normal, easy going behavior, erupting into sudden rage and violence. She turned back around and quickened her step as she tightened her jaw and growled, "Not this time you maniac—and never again."

Winter kept her eyes glued to the jungle on the opposite side of the bridge, as if it were a beacon in a storm. *Her escape.* A swarthy man emerged from the trees. Winter gasped and stopped moving as she felt her pulse quicken. *He looks like a local,* she thought. The man advanced to the edge of the bridge and looked right at her. She began waving wildly as she called, "Help me," and then started toward him. He placed one hand on each side of the rope railings and looked past her at Carson. A slow, deep nod, and then he looked back at her with his unwavering dark eyes. She froze and whispered, "I'm such a fool." *Trapped.* This was Carson's guarantee. *It is his game and his rules.* He didn't need to scout the area or pursue her quickly. He had efficiently closed her escape route. Carson did not like to lose.

She should have known he wouldn't come alone. He might be certifiable, but he was also smart and crafty. This man looked like a native island dweller instead of his usual bodyguards, but he belonged to Carson, of that she was certain. Winter turned toward her ex-husband. He was closer now and it wouldn't take long for him to reach her. She grasped the railing and leaned over it to examine the water below them. It churned as a white foam rose from the swirling surface. The boulders that rose above the mass of swirling water and foggy mist would be hard to miss in a jump.

"You would never survive," Carson said in a low voice. She kept her body close to the railing but turned her head to look at him. There was no indication on his handsome face of the monster that dwelled just below the surface. He smiled as he said, "I've missed you, Winter."

She shivered. *How had she ever thought that silky, deep voice was seductive?*

Winter kept eye contact with him, but gripped the rope with both hands, and began to ease her foot toward the edge of the wooden planks as she said, "I am not yours. Never was and never will be." She noticed her voice sounded much stronger than she felt.

He grinned at her words but his eyes held no mirth. They remained brown, flat pools and Winter had visions of a slithering snake. He whispered, "Silly girl, you will always be mine."

A coughing bark broke Winter's concentration and she glanced behind her ex-husband. The little dog, Pete, stood quivering at the edge of the falls as he stared in their direction. Indecision was written all over his scruffy face and twitching tail. Aiden appeared from behind him, but halted when he saw them on the bridge. He shouted, "Hey!" Then he surged forward with Pete close beside him until they were at the edge of the bridge. Aiden paused and called, "What's going on here? Are you okay, Winter?" His hands were balled into fists at his side.

Carson kept his body turned toward her and his back to Aiden. He smiled as he slipped a large hunting knife out of his waistband and held it close to his chest. He shouted over his shoulder to Aiden, "Are you the new boyfriend? Well, I'm her husband." He winked at Winter and whispered, "This is going to be fun." She shivered again and felt bile rise in her throat.

"Ex-husband," Winter growled through tight lips, then she looked around Carson toward Aiden as she shouted, "I'm okay. Stay back, he has a knife!" She moved both feet to the very edge of the bridge and then dropped into a squat. She would not be responsible for another man's death at Carson's hands. She turned her eyes toward the raging water below.

"No, Winter, don't try it!" she heard Aiden's voice call to her over the roar of the waterfall. She kept her eyes on the water, but she could still see him out of the corner of her eye. He turned to Pete and yelled, "Stay," then he placed a foot on the bridge.

Winter turned to look at him and shook her head as she mouthed, "No." Her eyes turned back to the dark swirling waters below her. The churning pool was mesmerizing. The sound of the waterfall filled her ears and she realized she might be slipping into shock. *Too much. Too much. Too much,* looped through her thoughts.

Carson took a step closer, lowered his voice and growled, "Don't you dare jump!" He was only two steps away from her now.

She took a sharp breath and pulled the lower rope railing up so she could duck her head and upper body under it. She felt the bridge sway as Aiden moved onto it, then Winter sat heavily on the wooden planks and her right foot slipped over the edge, so she dropped her left leg over, but she continued to keep her grip on the rope railing. Her eyes turned to Carson as she prepared to push off. She smiled and said, "I'm *not* yours." Carson's face contorted in rage as he raised his knife and surged forward. Winter leaned toward the water, but the bridge gave a violent shake that shoved her back a few inches. She squeezed her hands around the railing and murmured, "Aftershocks."

Winter tightened her grip even more as she stared up at Carson. His feet were in a wide stance on the rocking bridge and he looked like he was trying to ride a surfboard. She leaned over and glanced past Carson. Aiden was still upright, but bent at the waist as he held onto both sides of the railing and Pete was lying flat in the grass on the ground behind him.

The bridge lunged to one side and this time her bottom slid over the edge, but she kept her grip on the railing as her weight pulled her away from the bridge. She shifted her hands on the ropes and turned until she was facing toward the bridge. Her upper body was above the bridge surface as her legs dangled below it, high above the water. A glance down. Her legs and feet swung back and forth above the swirling water. She felt one of her hands slip, so she squeezed with all her strength until the rope cut painfully into her palms. It was like being on a wild carnival ride as the earth shook, stopped, and then shook again.

Her eyes went back to the bridge surface. Carson was now lying flat on his stomach with his legs spread wide behind him. His hands clutched at the wooden planks and Winter noticed he was no longer holding the knife. She turned her head, searching, and then spotted it on the opposite edge of the bridge. Carson followed her gaze and began to crawl on his belly across the planks toward the knife, but the bridge shook even harder, and Winter watched the knife slide closer to the edge. Carson scooted after it, but as the bridge pitched in that direction, he slid forward, and then tumbled over the side and dropped from her sight. She blinked. He was gone. Just like that. Winter turned her head back toward Aiden. He still clung to the rope railing, but he was now on his knees and staring in the direction where Carson had disappeared. He looked back at her and they locked eyes. "I'm coming. Hold on," he shouted to her. She looked down at the water, but there was no sign of Carson. Her head jerked back and forth, but there was only swirling water and rocks beneath her feet.

The rumble of the earthquake finally stopped, but the bridge still swayed with the rhythm of a swing that had been pushed into motion. Winter felt her hands slipping again, so she started swinging her body parallel to the bridge and kicked one foot, then the other, but she couldn't seem to get either of her feet onto the bridge. Her eyes were drawn back to the churning waters below. "No!" she said through clinched teeth, and with a determined push, she managed to get her right leg onto the bridge when Aiden appeared above her. She felt his hands grip her arm and leg and then felt him pull her the rest of the way onto the rough plank surface. Panting, she lay face down with her cheek flat against the boards as she tried to catch her breath. She pushed herself onto her knees and then Aiden helped her get to her feet. As she stood facing him, he gripped her shoulders and asked, "Are you okay?"

"I think so," she said. She clinched and unclenched her hands as she stared at her palms. They felt raw and sore, but were only a little red. The way they felt, they should be dripping blood. She looked up, grinned, and then said, "Yes, yes, I'm fine." Aiden nodded, then without a word they both moved to the side of the bridge where Carson had disappeared. They leaned over the railing in silence and examined the water below, but there was no sign of him, so they moved to the other side and Winter searched the river until it ran out of sight. She sighed. There was no bashed and bloody body resting on one of the rocks, only swirling water and a soft gray mist at the bottom of the falls. "Damn," she murmured.

They looked at each other and Aiden said, "No way he survived that fall. It's much too high, and with the rocks down there, there's just no way."

"I hope you're right," she said, but as she looked at the churning water she mumbled, "but it's really hard to kill the devil."

She looked at him and Aiden raised a brow as he said, "So, *that* was your husband?"

"*Ex*-husband, with the emphasis on *ex*," she said. Aiden remained silent. "Long story," she added, then turned toward the opposite end of the bridge. The man with the dark eyes had disappeared. He had probably slipped back into the jungle after the quake. "He had one of his henchmen with him."

Aiden laughed aloud and said, "*Henchmen? Seriously?*" Winter's eyes narrowed and his smile disappeared as he said, "Okay, you are serious. Just who was your husband? Uh, I mean, ex-husband?" He reached out a hand and touched her shoulder again as he said, "Wait, you don't need to answer that. It doesn't matter. I do know a little from the news, but save it for another time, when, and if, you want to talk about it. Come on, let's get out of here before, uh, the 'henchman' comes back." He didn't laugh this time, but the corners of his mouth twitched as he said, "Besides, Riley will be worried."

Winter did not move. "I have to make sure Carson's dead first," she said as she turned and her eyes scanned the water and its surrounding banks. Her shoulders drooped and she looked up at Aiden and said, "I have to get down there."

Aiden frowned and said, "I think we need to head back, but I see how important this is for you." His head turned toward the side of the bridge where the mystery man had stood. He shrugged and gestured in that direction as he said, "Well, okay. There's a path that leads to the bottom of the falls through the jungle on the other side of this bridge." He turned to Winter and continued with, "We can look for his body, but we need to be careful. That guy, whoever he was, has probably rabbited, but he may still be around." He took a step toward her, but then said, "Wait a sec," and turned around and walked back to the edge of the bridge where Pete was still waiting. The dog's tail began thumping with Aiden's approach. Aiden picked him up and then joined Winter in the center of the bridge. "Let's go," he said, then added, "his three-legged hop works fine on most surfaces, but I don't trust it on this rickety bridge."

Winter tore her eyes from the river below and said, "After what just happened, I don't trust my own two legs on this thing, either." She gestured toward the opposite side and said, "Lead on."

Aiden moved past her and she followed him as she kept her hands on the rope railing. Once they reached the opposite side, they entered the jungle and edged down the path. Aiden continued to carry Pete. The trail was rough and overgrown with vegetation and appeared to be seldom used. Winter wondered if this was also a part of Aiden's property. She kept her eyes on her feet as she followed Aiden, but would occasionally glance up and search the tangled greenery on either side of the path. She kept imagining seeing the two dark eyes of Carson's hired gun glaring back at her through the bushes. "Does this land belong to you?"

"No, I think it is owned by a corporation, but I hope they never develop it."

"I would think it would be too remote to be profitable. Especially if they can only access it by boat," she responded.

A movement in the jungle caught Winter's attention. Her head jerked up and she stopped moving as she stared at a dark patch of tangled leaves and vines. *Is there something there, or is it my imagination playing tricks?* It was only a few feet from the trail, but the light was too dim to see much in the middle of the towering trees. She kept her eyes on the spot but started following Aiden again. "Damn!" she uttered as she felt her foot catch on a tree root and she slammed into Aiden's back, then righted herself by placing both hands on his shoulders. He stopped moving and she took a step back and mumbled, "Sorry." Aiden glanced back at her, nodded, and then continued down the slope. Winter examined the leaves where she thought she saw movement, but couldn't see anything, so she took another step forward. Her foot was hurting like hell, but she kept moving as she tried not to favor it or get distracted again.

Winter pushed a thorny limb aside by wrapping the bottom of her shirt around her hand. What a difference in this path and the one she had followed to the falls. It was hard to tell which was path and which was jungle. "I need to know if he is really dead. I have to see for myself," she said as she glanced up at Aiden's back. *Too close.* She slowed her step until she was a couple of paces away from him again. She knew she was repeating herself, but she wanted to make him understand. She shook her head and wondered why she cared what this man thought about her, *but she did care.* She frowned and said, "I know you probably think I'm crazy, but you have no idea what he is capable of doing."

She saw the back of Aiden's head bob in a nod, and then he said over his shoulder, "I think I'm getting the idea. He seemed pretty crazy to me."

Winter tripped again, but was far enough back that she used a tree limb to right herself instead of hitting Aiden's back. "Crap," she mumbled as she felt a pain sweep from her toe to her ankle. It was the same foot and her big toe began to throb. Aiden turned to glance at her, but she shrugged and said, "Sorry, I stumbled again." She turned her eyes back to her feet. *Damn big feet.* He kept moving down the winding path, but Winter noticed his shoulders moving up and down. *Fine.* Let him laugh. She didn't care if he found her clumsiness hysterical if he kept leading her to the bottom of the falls.

She *had* to see Carson's body. Crushed on a rock would be good, or floating face down in the water, but *dead.* She sighed. It was hard to explain to someone who didn't know her situation, but she needed a definitive end to her long nightmare. The never ending bad dream had consumed her life for much too long.

Winter heard the roar of the waterfall and knew they were getting close. The forest felt wet and there was more moss growing on the ground and trees. She noticed water dripping from a branch and then they took one more step and were out of the jungle and at the base of the falls.

Mist floated around the large pool of water like a cloud and the sound of the falls was deafening. The base pool fed into a river of water that rushed vigorously over boulders and rocks until it ran out of sight. Winter frowned. The pool was spectacular, but there was no dead body floating up from the bottom or lying on the banks beside the river.

They walked around the edge of the water searching the banks, but there was no sign of Carson. Nothing in the water or on the ground by the river. Aiden stopped beside the waterfall pool and pointed at scarlet marks that slashed the top of a large boulder. "I am guessing he hit there and then was washed down the river." Aiden shouted over the noise of the falls.

"I hope you're right, but I would have felt better if we found a body." Winter sighed and said, "I'll never feel completely safe until I see him dead."

Aiden raised both eyebrows and said, "Okay, but if he was swept down the river, or even all the way to the ocean, there is a chance that there will be nothing left to find."

Winter said nothing. She knew he was curious about her story and she was sure she sounded heartless, but she wasn't ready to elaborate. *Her story. Two words.* How could her life with Carson be encapsulated into those two words? How could she articulate what brought her from a heart that was bursting with love, to the overwhelming desire to see the object of that love floating dead and broken in these wild waters? She looked at Aiden and only felt exhaustion.

Aiden cleared his throat and said, "Nothing stays in the pool for long." He examined the ground beside the water, then bent and picked up a small branch and tossed it into the center of the pool. Pete ran to the edge of the water and barked, but he stayed on the bank away from the rushing water. The limb swirled in a circle, then banged against the bolder with the scarlet stain, and then rushed over some smaller rocks, until it hit the river, where it flowed out of sight. "Pete, come!" Aiden said and the dog hopped to his side. Winter felt Aiden's hand on her elbow as she stared at the water. "Riley will be waiting, we better head home," he said. Winter allowed him to guide her toward the jungle. "He's most likely fish or croc food by now and you will never see his body."

Winter sighed and managed to say, "You're probably right." Her eyes kept darting around as she searched for any sign of Carson. As they entered the jungle she fell into step behind Aiden, but paused and stared at another clump of leaves when she thought she saw movement again. *Nothing there.* She was seeing danger in every shadow again. She moved on, but couldn't shake the chill traveling up and down her spine. Winter shivered and quickened her step. It would be just like Carson to keep stalking her in her thoughts even if he was dead. Damn man always had to throw the last punch.

***

The drunk American and Carson's woman searched the area around the pool at the base of the falls, then had a brief conversation, but Ricardo was too far away to hear what they were saying. The woman kept gazing in his direction, and at one point, they both turned and looked toward him, so Ricardo eased back and blended deeper into the jungle.

As he watched from behind a thick banana tree, they began to move away, but he stood motionless when the woman hesitated and looked once more in his direction. Ricardo waited. He was good at waiting. Even when a curious basilisk chose that moment to walk over his hand as he leaned it on the limb of the tree, he remained so still that the creature must have thought him a part of the tree, and his hand a brown limb. If he moved, it would have scurried away and startled the Americans. It would have been funny to watch the reptile run from the jungle and across the pond. The woman would have screamed at the sight of a lizard running upright on water, but Ricardo could not risk discovery, so he remained patient and still. A patient man gets paid. Ricardo was sure Carson had lied and had carried the rest of his money on him, so he needed to find the body and the cash. Ricardo was hungry. For food, yes, he could not remember a time his belly wasn't empty, but hunger for money was his driving force. Money meant power and power was everything in his world.

Ricardo emerged from the jungle about an hour after the gringos left.

He tied a rope to the banana tree and then around his waist before he waded into the deep pool at the edge of the falls. He eased into the water as he used his boots to feel his way over the uneven muddy bottom of the pool. When the water was waist high, he dove in and hovered just above the bottom with his legs kicking and his hands touching the mud and rocks. The current pulled at him and the falls pounded his back, but he persisted and only surfaced long enough to gasp for air, until he checked all the boulders and he was satisfied Carson, or more importantly, Carson's backpack and money, were not in the pool. His hope was that Carson or his backpack had gotten caught on one of the boulders but his usual bad luck prevailed and he found nothing.

Ricardo used the rope to pull himself out of the water until he was back on the bank. He sat for a moment as he caught his breath. He was soaked through to his skin and had bruises from slamming into the rocks. Sandy grit was jammed under his nails and in his hair and his mouth tasted of pond scum. He spat some of the water from his mouth and cleared his nose before he stood and removed the rope from his waist. He carefully wound the rope and stuck it into the pack he had found on the American's boat, then he sloshed along the bank until he reached the point where the water cascaded into the river. At least finding the pack had been a little good luck. But that luck was probably meant for Carson since it was his orders that sent Ricardo on board to disable the engine.

He watched the water flow for a while, then combed the bank and grass surrounding his side of the river, stopping several times to examine anything that looked out of the ordinary. A jabiru was standing on one leg and poking at something in a patch of tall grass. Ricardo approached it and the bird took flight as it soared high above the water, then it changed direction and headed toward the tree tops where it would probably scoop up an unsuspecting monkey.

Ricardo picked up a limb and used it to push the grass aside where the bird seemed the most interested, and then he saw it, a bloody blotch all but hidden by the reeds. He moved closer. There was an indentation in the grass and several small pools of blood had soaked into the sand. His eyes followed the trail of broken reeds toward a small opening in the thick jungle. "Alive," he mumbled as he shook his head from side to side. That was a disappointment, but at least there was a sign of him. Maybe Ricardo's luck was getting better. He didn't even have to venture to the other side of the river to find his prize.

Ricardo pulled out his knife and started toward the jungle. The sun on his back was drying his clothes, but his boots felt heavy with water. It didn't matter. Ricardo was used to discomfort. He pushed ahead but kept his eyes constantly roving. Extreme caution was what he needed now, not dry boots. Wounded and cornered animals were the most dangerous ones. If he was lucky, the jungle would have already finished the gringo off, but Ricardo was seldom lucky and the man called Carson seemed to be born under a lucky star. He crossed himself, spit, and then moved into the jungle as he used his knife to cut a path.

Chapter 14

Riley bounded down the steps and met Winter and Aiden half way across the yard. "Where have you guys been? That last tremor kind of freaked me out. When you didn't come back right away I didn't know what happened to you, and I wasn't sure where to look for you guys," she said, then punched Winter on the shoulder. Her eyes were wide and her words tumbled over each other.

Pete circled Riley, then sat in front of her on his haunches and barked. Riley laughed and scratched his head and said, "Sounds like you were a little freaked out too, right boy?" He quieted and flopped on the ground as he exposed his stomach. When she didn't scratch it right away, he wiggled his wiry body until she snorted and said, "Okay, okay," and rubbed his pink belly.

"Uh, a lot happened out there. There are some new developments, but I'll let Winter fill you," Aiden said as he turned to Winter.

Winter looked at Aiden, then back at Riley, blinked rapidly, and then looked around the property before she said, "Fine, but let's go inside the cabin first." She glanced around again, then brushed past Riley and headed toward the house as she said over her shoulder, "We're much too exposed out here." Riley glanced at Aiden, who shrugged, then they both followed Winter. Pete jumped up and ran ahead of them.

As soon as they were inside, Winter turned and hugged Riley. She moved away and said, "I'm sorry we worried you, but it was Carson. He is here. He tried to kill me, but we think he might be dead, at least, I hope he is."

Riley's chin dropped and her eyes grew wide again as she said, "*What? What* are you talking about? *Here*? He is here? I thought he was under arrest in San Francisco?" She didn't wait for an answer, but shook her head and then said, "Dead? What do you mean y'all '*think*' he's dead?"

"He *was* under *house* arrest instead of jail because his lawyers pulled some strings and he didn't even have to wear an ankle bracelet. Knowing Carson, that was simply a challenge. As far as being dead, he fell off the bridge by the waterfall. It was a huge drop, but we couldn't find his body, so I don't know for sure."

"Bridge? Waterfall? Where did you folks go this morning and why didn't you include me?" Riley asked as she looked from Winter to Aiden.

Aiden moved in beside the two women and the three of them formed a tight circle. "I think everyone seems to know more about this guy then I do. Don't you think it's time *I* get some answers?" Aiden asked. He turned to Winter and added, "Who exactly is this ex-husband of yours? I thought he was some big CEO or something, but the way he attacked you today, and with the accusations of murder, he sounds more like a gangster."

Winter turned toward him and said, "I'll give you the whole sordid story, but it's a long one. What I really think we need to do is get into town. I don't want to spend another night here. We are too isolated. Between the aftershocks, and the possibility that there are more of Carson's men around, we would be safer if we could get to civilization and law enforcement."

Aiden looked at Winter and said, "He couldn't have survived that fall. Seriously, with the rocks and height of the fall he probably died on impact, and if not, he most likely drowned long before he reached the ocean and became fish food." Aiden shook his head, then looked at Riley and said, "Even if by some slim chance he survived he must be seriously hurt." He looked back to Winter and asked, "Do you really think he is that dangerous?"

"Yes, absolutely! Extremely dangerous," Winter said, then rubbed her face with both hands. She turned toward Aiden as she said, "The abridged version is that Carson was my husband, but now he is my ex, and hopefully dead, husband. He is on trial for murder and I am the main witness. The prosecutor dropped dead at the trial, so we were delayed. Carson was supposed to be under house arrest and since I know the people who get in his way seem to die, I went into hiding. I can fill you in on more details later, but right now we need to get out of here. Again, *yes,* we are in danger. Carson doesn't give up and even if he is dead, he has probably arranged for someone else to deal with me, because he is also very big on revenge."

Riley put her hands on her hips and said, "Okay, folks, I want to know about this incident at the waterfall, but Winter's right, there's time for all this later." She looked at Aiden and asked, "What about that boat down at the dock? Is that what you had in mind?"

Aiden looked at both women and said, "Yes, that's how I thought we could get to town. The channel we are on meets up with the river past the falls, then we must navigate it through the mangrove swamps and on to the ocean. Once we get to the sea we hug the coast until we get to the other end of the island. It will be rough, but I've done it many times and it's our best shot. Grab your gear and I'll put out more food for Patch. I think we better take Pete with us."

"Do you leave her inside?" Riley asked.

Aiden smiled and said, "Yes, but she has an escape hatch so they can both come and go as they please." He winked and said, "I'll show you." He started toward his bedroom and both women followed.

The bedroom was spacious with floor to ceiling windows covering the two outside walls, it was as if the jungle was part of the room. The view mesmerized Winter. Banana trees, exotic flowers displaying vivid bursts of color, and a couple of monkeys playing chase until they noticed movement in the bedroom and disappeared into the tree tops. A nudge from Riley made her turn from the windows to take in the rest of the room. A large four poster bed with a canopy of mosquito netting was on the wall bordering the living room. The remaining inside wall contained two doors, one was a large double door that stood open to reveal a ridiculously orderly closet, the other, was a 3ft high door located close to the outside wall junction. The smaller door was shut but appeared to be for storage. Riley pointed to the little door and said, "Too cool!"

Winter looked closer and noticed a panel in the wooden door that appeared to move. Aiden grinned and approached the door where he bent and pushed on the panel. It swung freely. It was mounted on tiny hinges and painted the same brown as the wood. He twisted the nob on the actual door and pulled it open.

"Wow!" Winter said as she leaned over to view the inside of the cubicle. A cat box sat on one side of the space with a tiny night light mounted just above it. The back wall of the enclosed space held what appeared to be another movable panel. Aiden got on his knees and pushed at the back-wall panel. Winter could see a ramp that led to the cabin's crawl space in the dim light. She asked, "Don't you worry about critters other than Patch or Pete getting through that door?"

Aiden dropped the flap and looked back at her and said, "Honestly, a little. I enjoy the monkeys playing outside the windows but I don't want them coming in here. So far, it hasn't been a problem, but maybe the smell of Patch's potty room isn't as appealing as the kitchen smells might be to them."

"Good point," Winter said.

Riley stood with her hands on her hips and said, "I am impressed! Did you do all this yourself?"

"I can't take all the credit. The basic structure was here when I bought the place. I simply made a few modifications, like Patch and Pete's closet," Aiden said.

They exited the bedroom and Winter and Riley packed up their personal belongings, then picked up some water and food from the kitchen to stuff into their packs. Winter grabbed a peanut butter jar and made a sandwich and wolfed it down. "What? I'm hungry." She said when Riley laughed at her.

"You are always hungry, sweetie. I don't know how you stay so slim." Riley said, but she followed Winter's lead and ate her sandwich as she headed for the door.

Aiden did the same thing after he filled Patch's water and auto feeder to the brim, and then they left the cabin and headed toward the dock. Aiden climbed onboard the boat, then reached for their packs. The boat was a mid-size center console and was filled with fishing gear. A small boat to have on the ocean but Winter imagined it would be easier to steer through the narrow river channels and mangrove trees on the way to the sea.

Aiden placed their packs under a bench running along the side of the boat, then moved to the console and started the engine. "Could you ladies untie the ropes and hop on?" he asked as he nodded at the ropes tethered at each end to the dock. Aiden whistled and Pete came to the edge of the dock. He grabbed the dog and he lifted him onto the boat. Pete jumped up on the bench and perched his one front leg on the side so that he had a view of the water at the front of the boat.

"I take it he's done this a few times before?" Riley asked.

"A few times," Aiden said with a laugh.

Winter smiled, but it slipped away as the boat motor sputtered and chugged to a stop. "What's wrong?" she asked.

"Not sure," Aiden said as he examined gauges. "I know I had plenty of gas but the gauge shows empty." He removed a panel exposing the engine. A strong smell of gasoline rose from the chamber. "Damn," he said.

"Look!" Riley said as she pointed toward the water at the side of the boat. An oily blue-green substance floated around it.

"Someone has been messing with the motor. I'm surprised it even started," Aiden said, then he got closer and examined the engine. "Looks like puncture marks. Maybe from an icepick or screwdriver?"

"Carson," Winter mumbled.

"Well, this boat's not going anywhere without some serious repairs," Aiden said, then moved to the side of the boat and patted his leg. "Come on, boy, no boat ride today," he said. Pete whined, looked at the water, then hopped down and approached Aiden as he allowed himself to be lifted back onto the dock. Both women moved closer and accepted their packs before Aiden climbed out of the boat.

"What now?" Winter asked.

Aiden stared down the river and then looked back to the house.

"Can it be fixed?" Riley asked.

"Not by me. They did a real number on it, so I would have to have new parts first, and anyway, I'm not sure I have enough extra gas stored for the trip," Aiden said.

"Maybe we could take your jeep to the sinkhole, then walk the rest of the way?" Riley said.

Aiden shook his head before he said, "That might be very risky going through the jungle."

"It's risky staying here and it's not like someone will be coming to rescue us," Winter said, then continued with, "and, I assume we won't have phone or cell service for a long time." She gazed at Riley and said, "I would like to get word to someone about the yogis, also."

Aiden frowned at her, then swung around and looked back at the cabin and said, "I have an idea." He left the dock and headed toward the house with Pete following close behind him. He stopped and gestured with his hand as he said, "Come on," so both women followed.

When Aiden reached the house, he moved around to the side of it instead of climbing the steps to the porch. A bulky green tarp covered something large stored under the front porch. Aiden began tugging at the tarp, so Winter and Riley moved in to help him. Under the dusty tarp were two kayaks. One was a double seater and the other a single seater. "This could work," Aiden said as he grinned at them.

"On the ocean? You think we can manage those things on the ocean?" Winter shook her head and continued with, "On the river, fine, but not with ocean waves. We'd be toast."

"Got a better idea?" Aiden asked.

"Okay, no, but do you think we can really do this?" Winter asked.

"We have to do it, so we will," Aiden said, then added, "But, maybe we should spend the night here and start first thing in the morning."

"I really don't want to spend another night here knowing there might be someone out there watching and waiting, and by someone, I mean Carson, or his hired help. I wouldn't sleep, anyway," Winter said.

Riley said, "I get it and I agree. Let's get this show on the road, or river, so to speak."

"Okay, let's do it," Aiden said as he began to tug at the larger of the two kayaks. He added, "You two get the smaller one down to the water and I'll pull this one out, but first, let me hose them out and check for snakes and spiders."

"Snakes and spiders?" Winter said as she took a step back.

Riley laughed and said, "Winter, I think that a few spiders are the least of your worries and you've already dealt with a giant snake."

Winter laughed and said, "Riley, you have a way with words." She moved in to help Aiden clean the kayaks.

After cleaning them out, they moved them to the river's edge and then packed some supplies into the hatch of the larger one. Aiden used the hatch of the smaller one for a makeshift bed for Pete. He looked at the horizon and said, "It's getting late to make a start, but we can stop and camp somewhere for the night if we need to. Once we get on the ocean, there are a lot of little beaches," he said. "I hope we get to a beach before the sun goes down. I don't want to get caught in the open ocean in the dark."

Winter gazed across the yard at the cabin and said, "Thank you both for understanding. I really don't want to stay here another night. It would feel like we were sitting ducks."

Aiden looked at the women and said, "Okay, then, let's get going, the sooner the better." He patted the bed on the smaller kayak and Pete jumped into it. "We need to get through the mangroves and make the ocean before dark if this is going to work. Once we are on the ocean, stay close to the shoreline and as soon as we see a spot with a wide enough beach, we'll camp for the night." He checked two large flashlights and then he tied them to each kayak within reaching distance. "Just in case," he said. He handed Winter and Riley life vests from the center console boat, then he slipped a small one on Pete, as he said, "I got this one when I first started taking him out on our excursions."

"I've kayaked on lakes and rivers but never on the ocean." Winter said.

"Well, I've never been in one of these things, but I've paddled a few fishing row boats," Riley said as she tugged at her life jacket.

"Okay, Riley, you're with me in the double and Winter, you take the little one with Pete," Aiden said.

Winter frowned and said, "Okay, but I'm a little worried about tipping him out."

Aiden smiled at the dog and said, "No worries, he is a great sailor, right, Pete?" The scruffy dog coughed a reply and they all laughed. "He is a good swimmer, but I always watch him around crocodiles," Aiden said as Winter stepped into her kayak.

"Crocodiles?" Winter asked. She looked at him and said, "You're just messing with me, right?"

Aiden smiled and said, "No, I'm serious. There are crocs in the swamps and along the river, but they won't bother you if you are in the kayak and keep moving. Pete doesn't like them, though, so make sure he doesn't decide to take one on." He winked at her.

"Good to know," Winter said. Aiden pushed her kayak into the river before helping Riley into the front of the double. Winter floated in place getting used to the weight of the boat and the double headed oar. She watched him get into the back of the larger kayak and use his oar to push it free. He was quite graceful, but his muscles rippled as he began to paddle.

"Don't go there," Winter mumbled to herself.

"What?" Aiden asked.

"Nothing," Winter replied. "I was just telling your little dog to hold steady," she said as they headed out to the center of the river. Pete turned his shaggy head and brown eyes on her. "Keep your thoughts to yourself, Pete," she mumbled. Winter put her paddle into the water, but paused as she thought she heard something coming from the jungle. Her head turned and she studied the trees, then asked, "Did you guys hear that?"

"What?" both Riley and Aiden asked at the same time.

"I don't know---it sounded like a muted crack," Winter replied.

"Maybe a tree limb broke in the earthquake and it just snapped?" Riley asked.

The kayaks pulled up side by side. They remained quiet and listened, but nothing unusual came from the jungle. "I guess it was nothing," Winter said as she shrugged.

"Want me to check it out?" Aiden asked as he stared back toward the shoreline.

"No, it's probably just my nerves. It's getting late so we better keep going," Winter said.

Aiden shrugged and he began paddling once more. Winter followed them and gazed at the sky as the sun sank a little lower toward the horizon.

Chapter 15

Carson crawled over a tree root and bit his lip to keep from screaming. He stopped crawling and sat up. A thick, tangled veil of green hid him from the river area, so he scooted on his bottom across the uneven ground until he could lean against the tree, then he shifted the weight off his injured leg. His right leg was severely damaged and his left arm dangled at his side; both were completely useless.

He thought the reeds by the water were difficult to maneuver, until he reached the forest, and he found it almost impossible to navigate by crawling, and crawling was all he could manage in his current state. Carson winced as he eased his right hand over his left shoulder and felt it sagging away from the socket. He must have dislocated it when he hit the water. It was an old college football injury that still haunted him when it was stressed, and hitting the water from the height of the bridge must have done the trick. He was lucky he hadn't broken his neck when he had smacked into the water's surface. He blacked out on impact, but woke as soon as his desperate lungs began to suck water in through his windpipe. Drowning might have been less painful than what he felt now, but it was not an option. He had to finish this. He was not afraid to die, but if he went, Winter had to go first.

Carson examined his injured leg. It was bleeding where he had knocked against a boulder as he tumbled in the current, but he didn't think it was broken. He had trouble putting weight on it, though, so a bone break was still a possibility. Blood oozed through the rip in his shorts in a slow but steady ripple. Carson pulled off his backpack and rummaged around in it until he found a clean t-shirt he could use as a makeshift bandage. He wound the shirt around his thigh and made it just tight enough to stop the flow of blood. No use sending out a signal that dinner was served to an animal high enough on the food chain to take advantage of his injuries. Something screeched at the top of a tree and it was answered by another beast on the ground. Being steadily torn and gnawed at by sharp teeth was not how Carson wanted to go out.

He pulled the gun from his backpack and slipped it under his injured right leg, then he eased the backpack across his lap. He had to watch out for animals, but also two legged predators. He examined the crushed grass and weeds dotted with crimson in his wake. It would be easy to track him, but there wasn't much he could do about it right now. He sighed. He knew he was going to pass out with what he had to do next, so all he could do was hope for the best.

He placed the shoulder strap of the backpack in his mouth and bit down. He scanned the clearing, then he took a deep breath, and slammed his shoulder against the tree trunk. He heard a satisfying snap as the ball went back into the socket, but then the world went black, as he knew he would.

***

Ricardo used his knife to slash into the jungle's tangled limbs and vines. He stopped every few steps to look for the blood trail. The gringo was leaving a wide trail of blood drops and crushed grass and leaves on the forest floor, but nothing higher up. Ricardo smiled. *Crawling not walking.* Maybe Ricardo was finally getting his own lucky star. He was stealing it from the man known as Carson. Once he had taken the American's life, the man's luck would belong to him.

As Ricardo entered a small clearing he stopped and stood perfectly still. *At last.* The rich American was on the other side of the clearing. He leaned against a tree trunk with his eyes closed and his head slumped on his shoulder. *Dead or asleep?* Ricardo shrugged and grinned so hard his cheeks hurt. It felt strange. His face was unaccustomed to smiling, so the sensation made his lips crack, but he couldn't seem to stop. "Finally," he said in a quick breath. *Luck.*

Luck was an important commodity in Ricardo's world where the birthright was poverty and an early death. Having luck was even better than being born into a wealthy family. With luck, anything was possible. The gringo was holding his backpack on his lap in full view. Ricardo took one step forward and then stopped as he felt a familiar seed of doubt tap him on his shoulder. The grin disappeared as he thought, *Is this too easy?*

Ricardo kept moving forward, but stopped every couple of steps to gauge the injured American for any sign of life. He felt like a cat stalking his prey. He gripped his knife and felt the power flow up his arm as he puffed out his chest. He stopped a few steps from the body and stood very still. Carson didn't blink or twitch his eyes, but his chest still had some erratic movement. Ricardo moved forward and nudged him with the toe of his boot as he held his knife poised high in the air, but the downed man kept still. Ricardo leaned forward and gazed at the American. There was a t-shirt tied around his injured leg with a tinge of blood seeping through it. *The source of the blood trail,* Ricardo thought, but then his eyes stopped at the prize on the man's lap and he nodded as his knife dropped to his side. *The American is done,* Ricardo thought as he leaned over the inert man and eased the backpack off his lap. He took a step back and rummaged through the pack. *No money.* Ricardo frowned and shook the backpack violently until everything was scattered on the ground. *Still, no money.*

He moved in and stood over the unconscious man. Ricardo felt the heat of rage almost blind him as he raised his knife to strike, but then he noticed a slight bulge around the gringo's otherwise slender waist. He knelt on one knee and eased the man's shirt up. *Clever American.* This time instead of a gun under the snake tattoo, a money belt rested. Ricardo squatted and used his knife to cut the belt free. His hands shook as he unzipped the belt. It was filled with green American dollars. *Twenties, tens, fives, wads of cash.* Ricardo's eyes glistened. More money than he had seen in all his years of picking pockets and rolling turistas. More money than he could have imagined, and it was his. *All his.*

He zipped the belt closed and stuffed it into his waist band, then he sensed something. *Movement.* He gripped his knife and his eyes shifted back to Carson. He swallowed hard and sat back on his heels. *He has his gun.* The barrel was pointed at Ricardo's chest and the butt rested on the snake on Carson's belly. The gringo's eyes were open and glaring at him as he said, "Hello, Ricardo. I think you have something that belongs to me."

Ricardo scrambled to his knees and raised his knife, but it felt like he moved in slow motion. Why had he not cut the American's throat the moment he saw him? That's what you do when you come upon a snake. Ricardo knew in his heart that he was too late, but he really wanted to kill the American. *Don't bring a knife to a gunfight.* Ricardo had never been lucky. Why should that change now? One could not steal another man's luck. You were born under a lucky star or you weren't.

The explosion of the bullet slammed Ricardo in the chest and he felt his body go limp as he fell forward and landed on Carson's injured leg. He heard a groan from the American then felt a hand shove him to one side. As he lay on his back he felt a wetness flow across his chest and he had a strange sensation of no longer being connected to his arms or legs. He tried to move his head to see what the American was doing, but it took too much effort and he felt so weak and cold. *So cold.*

Ricardo felt the knife pulled from his hand and the money belt tugged from his waist. *Good bye wealth.* He could see the tree above the gringo without moving his head, but then his vision started to grow dark around the edges. The American appeared in his line of sight. He was using the tree to stand. It was a strange and magical sight as Carson eased upright with a dark outline around him like a frame. The gringo had the knife in his hand and at first Ricardo thought he was going to feel the impact of a blow, but instead, the American used it to cut a limb from the tree.

Ricardo watched Carson use the limb for a cane as he limped away and disappeared into the jungle. He was wearing his backpack and his money belt was probably in it. Ricardo could almost see the lucky star hanging above the American's head. Ricardo sighed and closed his eyes.

Chapter 16

Winter flinched as hanging moss grazed her shoulder and then she swatted at a mosquito feeding on the opposite arm. She glared at the stagnant water and tried to concentrate on keeping her paddle low enough that the liquid wouldn't run back down her arm. It was a losing battle and her shirt and shorts were getting soaked. The waterway was narrow, it was only about six feet between the river's muddy banks. Mangrove trees guarded the banks with their exposed gnarly roots fighting for real estate at the water's edge. It felt like they were paddling through a narrow tunnel and Winter crinkled her nose as she sniffed at the air; the smell was somewhere between rotting fruit and open sewer lines.

"Are you sure this goes all the way to the ocean? You said you've traveled through here before?" Her voice sounded eerie as it echoed in an area where a canopy of trees was almost touching from bank to bank. It was claustrophobic and felt like a different river than where their journey started. It was as if they had taken a wrong turn, even though logically she knew there had been no turns or other channels to take. She lifted her oar out of the water and glanced around as she asked, "What on earth is that smell?"

She heard Riley laugh and Aiden said, "This area is close to being a swamp. The smell is moist forest, stagnate water, algae, and fungus. Basically, it's rotting plants and animals." He glanced at her over his shoulder then turned his head forward and kept paddling as he continued with, "I've traveled this way a lot when I don't want to dock my boat in town for fishing tours. This channel is deep enough in the middle, but it's a lot trickier to maneuver with the fishing boat than with these kayaks. The higher boat makes it hard to duck all the low hanging tree limbs and I have to keep it in the absolute middle to avoid the shallow water and roots by the banks." An audible sigh and he said over his shoulder, "We aren't far from the ocean now."

Was that exasperation she heard in his voice? Winter had to admit that she may have sounded a little whiney in her questioning, but then again, she felt like she had every reason to feel frustrated and grumpy. This trip to find serenity was anything but serene. She frowned and thought, *Okay, Winter, it's no picnic for them, either, so suck it up.*

Winter watched Aiden's back as they paddled through the murky waters. He had insisted on keeping the lead, even though there was nowhere in this waterway they could have gotten lost, and he was moving impossibly slow to boot. She snorted. *Typical male behavior.*

She looked at Pete in the front of her kayak. The little fur ball seemed calm enough as he curled into his makeshift bed, so maybe she was the only one feeling impatient. As soon as the thought floated through her mind, the dog lifted his furry head and cranked it toward the bank and growled. Winter followed his gaze and saw something shift between the roots of a mangrove tree. The hairs on the back of her neck stood up. Winter pulled her paddle out of the water again and floated as she stared at the area. She gasped as the movement took form. A crocodile rose and adjusted his place in the mud, then eased down and blended with the gnarly tree roots. If she hadn't seen him stand she never would have guessed there was something there. It looked like some prehistoric beast from another era.

Winter shivered, eased her paddle back into the brackish water, and pushed harder than before. "Uh, let's get a move on, folks. We have some company on the banks," she said as she closed the gap between the kayaks. Her eyes shifted to the ripples in the dark surface of the water as she looked for any sign they had company in the river. No long reptilian back or beady dark eyes surfaced. A glance up and Winter realized how fast she was closing on the lead kayak, so she used her paddle to slow her movement.

"They rarely bother with boats," Aiden called, but Winter noticed his kayak slid forward a little quicker than it had before.

"Yeah, but 'rarely' means sometimes," she mumbled.

They rounded a narrow bend and the river opened to a much wider waterway. The mangrove trees were replaced with conifers intermingled with tropical broadleaves. Winter took a deep breath of fresh air. The clean forest scent was amazing after the rotten stench they left behind. A pull in the current made paddling easier as her kayak glided forward. She enjoyed the open space and fresh air until she heard a sound that she didn't recognize. Winter cocked her head to one side and listened, then frowned as it registered in her memory banks.

"Strong currents ahead where the channel narrows again, but don't worry, it isn't anything we can't handle," Aiden called back to her. "Just stay in the middle where the water is deeper and follow my lead."

"Should I do something with Pete?" She called to his back.

"No, his balance is great, even with only three legs," he replied, then added, "besides, there's no time."

Winter sighed and thought, *Okay, feminist thoughts aside, maybe it is better Aiden is in the lead.*

She concentrated on staying a few feet from the lead kayak and imitating the way Aiden handled the strong current and occasional white tipped rapids. They surged through the water as they used their paddles more for pushing off rocks than paddling. *Right again*, Winter thought as they slid into a wider section of the river. The rapids had not gotten strong enough to be dangerous, and Pete hunkered down from the minute they started until they were through the rough waters. Once they were on the other side of the surging water the little dog stood and wagged his tail. In the distance, Winter could see the river channel empty into the vast ocean with no horizon in sight. *At last,* she thought as her heartbeat quickened.

As they got closer to the sea, Winter felt herself struggling more with the current. The river was wide enough that both kayaks were now traveling side by side, so Aiden called across to her, "Go left at the cliffs and hug them as close as you can." She nodded and fell in behind him. As she gazed ahead at the vast rolling ocean and white tipped waves, she swallowed hard and her lips clamped into a tight line.

Winter managed to make the turn at the cliff's edge but had to use all her strength to keep the kayak from flipping over with the first wave surge. She kept looking up at the sheer cliffs as they paddled by them. They rose like a jagged wall out of the blue-green water like a gigantic skyscraper. It made her feel small and vulnerable. To stay close to them without bashing against the jagged rocks was not easy. Winter's muscles screamed with the strain and they still had a long way to go. Pete curled deep into his bed, and after one glaced at the cliff wall, he buried his face and refused to look up.

Winter was too stubborn to admit her fatigue and continued to keep pace with Aiden and Riley. Her brow furrowed as she stared at the double kayak. At least they had two paddling through the treacherous waters. Pete glanced at her as if he read her thoughts. "Freeloader," she whispered. His tail thumped in response. "Yeah, you just rest, little guy. I'll get us there in one piece," she mumbled as she gritted her teeth and pushed harder against the strong ocean current.

When they finally left the cliffs behind, Winter stopped picturing herself crashing into the jagged rocks. The paddling became even more difficult. They had to stay as close to the coast as possible without getting caught in the waves that were charging toward land.

It required constant paddling to fight the waves, so there were no more rest periods of simply floating. Winter's shoulders and arms ached. Each time she pulled her paddle out of the water she was immediately pulled toward the tree lined shore.

"It's getting hard to see," she called as she peered toward land. The shore was fast becoming a shadowland of dense forest. She kept searching for a break in the trees, but the jungle forest was uninterrupted, and it would soon be nothing but a dark silhouette.

"I think there is a beach on the next cove that will work, so let's pull in there for the night," Aiden said.

As they came around the next bend, Winter spotted the cove. It was a small strip of sand surrounded by jungle. She shivered. She knew they would have to spend the night on a beach, but she still had held the hope that they would reach some sort of civilization before disembarking the kayaks. The thought of sleeping out in the open on a beach so close to the wild, uninhabited jungle was a bit intimidating. Her shoulders slumped. She was much too tired to go on any longer, so it would have to do. "Is it high tide or are we going to lose that strip before morning?" she called. As scary as the beach might seem, spending the night in the jungle would be worse.

"It's high tide, so we're good," Aiden said.

"Let's do it before my arms fall off," Riley said as she rotated her shoulders. "This paddling in these ocean waves is ridiculous. I can't believe folks do this for fun."

Aiden laughed and jammed his paddle into the water as they turned and rode a wave toward the shoreline. Winter watched them glide forward, then rise on another wave, and shoot closer to shore. She followed their lead and pushed hard into another wave as the kayak rose in a swell, then surged forward. "Try doing it by yourself for a while, Riley," Winter mumbled as she felt the protest coming from her upper back and shoulders. Her words were lost in the sound of the surf as a mist of salty water splashed over her. She blinked rapidly when the salt burned her tired eyes, but the mist felt cool, and she pushed even harder to reach the promise of the shoreline. By the next wave, a smile and a giggle rode with her. It felt like body surfing in a boat.

Aiden and Riley reached land first and nosed onto the sandy beach.

Aiden jumped out and waded calf deep in the water until he was in front of the kayak, and then pulled it the rest of the way onto the sand. Riley stood and stepped out of the boat. She stretched and headed across the sand toward the jungle. "I'll be right back. Nature's calling," she said.

"Be careful," Aiden called.

"Country girl, here," Riley said. A wave of her hand and she disappeared into a wall of greenery.

Winter felt her kayak hit bottom as its nose embedded in the sand. She scooted it a little further simply by shifting her bottom forward on the seat a couple of times as she dug the paddle into the sand.

Pete stood and gave a hefty shake, then jumped out of his makeshift bed and hopped to the edge of the kayak. He jumped from the tip and made a graceful three-legged leap onto the dry sand. He ran in tight circles as he did his coughing bark, then stopped and gave a quick dig in the sand with both back paws. He hopped over to a tree and lifted his back leg to relieve himself. Aiden laughed as he watched his pooch and then moved in to help Winter pull the smaller kayak the rest of the way onto the beach.

Winter got out of the kayak and together they pulled it close to the tree line and then they did the same with the longer kayak. Riley emerged from the jungle and said, "Much better." She had a handful of twigs that she dropped on the beach by the kayaks as she said, "I'll get some more firewood." She began to walk the beach looking for driftwood and dry limbs.

Aiden pulled out a small collapsible shovel from the front of the larger kayak and began digging a pit in front of the kayaks. He glanced at Winter and said, "For the fire."

"Okay, I'll help Riley with the wood," she said.

Once they had the fire lit and the kayaks acting as a barrier to the jungle, they spread some beach towels in front of the boats and plopped down. Aiden dug into his backpack and pulled out water bottles and sandwiches and passed them around. He rested against one of the kayaks with his long legs stretched out in front of him as Pete leaned into his side. He rubbed the dog's neck and handed him half of his sandwich. The dog ate it in two bites, so Aiden reached into his bag and pulled out a rawhide bone. The dog barked his approval and settled down to gnaw on it.

Winter smiled at the domestic scene as she munched on her sandwich and sipped her water. The night was warm and humid but the fire still felt good close to her feet. She pulled off her soggy tennis shoes and socks and wiggled her bare feet. "The fire seems to be keeping some of the mosquitos away," she said as she eased back against the smaller kayak. She felt it slide backwards until it jammed against a tree, so she moved with it and readjusted her position.

Riley yawned and said, "I feel better sleeping with a good fire. Might keep the bigger beasts away, too."

"Bigger beasts?" Winter asked as she glanced at the darkening jungle.

Aiden chuckled, finished his sandwich, and took a long draw on his water bottle before he set it down and said, "There are a few bigger predators in the jungle but they won't bother us." He leaned forward and poked the fire and turned toward his dog as he said, "Pete here would be a delicious morsel for them, but we won't let that happen, will we boy?" The dog gazed up at him and Winter would have sworn that he was smiling again as his tail thumped against the beach towel. She chuckled and Aiden looked at them and said, "You ladies can catch some sleep if you wish and I'll keep the first watch."

"Sounds good to me," Riley said as she turned and curled into her beach towel with her back to Winter and Aiden. Within moments a soft snore mingled with the jungle sounds.

Winter scooted down on her towel and shoved her backpack against the kayak, then eased her head into the makeshift pillow. She tried closing her eyes, but her mind began playing a reel of the day's activities, mixed with images of her life with Carson, so she opened them and gazed at the sky. It was completely dark now and the black canvas was covered with twinkling dots of light. The massive number of stars made her problems feel smaller somehow. She sighed and turned her head toward Aiden and noticed he was staring at her. "*What?*" she whispered.

"Caught me. Can't sleep?"

She sat up and leaned against the boat. "No," she said as she ran her hand in the sand. The grains felt soft and a little moist. "Too much going on in here." She reached up and tapped the side of her forehead.

"Like your ex on the bridge?" Aiden asked.

She looked at him and said slowly, "Him, a friend back home, my life in general. A little bit of everything."

"Want to talk?"

"I don't know." She looked up at the sky again and said, "It's really beautiful out here, isn't it?"

"It is. I came to the island for a small escape, sort of an extended vacation, but I got a little lost and stayed. I'm not usually that impulsive, but this place grows on you."

Winter turned toward the fire. "I can see how that could happen. I was a little lost when I got here, also." She sighed deeper, paused, then said, "I just don't know how I got here, not the island, but this place in my life. Sometimes I feel like I'm watching a movie about someone else because the things that have happened in my life simply couldn't have happened to me. If you asked me at twenty where I would be now, it wouldn't be here, *you know*?"

Aiden leaned forward and poked the fire with a stick and then said, "Actually, I do know what you mean."

Winter cocked her head to one side and asked, "Really?" As their eyes connected she saw pain reflected in his. With a flash of guilt, she wondered what demons delivered him to living such an openly self-destructive way of life. Who was he and how did he get here? Had she become so consumed with her own reality that she couldn't have empathy for someone else's pain? Even worse, had Carson made her so cynical that she put the entire male population in the same category?

Aiden broke eye contact and returned his attention to the rekindled fire. The flames were shooting up vivid colors of red and orange as they greedily consumed the tumble of limbs stacked loosely in a pyramid. He leaned toward it and held his hands up to warm them as he said, "I wouldn't change any of my choices. Granted, I would like things to have had a different outcome, but I wouldn't have changed the road I chose. Not one bit."

His shoulders slumped and Winter recognized that look. She asked, "Are you talking about your girlfriend? Your wife?" He looked at her and his lips tightened. He said nothing and she couldn't read his expression. *Anger, longing, despair?* She knew she had hit a nerve, but which one? Her mouth may have gotten her in trouble one more time and shut this man down. She said in a low voice, "Did someone leave you?"

"In a manner of speaking," he said. His lips relaxed into a shadow of a smile. "My wife, Michelle. Ovarian cancer took her from me." He looked at Winter and said, "Our brief time together was worth any pain I feel now."

Winter gasped and said, "Oh, I'm sorry, she must have been very young."

"Thirty-four," he said with a sigh as he leaned against the kayak. "She was symptom free and they caught it on a routine exam." He seemed to look through Winter, instead of at her. "We kept getting bad news from test results, but my mind believed it couldn't be happening, not at her age. Six painful months later she was gone."

Winter reached out and touched his shoulder, "Hey, I mean it, I'm really sorry."

He smiled and his eyes focused on her as he said, "Me, too. I came here," he gestured with both hands at the ocean, "and I stayed drunk for my three-week vacation, then I got a place and just stayed. I bought a boat and put my life on hold in the States. I run an occasional small charter for fishing or snorkeling, and keep my hand in my stateside tech business, but mostly I bum around every day. I know it sounds destructive with all the alcohol, but it's what I needed to survive." A deeper sigh and he raised his eyebrows and said, "I dropped out because I wanted to get away from any reminder of Michelle, but somehow, everything here reminds me of her, even though she was never here." He poked the fire again as he continued, "I have to admit, the drinking has gotten a little out of hand." He shook his head as if to clear it and said, "I've never had a problem before, but lately I have spiraled more then I should." He shrugged and said, "Okay, I've spilled, so enough about me. Now it's your turn."

Winter scowled and said, "Well, you met my ex-husband, or I should say, hopefully, my dead ex-husband."

He said, "You still don't believe he's dead?"

She shook her head, "I don't know. I hope he is, but he has a way of popping up just when you think you are safe." Winter glanced at the dark jungle behind them.

"Tell me about him." Aiden said as he flicked at the fire with his stick, then he broke a limb with his knee and threw it on the campfire. The limb caught and another blaze shot up. It was too green because the fire popped and Winter jumped. She scooted a little farther from it and pulled her beach towel and backpack to her new position.

Winter gazed into the fire suddenly wishing for a glass of wine. *Was she so different from Aiden?* Her stomach clinched like it usually did when she thought of Carson.

Aiden whispered, "It's okay if you don't want to talk about him."

Winter felt a tear run down her cheek and reached up to touch it. *Funny*. She hadn't cried about Carson in a long time, in fact, she thought that was not possible anymore. Anger had been her silent companion for a very long time and it didn't leave much room for anything else. She took a breath and squared her shoulders. "It's okay. How much do you know about me from the news?"

"Not a lot. I've been pretty out of touch. I did read a little about him going to trial and that his wife, uh, ex-wife, uh, *you*, are the prosecution's witness." He leaned toward her and continued with, "Even before I met you, and both of you were simply names on my 'what's trending on the web' news service, I assumed he was a rich, society golden boy who pretty much had everyone fooled."

"Well, kudos to you, because it seems the rest of the world believes his bullshit image." Winter glanced at Riley. The redhead still had her back turned toward them. Winter smiled and said, "Except for Riley. She was a stranger until two nights ago and she has been unbelievably supportive." A snore punctuated the night and Winter chuckled. The fire drew her back and she gazed at the crackling flames. Winter knew she was stalling. If she stared into the campfire and concentrated on the red and orange dancing flames, and the smell of the smoke washing over her, she would not cry. She bent her legs and hugged her knees to her chest and asked, "Did you know who I was when we met?"

Aiden frowned and said, "I honestly didn't connect you with the news story. Even with your unusual name. Blame it on my soggy brain at the time, or the remote chance someone from the news would be on this island, but I didn't know you were *that* Winter. He shrugged. "By the way, how *did* you get your name? Was your mom a bit of a bohemian?"

Winter managed a smile, "You would think so, but sadly no. She was very traditional. I'm not sure where I got my drive to be an artist, but it certainly wasn't from my down to earth, hard working mom." An inner vision of her mother's ruddy cheeks and rough, red hands made her smile. "After having eight children before me, I think she was simply tired of coming up with names. I was born just before Christmas, so I am grateful I didn't wind up with Merry, Holly, or even Christmas. I guess Holly would have been okay. I knew a Holly I liked and I suppose it might have been better than *Winter*."

"I like the name, 'Winter'. It sounds like you are in the arts and it's a little, well, mysterious." Aiden leaned against the kayak and turned his chin toward the sky. "How about in the beginning? How did you first meet Carson?" he asked.

Winter's mother and family faded from her mind. An inner vision of Carson and the first time she met him replaced it. She was surprised when her features relaxed and her stomach was no longer clinched. She sighed and said, "You know, the first time I saw him it really was magical. He was perfect, but isn't that how a lying trickster appears, as perfect?" She shrugged her shoulders and said, "*And, after all, what is a lie? 'tis but the truth in masquerade.*"

Aiden laughed and asked, "Shakespeare?"

A tug at the corner of Winter's mouth as she said, "No, Lord Byron." Then she continued with, "I was a young artist. I had just gotten my first show in New York and I was feeling pretty cocky, maybe even invincible." She leaned toward the fire. Goosebumps rose on her bare arms and she felt chilled, even though the night was warm and muggy. Her eyes glazed as she played the memory in her mind. She said, "When he came into my show he made quite an entrance. Every eye was on him, both men and women. He was disgustingly handsome and he seemed as if he didn't know it. He moved along my paintings studying each one, then he approached me and said he had to meet the artist of such exquisite works. After that he left. Just like that." Winter snapped her fingers and sat quietly for a moment.

Aiden nodded at her, but said nothing. She glanced at him, then back at the fire. She reached up and pulled the clip from her ponytail and shook her head, then she ran her fingers through her tangled hair and tossed it over her shoulder. "The next day I received a huge bouquet of gorgeous flowers and an invitation to lunch. Lunch turned into dinner, and well, honestly breakfast." She dug her chin into her knees and a vail of dark hair fell across her face as she kept talking. "Anyway, we were inseparable after that. He was the perfect suiter, attentive, but not smothering, interested in my work and friends, as I said, *perfect*. At least until the ring was on my finger." She shook her head and pushed her hair back and turned to look at Aiden as she said, "It was gradual, but after we married it all changed. First, he began to find something wrong with my family and friends, one by one, until he had almost all of them out of my life. Next was my work, he didn't want us to be separated, so it became a hobby, then an inconvenience that wouldn't be tolerated. He strategically eliminated everything in my life that gave me self-confidence and made me feel loved, except for him, of course."

Winter closed her eyes and leaned back. She made a sound that rumbled from deep in her throat until it reached her mouth as a low growl. "Geeze. It was classic." *How could I have not seen it?* she thought, and then said, "I was so naive and stupid!" She struck her leg with her fist and felt a familiar heat rise to her checks. Her eyes narrowed as she said, "There was the Carson who was presented to the world and the Carson that I lived with privately. Private Carson turned out to be a monster." She sighed and said, "He told me later that he never liked my paintings. He pretended to be impressed as part of the game."

Aiden said, "Wow, that's enough to put you off men altogether."

Winter looked at him and laughed but she felt no humor. "Yep, that's kinda where I've been living lately. Anger has been my best friend."

"Okay, now I understand that prickly exterior a little more," he said.

Winter raised one eyebrow and said, "Uh, no, that has pretty much always been there." Her mouth twitched at the edges as she added, "And the snarky humor."

"Whoops," he said.

"Okay, enough. This is draining." Winter slumped against the kayak and yawned. "I'm exhausted. I don't know what's happening, but that's the most I've talked about myself in a very long while, at least, without having a bottle of wine involved." A glance toward the sleeping Riley.

Aiden tossed her another towel and said, "You better get some sleep while you can. Tomorrow is almost here."

Winter mumbled, "Uh-huh," but her eyelids were already closed as she snuggled into her backpack. She felt the towel being adjusted until it covered her upper body and she thought she mumbled, "Thanks," but wasn't sure if it was only in her head. Soon her mind faded into a deep, dreamless sleep.

***

Six steps. That's all - six wide plank steps with a sturdy railing for him to grip. Carson contemplated the single flight of stairs and emitted a deep breath. The climb to the front porch of the cabin seemed insurmountable. He was so tired and his body felt broken. He dropped his head and closed his eyes, then raised it and glared at the porch. Gritting his teeth, he placed the branch he was using as a crutch on the first step, gripped the railing, and then hopped up one step. Pain shot through his injured arm and leg, and sweat popped out on his forehead, but he narrowed his eyes as he stared at the top step and growled, "You can do this!"

Carson hopped up another step, then another, starting each one with his good leg. His PT nurse had told him when he was working through his ACL injury to go up with the good, down with the bad. "Think heaven and hell," she had said. It was an effective way to remember, even though he had wanted to throttle that nurse most of the time.

He kept going until he was standing on the porch. Sweat soaked his shirt and his head roared, but he made three more quick hops until he was at the front door. He swayed for a moment, then grasped the door handle and twisted, but the door didn't budge. *Locked. Damn!* Why would anyone lock their doors out in this wilderness? Like there was going to be a crime spree of burglaries? *By whom? Monkeys?* There was no one around for miles in this God forsaken place.

He scooted over and sat heavily in a rocker placed just to the left of the front door. As he searched the grounds he spotted the disabled boat tethered to the dock. There might be a hidden key to the house on it, but there was no way he was going to make it to the boat and back again. Maybe he would find medical supplies and food there and could camp out for a while. Carson shook his head as he calculated the distance to the dock. He wasn't going to make it there, at least not for a while.

As Carson rocked and thought about his options, a bit of blood dripped from his leg onto the porch. He gazed at the bubbles of red and his head started feeling funny. He had lost a lot of blood and he couldn't afford to pass out before he took care of his wound, so he pushed himself up and hobbled over to the window by the front door. *Cheap windows. Easy latch.* He averted his face and took a hard swing with the branch. A loud thump sent a vibration down his arm, but nothing happened. The glass must be a little thicker than he first thought.

Carson turned to examine the porch and his eyes locked on an iron boot cleaner at the top of the stairs. It wasn't attached to the floor and it looked heavy. He hopped over, grabbed it, and then returned to the window. This time the upper window smashed easily with his new tool. He used his branch to knock out the rest of the glass, then unlatched the window and slid the bottom half up.

After he brushed the glass shards away from the window sill, he sat on it and swung his good leg through first, then followed by lifting the injured leg over the sill. Once inside he closed the window and pulled the shade down to cover the exposed space. Finally, a little luck. Well, waking up before Ricardo could finish him off and not dying in the tumble off the bridge, could be considered good luck, but he needed a little more if he was going to get through this.

He grinned. *What am I thinking?* Carson didn't need luck. Ricardo was the one who babbled on about getting a lucky star the whole time he was with him. *Boring idiot.* Why on earth should he be listening to that backward waste of skin? Carson had been lucky his entire life and what luck he didn't have, he made, or bought. He snorted. *What a fool.* Who needs luck when you have money and power.

Carson called, "Hello?" *No answer.* He hopped across the cabin into the kitchen and opened the refrigerator door. "Yes!" he said as he grabbed a bottle of cold water and gulped half of it down. Shutting the door, he leaned his back against it, and looked around the cabin. A door on the other side of the room was cracked open and looked interesting, so he decided to explore.

The master bedroom. He stiffened. What a tiny primitive space. *What can Winter possibly see in the simpleton that lives here?* He glared at the queen size bed. It was neatly made, but he could see a dent in the covers where someone had sat on it. The corners of his mouth drooped and his eyes narrowed. *Was Winter the one sitting there?* She had had the best. How could she settle for something as crude as this? *Had she slept here?* He felt a familiar fire rise from his stomach to his mouth. Had *they* slept here? His hands clinched and he backed away from the bedroom and turned his attention to the rest of the living space. A door stood open to a small bathroom and he could see a medicine chest mounted on the wall. *Perfect.*

The medicine chest held all the supplies he needed: peroxide, bandages, antibiotic ointment, and even a bottle of Tylenol, not as good as some oxy, but it would do for now. He spread a towel on the counter and filled it with what he needed, plopped his water bottle on top, then squeezed it all under his arm, and hopped back to the bedroom. He hesitated at the door, then snorted and went in. It didn't matter what had taken place here. It would all be rectified soon. That was a promise.

Carson sat on the bed and eased the t-shirt bandage off his damaged leg. He pushed his shorts off and kicked them away with his good leg. Lifting his injured leg with both hands, he scooted around on the bed until his back was propped against the headboard, then he opened the towel and spread out his supplies. Blood oozed out of the wound and dripped onto the bed cover as he bent to examine the gash, so he placed the towel underneath his leg.

His thigh was black and purple and a jagged tear ran through the center of the bruises. The ragged wound had patches of dirt peppering the entire area. His brow furrowed. Infection and the loss of his leg was a strong possibility. The thought of going back to the bathroom to wash it made his stomach churn, so he picked up the peroxide bottle. He paused, took a deep breath and held it as he poured the clear liquid over the open wound. Carson screamed as the white bubbles churned. The pain the peroxide caused felt like an electric shock radiating from the cut in his leg to his chest. A dark veil edged in around his sight, but the blinding agony soon subsided and the searing pain was replaced with a burning ache localized only to his thigh.

When Carson's vision cleared, he poured some of the peroxide on his hands and rubbed them together. He patted at the area surrounding the wound with a pad of gauze until it looked clean, or at least as clean as it was going to get. Gritting his teeth, he squirted large globs of antibiotic ointment on the gaping wound. He pulled out some more gauze pads and eased each into a line down the ragged gash. He used a box of gauze to loop around his leg and pull the tear together. Last, he picked up a spool of white tape and covered his handiwork.

The bandage looked good. He grabbed the bottle of Tylenol, bit off the cap, and dumped four into his mouth, washing them down with the rest of the water. He pushed the wet towel and the bedspread into a big ball and tossed them onto the floor.

Carson scrunched down on the cool sheets. His eyes fluttered, but sleep wouldn't come, so he opened them wide. Something, or someone, was watching him. He could feel it. He leaned forward and peered into the living room. *Nothing.* He turned his head back to the bedroom and stared at the multitude of windows. *No movement.* Goosebumps rose on his arms and the back of his neck. He turned his head from side to side as he looked around the room. There was a large wooden armoire on the opposite wall. Carson studied the ornate carvings on the front. The doors were closed. He cocked his head and listened, but it didn't sound like someone was hiding inside. His eyes edged up it until he was staring at the top of the tall cabinet. A huge, yellow, one-eyed cat sat as motionless as a statue. Carson shivered. He hated cats. *Horrible creepy creatures of the night.*

The beast watched him through its one unblinking yellow eye. Damn thing hadn't made a sound the whole time he had been in the bedroom. Carson grabbed a pillow and threw it at the animal. It fell just short of the top of the armoire. The cat hissed at him and flattened its ears as it emitted a deep, low growl. "Get out of here!" Carson screeched at it. He reached around on the sheet and his hand found the closed bottle of peroxide. He gave it his best throw, but missed, and the bottle bounced off the wall close to the monster's head. The cat yowled, leaped from the armoire onto a table, and then flew from the room in a yellow flash.

Carson pushed up from the bed and hobbled over and slammed the bedroom door. "Damn cat," he mumbled as he scooted back to the bed and fell onto it. Now he really hated the owner of this cabin. *What kind of real man keeps a cat? Filthy, messy devils.* After a glance at the closed bedroom door, he eased his leg onto a pillow, lay back and closed his eyes. He lifted one eyelid and checked the bedroom door. *Still closed.* He shut both eyes, crossed his hands over his chest, and slipped into a deep slumber.

Chapter 17

Winter was lying on the bed with nothing but a sheet protecting her from his view. Carson gripped the bottom of the sheet and pulled it back a few inches. She stirred, so he paused until she settled. He gave it another playful tug. As her bare shoulder emerged from the sheet, she flipped onto her back, but her eyes were still closed, and her face looked flush. He could see the curve of her body beneath the thin sheet. "Winter," he whispered. *Awake and playing, or asleep and in some pleasing dreamscape?* He felt a familiar heat rising in his chest. *Who was she dreaming of?* he thought as his fists clinched, but Carson paused and glanced around. There was a muted tapping on the roof and window. He mumbled, "*What?*" Opening his eyes, he blinked. *A dream, only a dream.* The dream vanished like a puff of smoke as soon as his eyes opened. *Pity.* It was just getting interesting. He stretched and looked out of the windows. Gray morning light backlit the jungle and, surprise, it was raining. The tiny drops hit the windows and ran in rivulets down to the forest floor. Giant leaves glistened and bounced up and down in a bizarre morning wave to him. *Freaking rain forest.*

Carson sat up, winced, then leaned forward as he flexed his muscles. *Man, am I stiff,* he thought. Every time he flexed, his body protested. *The fall.* It had to be the fall. It must be how it feels to be hit by a car and live. He pulled up his t-shirt and there was a cluster of bruises lining his side and rib cage. He dropped his shirt and turned his attention to his injured leg. It felt as if a wide band surrounded the wounded area in a tight vice. *It must be the swelling*, he thought. He examined his legs and his right thigh was noticeably bigger than his left. A burnt orange circle in the middle of the dressing showed seepage, but at least there were no dark red stains. His bandage was holding.

He rolled his hurt shoulder. It was sore, but the pain was not debilitating, and the ball had stayed in the socket. He squeezed his fist. The arm and hand would work good enough for him to do what he needed to do. He edged over the side of the bed and put some weight on the damaged leg. When it held, he attempted to stand, but fell back onto the bed. *Not yet.* He grabbed the bottle of Tylenol and shook four out into his palm then swallowed them dry. Too bad the jerk who lived here didn't have something stronger in the medicine cabinet. He picked up the limb he had been using as a crutch and hobbled to the bedroom door.

After he eased the door open, he glanced around the big open room. No sign of the cat, so he headed for the bathroom. Once he was in the small room he shut and locked the door. Logically he knew the cat couldn't unlock the door, but it still made him feel better. Cats really freaked Carson out.

Bloodshot eyes reflected the pain he felt. Another forage in the medicine cabinet produced eye drops and he applied them generously to both eyes. "Shit!" he shouted as he squeezed his eyes shut. *Damn that burns*, he thought. After a few minutes, he blinked and gazed at the mirror again. The image staring back at him was still pale and scruffy, but his eyes were clear. The scruffy beard needed to stay. He didn't want to look like the image splashed across TV and in the tabloids.

Carson shed the rest of his dirty and tattered clothing and used the limb to push them into a corner, then he scooted over to the shower and adjusted the tap until it registered hot. He moved under the water as he held onto a towel bar with one hand and used the other hand to run a bar of soap over the rest of his body. It felt great to scrub away the grim. Carson gently removed the bandage on his leg and yelled when the water contacted with the wound, but he let water run over it for a minute before he shut the shower off.

After he got out of the shower and dried off, only a trickle of blood was oozing from the leg wound. He sat and redressed it, then returned to the bedroom and rifled through the drawers until he came up with some clean clothing to wear. "This asshole is such a bum," he mumbled as he pulled on a t-shirt and shorts. "No taste in clothing and living in this dump. What could Winter be thinking? To go from a penthouse to this crap hole?" he said aloud as he shook his head.

Carson used the makeshift crutch and headed for the living room. Just as he exited the bedroom he heard a loud screech and something knocked hard against his leg. He went down with a thud and screamed, "Son of a bitch!" He lay on the floor until the pain subsided, then eased himself up by holding onto the door frame. He had forgotten about the stupid cat.

After he got up, he bent at the waist to retrieve the limb and the beast leaped onto his back. He felt sharp pain as the cat's claws dung into his back then slid down his side. "Aaaaaaawwww!" he yelled, but as he swung around with the limb, there was no sign of his furry roommate. "You are going to regret this, asshole! You are dead!" he screamed as he glared around the room, but when he heard a hiss above his head, he looked up to see the devil cat perched high in the open log rafters.

Carson edged over to his backpack and eased out his gun. He leaned on the limb and used both arms as he pointed it toward the ceiling, "Gotcha, asshole," he whispered, but as he was about to squeeze the trigger, there was a loud knock at the front door. He jumped and jerked his head toward the door, but then swung it back toward the ceiling. *No cat.* "Damn!" he muttered as he stuck the gun into the back of his waistband and shuffled toward the door.

Carson edged the door open about four inches, but kept his hand hovering just above the gun behind his back. An older Hispanic man stood on the porch. Carson's mouth twitched. The grizzled old man was about as tall as a 6th grader. "Ola, Is Señor Aiden okay?" he said.

"Uh, he's not here," Carson said as he looked over the man's shoulder. His visitor was alone, but he had a horse tied to the front porch post. *Interesting.* A perfect mode of transportation with the infrastructure in utter chaos. It didn't need gas and could pass through areas even a scooter couldn't manage.

The man frowned and tried to see around Carson into the house. "I'm his friend and wanted to see if he okay from the quake." He looked toward the boat dock and said, "His boat here and his jeep was on the road, so where he go?"

Carson smiled broadly and said, "Well, I was injured in the quake, so he and my wife went to get some help."

"How they go to town?" The man shook his head and then said, "That make no sense. They would have taken his jeep or boat." His eyes narrowed as he stared at Carson.

"That's a good question, but with the roads in such bad shape, they were worried they wouldn't make it in the jeep." Carson replied.

The small man's head bobbed up and down as he said, "Okay, they right about that, trees and cracks everywhere. That's why I ride my *caballo,* Molly here." He pointed at the horse. The animal whinnied and flicked her tail, as if she knew she was the topic of conversation. "But why not take his fishing boat?"

Carson pulled the door open wider and said, "Why don't you come in." He noticed the man hesitated, so he pointed at his injured leg and said, "I'm getting tired standing and I'm not moving around too well."

The man smiled and said, "Okay, okay sure." He walked through the door but stopped just inside. He faced the bedroom and stared at the rumpled bedspread on the floor as he began to say, "What happened here?" but Carson's stick silenced the little man as it connected with the back of his skull. The old man fell forward and hit the floor with a loud crack.

"Guess you won't get your answers. Not that it matters. You are both dead men, anyway," Carson said. A pool of blood began forming a scarlet pillow around the man's bald head. It was only a small wound in the base of his skull, but it was producing a lot of blood. Carson bent and examined him, he was still breathing but out cold. As Carson raised his stick to finish the job, a blur of yellow fur whizzed past him and flew down the front steps. Carson turned and stormed onto the porch. The cat sat in the yard, calmly washing its face with its paw, as it stared at Carson with that weird one-eyed stare.

"You little shit," Carson said as he eased his gun out and took aim at the furry beast, but before he could squeeze the trigger, something else caught his eye. The horse was dancing in place and her eyes rolled as she tugged at her leash. The reigns begin to pull away from the railing. He needed that horse. The cat stood, twitched its tail, then strolled across the yard toward the jungle. "Shit," Carson said, but he stuck the gun back into his belt and moved down the steps to calm the horse. After he had the animal settled and made sure she was securely tied, he looked around but the cat was gone.

Carson hopped up the stairs and re-entered the cabin. He moved around the prone man and headed straight for the bedroom. The old guy was most likely going to bleed to death anyway. No need to waste time or any more effort on him. His backpack, the Tylenol bottle, and a couple of bottles of water was all he grabbed, then he was back out on the porch.

Carson eased down the steps and approached the horse. "Easy girl, easy," he said in a gentle voice. "We are going to take a little trip to town, then you will be a free girl." He rubbed her jaw and behind her ears, then moved to her side and grabbed the saddle horn. A deep breath and he shoved his good leg into the stirrup while using the stick to support his bad leg. He managed to pull himself up onto the saddle without screaming and lifted the bad leg over the horse and let it dangle. After he jammed the stick between the strap and blanket, he pulled the reigns free and turned the horse toward the road. He was suddenly glad his bitch of a mother had insisted on a childhood filled with riding lessons. Motorized vehicles couldn't make it all the way to town, but this horse would. "Brilliant!" Carson mumbled. "See, Ricardo? some folks are born with luck and some aren't." He eased his good heel into the horse's side to urge her along. *Piece of cake*.

***

Winter felt something hit her forehead. Plop. Plop. She opened her eyes and a blob of water momentarily blinded her. She bolted up as the sky opened to a deluge of rain washing over her. Everyone bounded up from their makeshift beds and scooted to the relative shelter of an overhang of tree branches. As they crouched together, the rain made its way through the lacy cover of trees and leaves, so Aiden dashed back and grabbed their rain jackets from the kayaks.

"I'm already soaked," Winter muttered as she caught the jacket he tossed her and pulled it on. "Well, I guess we *are* in the rain forest," she said as she wiped the moisture from her face with her sleeve, "but, what an alarm clock."

"Look," Riley said as she pointed toward the sea where the gray sky met the ocean. A mass of churning waves made the horizon impossible to determine. They watched white capped waves rise several feet into the air, and then smash onto the beach.

Aiden frowned, then scurried over and grabbed their backpacks, pulling them under the tree overhang as well. He squatted and got some jerky from his pack and tossed it to Pete. The little dog caught it, chomped it down in two bites, then huddled against a tree trunk. "I don't think we will be able to use the kayaks anytime soon. This section of the sea can be challenging even without a storm, and I don't think any of us want to try it when it's like this," Aiden said. He took a bite of a of jerky, chewed it a moment, and added, "Some tourists in sea kayaks were recently lost when a storm popped up. The searchers gave up on them after a week and one of the kayaks washed up empty. Never did find the bodies. These winds and waves can toss a kayak around like a toy."

Winter shivered and perched on a jagged rock, then shifted her weight until the sharp edge was tolerable. "Any suggestions?" she asked as she reached into her own backpack and pulled out a peanut butter sandwich she had stowed away. "I really don't want to sit here for the entire day," she added with a mouthful of peanut butter.

Riley sat beside her and grabbed an apple out of her bag and took a bite. "I'd kill for a shower and some real breakfast," Riley mumbled over the apple as she chewed. She scratched at her leg and asked, "What *is* this?" She had large red whelps covering one calf.

Aiden moved over and examined the bites. "Sand fleas. They can be really nasty here," he said, then rummaged in his backpack and pulled out a pill bottle. "Here, take some Benadryl. It will help a little, but you are going to have those bites with you for a while." He shook his head. "We can get you some ointment when we get to town. Sorry, you must have slept on a nest of them."

Winter gazed at Riley's leg and started scratching her arm. "I only have a couple of places on my arm, but let me have one of those." She frowned and downed the pill. "Aiden, how can we get out of here if we don't go by sea?" she asked as she turned to look at the tangle of growth behind them.

"Only a couple of options and neither are desirable," he said and took a swig of water. "We can't go by sea now, but we could wait out the storm and see if the waves calm down, or we can try to make it through the jungle." He shrugged and looked over his shoulder at the dense mass of trees. "Good news is that we are probably not that far from other houses by now, but the bad news is that the forest is thick and wild, and we have a small mountain between us and any kind of road. Also, there are lots of species much worse than sand fleas living in there and we may hit some swamp areas before reaching civilization."

They all sat in silence as the rain pelted them and the waves continued to crash the shoreline. The beach had widened as the tide receded, but the ocean looked wild and furious. Winter shook her head and said, "I don't want to spend another night on this beach. If you think we are close enough to reach some houses by nightfall, I vote for attempting to make it to a shower and a dry bed."

The downpour had diminished to a steady drizzle, but when Winter looked toward the sea, the waves appeared to have increased in intensity.

"I don't think I want to try to sleep with fleas for another night," Riley said as she rubbed at one of the bites. "Sand fleas? Give me a break."

Winter turned from Riley to Aiden and asked, "Well?"

He sighed and said, "I can't guarantee town by nightfall, because I haven't trekked through this section of jungle, but I do know it doesn't look that far on a map to a cluster of houses on the coast."

Riley stood, bent to scratch, but pulled her hand back and balled it into a fist. "I know, I know, don't scratch." She sighed, shrugged, and said, "Okay, let's do it. I haven't navigated an uncharted wild jungle yet, so it will be just one more item to add to my list of things I couldn't have imagined myself doing when I was in Oklahoma." She placed her hands on her hips and said, "The real reason is that I want to make it to that shower and ointment before these bites drive me bat crazy."

"What about the kayaks? Do you think we will hit a river where we could use them?" Winter asked Aiden.

Aiden shook his head as he stood. "No, it would be much too hard to carry even one of them through the jungle. Besides, you will need both of your hands free. You need to carry something to use with the jungle, and as a weapon."

"Weapon? What do you mean?" Winter asked as her brows edged toward each other.

"A stick, a machete, or a knife to push the vines back, and for critters," Aiden said, then bent and pulled a harness from his backpack. He slipped the harness over his arms and cinched the belt to a canvas sack hanging mid-chest. He whistled to Pete who hopped over and jumped into his arms. After he tucked the dog into the harness, he slipped his backpack on, then picked up his machete and said, "We will need to cut a path as we go. I have the machete, so I'll lead. We can leave most of this stuff with the kayaks, but take food, water, and your jackets."

Winter and Riley laughed and Winter said, "Sorry, what you said is very serious, but you look like the cover of *The Great Outdoors* magazine meets *All About Pets.*" She picked up her backpack, broke off a sturdy limb, and then fell into line behind Aiden. She said, "Lead on," and gave him a mock salute.

Aiden said, "Very funny." Then turned and began to slash a path through the jungle. Winter kept chuckling, but used the limb to push aside vines at her feet.

"What a group! If we make it to civilization, it will be a miracle," Riley mumbled behind her. Winter laughed but kept moving.

Chapter 18

Winter mopped the sweat on her face and forehead with a kerchief. Her sodden t-shirt stuck to her back and chest, but there wasn't anything she could do about that. If she changed the shirt, a new one would be in the same shape within minutes. She stopped walking and took a long swig from her water bottle. The jungle felt as if it was pressing in around her and the humidity made it difficult to breath. Aiden had cut away the largest foliage blocking their path, but beside her green and brown walls rose to block the sky. Her ears rang with the constant sounds of disturbed insects and birds. Kayaking on the raging waters of the ocean was starting to seem a lot more attractive. She snorted as she thought about the web page advertising an "Island Paradise," but then sobered when the thought spurred the memory of the falling pagoda and the unfortunate yogis. "Something wrong?" Riley asked from behind her.

"Uh, no, sorry," Winter said as she stuck the water bottle into her pack and began moving again. "Just a quick water break," she added. How long had they been walking? It felt like hours, but she refused to ask. Her internal questions and complaints were irritating even her, so she didn't want to put them out there to everyone else.

As she trudged along the path, she gazed at Aiden's back above and below his heavy pack. His shoulder and arm muscles rippled under his wet t-shirt where it stuck to his slender frame. *Now that is just ridiculous*, she thought. How could he make sweat look good while he carried such a heavy load, when she felt, and was certain she looked, like a damp dish rag? He even carried the dog on his chest while he hacked their path through the jungle. He hadn't stopped to rest even once. Winter shook her head and a drop of sweat flew off her forehead and landed on her arm. She frowned. *Ridiculous.*

Winter turned her head toward the sky but couldn't see anything but the convergence of green. She wasn't sure if Aiden knew where he was going, but they kept following him like a couple of sheep. *What is that about?* Some sort of primal instinct that made women follow men? She frowned. She thought she had learned her lesson after Carson, but here she was again, blindly following a man. Of course, Aiden was a different man than Carson. She was just beginning to see how very different they really were. That dog would have been history with Carson. Not only would he never own a dog, it would be looks over substance any day with him.

Winter felt her ponytail fall and her hair fanned out over her moist shoulders. "I'll catch you guys in a sec," she said as she took a step to the side of the path and waved for Riley to move ahead of her. Riley nodded silently and kept moving. The woman put her to shame. *Tough lady.*

Winter reached into her tangle of black hair and found the errant hair clip, then pulled the mass of damp curls into a ponytail at the top of her head and struggled with wrangling it back into the clip. Her lower back pressed into a tree as she wrestled with her hair, but she paused as she thought she heard a rustling noise to her left and behind her. The small hairs on the back of her neck stood to attention and she clipped her hair in place as she eased away from the support of the tree. When she was a few steps away, she turned to watch as a fat green snake slithered along a branch beside the place where she had just been standing. She shivered as it disappeared into the thick wall of leaves and vines. Invisible once again. *Nature's camouflage.* Winter shook her head and scurried along the path until she was close on Riley's heels and nearly knocked into her. At least she hadn't humiliated herself with a high pitched girly scream, although screaming had been her first instinct. Riley glanced back at her and asked, "You okay, darlin?"

"Yes," she said as she glanced from side to side. "Just watch out, okay? Some of the branches aren't branches."

Riley laughed and said, "Well, okay. Noted."

Aiden stopped and said, "Ladies, looks like we have a swamp coming up ahead. Watch your step and try not to get too close to the water's edge." With that he began slashing at branches as he seemed to move away from the direction they were originally heading.

"A swamp?" Winter mumbled. As they got closer she understood the warning and direction change. The swamp water was dark green and stagnant. Trees lined the banks and grew throughout the shallow water. Moss and vines hung from the tree branches to the water's surface. The soil around the water looked like wet mud and Winter could picture it sucking the shoes from her feet, so she kept close to the jungle side of the path. "Creepy," Winter mumbled as she stayed close to the others and watched the water for movement. She swatted at a mosquito that seemed unusually large as it buzzed around her ear and then asked, "Is this the part where the 'crocs' you mentioned might appear?"

"It's a possibility," Aiden called.

She kept a watch for 'moving branches' and crocodiles as they kept a brisk pace for such a difficult path. Winter didn't want to spend any more time here than necessary. The stench rising to greet her nostrils was something between rotten eggs and that time a mouse had died in her condominium walls.

"Uh, Aiden?" Riley called as she stopped dead in her tracts. They all paused and followed her gaze. The bank on the other side of the swamp moved. There were several large crocodiles catching a little sunlight that was filtering through the canopy of trees and one of them had his big snout pointed right at them. His beady little black eyes blinked, then he waddled forward and slid gracefully into the water. Winter realized she had found something she disliked even more than snakes.

A low growl came from Pete and the dog's legs pawed at the air as if he was running. Aiden said, "Let's move ladies," as he turned and headed forward. His arm swung from side to side with the machete leading the way. Winter felt a bolt of energy and surged ahead. She blushed when she realized she had slid into second place behind Aiden and felt a flash of guilt. She turned and gestured for Riley to move ahead of her, but the redhead frowned and shook her head before placing a hand on Winter's back as she gave her a gentle shove. Winter got the message and quickened her step.

Gradually the smells changed from rotten swamp back to damp jungle. Winter felt the flat incline begin to slope upward. Aiden was in front of her, and she noticed his calves tense with the increased effort. They were heading straight up the side of a hill and it was getting steeper with each step. As she climbed, Winter resisted the urge to grab branches for assistance. The snake was still fresh in her mind. A throbbing rhythm nagged at her foot and her thighs screamed, but she clinched her jaw, and kept moving.

How is he charging up the hill like that? Winter thought. Aiden was swinging the machete with a vengeance and was keeping a brutal pace. Her view of him as an out of shape drunk kept moving farther away from the mental box she had first placed him in. Just when she felt she was going to have to stop, she noticed Aiden break free of the woods and step into sunlight.

Winter pushed the rest of the way out of the jungle and followed Aiden to the center of a meadow. They stood on a hilltop clear of trees. Winter turned in a slow circle then stopped and stood beside him. The vantage point gave her a view all the way to the sea, and the cluster of houses they were searching for. "It's breathtaking," she said.

Riley approached and said, "Damn!"

They stood for a moment in silence. The meadow was surrounded by jungle in every direction, but they could see beyond it to the bottom of the hill where the ocean sparkled a clear turquoise blue. The coast line beyond the jungle was scattered with docks, boats and some isolated roof tops. *Civilization.* They were almost there. If they could get through the wild, tangled jungle on the other side of the meadow without mishap, they would be home free.

Aiden put Pete on the ground. He ran around in a tight circle, stopped, and relieved himself, then ran back and sat at his feet and barked. Aiden scooped him up and dropped him back into the harness, then gazed at their distant target, turned, and said, "Almost there." He started walking toward the first stand of trees.

Riley shrugged and headed after him. Winter groaned and mumbled, "Really?" Then dropped her head and started after them as she called, "Okay, okay, wait up, will you guys?"

***

The downhill trek was as bad as the uphill climb, but longer. Winter's muscles cramped from constantly attempting to slow her pace on the steep incline, and her injured toe kept hitting against the front of her tennis shoe. Momentum made her want to run down the hill, but logic told her that would be a complete disaster. As the path finally leveled out, Aiden stopped and turned toward them and said, "Do you want to take a break or keep pushing it?" He glanced up at the sky, but with the trees, it was impossible to see the sun. He checked his watch and said, "We have a couple of hours of daylight left, but it's going to be tight." He placed Pete on the ground and allowed him to take another break.

Riley stopped chugging on her water bottle and a trail of moisture dribbled down her chin as she said, "I vote we keep going. We'll be sore later, but we will be anyway, and at least we will be out of this jungle before nightfall." She stuck the bottle into her pack and wiped her chin with the back of her hand. Her eyes swung from Aiden to Winter. Fatigue showed in the pure green orbs, but her stance and the straight line of her mouth and jaw screamed determination.

"I agree. I know we are all past the point of exhaustion, but I really don't want to be caught here after dark," Winter said as she glanced at the trees and bushes. Nothing moved but she didn't trust the tangle of green.

"Okay, let's go," Aiden said as he picked up and secured Pete. He turned and started moving forward. "I think we are at least through with the hill," he said as he chopped at a vine. Winter knew he had to be getting tired of cutting through the tangled brush, but somehow, she couldn't bring herself to volunteer for his job. *Maybe he likes being the tough one.* The justification was thin, still, she couldn't find her voice, so she sighed and kept walking.

Winter pulled her shoulders back after a few steps and said, "Aiden, I'll take your place with the machete."

"Good timing, Pappas," he said with a laugh.

Winter glanced up and felt her spirits rise. Aiden was no longer using the machete but walking freely. She could see bright sunlight and blue sky. She stopped and tilted her head back, closed her eyes and let the warm sun play over her face. When she opened her eyes again it no longer felt like walls surrounding her on all sides. They had to be getting close to the houses near the ocean. Sniffing at the air, she couldn't detect salt, but the sea had to be close. She moved her newly energized feet and found herself almost on top of Riley, then laughed. Her friend was right on Aiden's heels. All of them were getting anxious to finish with this journey.

Aiden rounded a particularly large tree and disappeared. "What happened?" Riley said as she surged forward, but screamed as she slid out of sight also. Winter paused, then edged around the tree as she risked putting her hand on it to steady herself.

On the other side of the tree, Winter found herself at a ledge that gave way to a steep hill of tumbled dirt, rocks, and tree limbs. It must have been formed by the recent earthquakes, because there was no new growth in it. It looked as if a backhoe had come through and dug the hill away, leaving jungle debris everywhere. Aiden lay at the bottom of the hill. He was on his back tangled in some bushes and cradled Pete on his chest. Riley was just above him clinging to a tree stump. "Are you guys okay?" Winter called down to them.

Aiden sat up and looked around and said, "I am, and Pete thought it was a fun ride." The dog barked, then panted a dog smile. Aiden winced as he reached for the machete that was laying close to him. "I think I might have twisted my wrist, but everything else feels okay. How about you, Riley?"

Riley pulled herself up until she was sitting on the stump. She moved her arms, and then her legs, but said, "Ouch. I think I might have turned my ankle." She stood and put weight on it, then did a step hop the rest of the way down the hill until she reached Aiden and sat beside him. Aiden released Pete who hopped over and licked Riley's face. She laughed and stroked his wiry back as she said, "It's okay. Hurts a bit, but I can keep going."

Aiden looked up the hill at Winter as he called, "Can you get down to us?"

Winter studied the hillside and formed a path in her mind. "Yeah, I think so," she said as she eased her way down the chosen path with the help of a few downed trees. Once at the bottom she bent and removed Riley's boot and examined her ankle. "It's swelling," she said.

Aiden pulled a cloth out of his backpack and handed it to Winter. "Wrap it tight and get the boot back on before it blows up too much."

Winter wrapped it, but before she could ease the boot on, Riley grabbed it and said, "Let me." The redhead jammed her boot on with only a slight frown and no curse words. "Best to do it quick. No point in prolonging the pain," she said.

"Uh, okay," Winter said, then added, "look, we've got to be close. Do you two want to wait here and I can go get help?"

Riley snorted and then said, "Nonsense. I don't know about Aiden, but I am perfectly capable of getting there on my own two feet." She stood, grabbed a limb and used it like a walking stick. Her first steps were slow on one side, fast on the other, but she gained momentum until she had almost a normal gait. She paused and turned as she said, "See, no problem."

Aiden and Winter looked at each other and shrugged, then both stood. Aiden picked up the dog and tucked him into his pack, but Winter noticed he winced with the effort. He tucked the injured wrist into one of the pack's straps keeping it immobile and then nodded at her. "All set."

"Well, all right then," Winter said.

Aiden said, "Wait." He pulled out a compass and said, "This way." As he started down a wide trail.

Winter nodded. The compass explained his sense of direction. Since they had no phone reception, Aiden had prepared by going old school. As she walked she looked ahead at the path in front of them and grinned. *People have used this path a lot.* They walked easily on flattened grass and exposed earth from a lot of footfalls. *People.* It would be good to see people again.

Chapter 19

Not much had changed since Carson and Ricardo had driven out of the village on the mopeds, but to be fair, it had only been two nights. *Hard to believe*, Carson thought. So much had happened in those two nights.

People no longer walked around dazed and bleeding, but the buildings and streets still looked like a war zone. Carson rode down the middle of the street on horseback, but he didn't draw a single glance. The village was still too chaotic for anyone to notice. As he rode by a group of villagers working furiously to dig through the debris, he raised an eyebrow in their direction. The simpletons almost appeared to be organized. Carson pulled on the horse's reigns and came to a stop. He pulled out his phone. Still no signal and he was down to 15% power. "Guess Ricardo was right about the cell service," he mumbled, so he stuck his heels into the horse's flank and moved further down the block.

Men, women, and children were working together. One group at the end of the block had formed a human chain to lift debris by passing it from one to another, with the last one tossing it onto a huge pile of rubble in the alley next to the building. Someone at the front of the line yelled, "I found someone!" They all froze and turned toward the voice. "Alive!" the same voice shouted. The entire line rushed toward the voice. It was like ants heading to sugar, and then they began to throw aside rocks and timber. As Carson got closer to the area, he strained to see the object of their search, but it was impossible through the wall of people. They stopped digging as a unified shout went up from the entire group. Another villager had survived. *Big Whoop*, Carson thought as he moved on and turned the corner next to the building.

As he rounded the block he found himself behind an ambulance. The lights were flashing, but the vehicle was moving slower than his horse. "Oh, come on!" Carson called as the emergency vehicle came to a complete stop. They were in front of a building that was still intact and appeared to be an apartment building. Some of the residents were leaning out of the second story windows and shouting for the attendants to hurry.

Carson sat high in the saddle looking for a way around the wide vehicle, but both debris and abandoned cars blocked his way on all sides. He was about to turn his horse around when four people emerged from the building carrying a stretcher with an unconscious little girl lying on it. "It's about time," Carson mumbled as he glowered at the group.

They opened the doors to the ambulance and it was already full. The injured sat in the isles and some lay side by side on stretchers, and there was even one small boy crouched between the driver and front passenger spot. Carson shook his head. There was no way they would get the newest casualty into that vehicle, but as he watched, they did it. The people sitting in the isle lifted the child over their head until she was completely inside and resting horizontally across the folks on the stretcher, then they shut the doors and the ambulance began its crawl forward again. "No way," he mumbled.

Instead of finding an alternate route, Carson decided to keep following the ambulance. They might lead him to whatever they were using as a medical facility. He needed treatment for his leg and it would be a good place to start looking for Winter and her party. It was likely at least one of her group was injured on their long trek into town.

After following it for almost an hour, Carson said, "Okay, enough of this crap." He began to tug on the reigns to turn the horse away from the ambulance, but the vehicle turned and pulled into a parking lot.

Carson stopped the horse and stared. *What a curious sight.* Across the parking lot was a small clinic, but the asphalt parking lot in front of it looked like a circus. Tents and open-air cabanas covered half of the lot and the other half was covered with folding chairs, picnic tables, and a couple of food trucks. A lengthy line of people was standing in front of the main tent, and a steady stream of medical personnel ran back and forth from the tent to the clinic building, either carrying supplies or escorting the injured into the building.

Carson slid off the horse's back and tied her to a lamppost, then looked around for someone who appeared to be in charge. *Ah.* A large Hispanic man with gray hair fit the bill. As the man walked, he was surrounded by a rotating group of younger men and women in white coats. They would ask him a question, or present him with some paperwork, get a reply, and then scurry off. Carson watched the man disengage himself and head for a coffee urn at one of the food trucks, so he hobbled over. He stood right behind the older man until he turned with his Styrofoam cup in hand and he almost sloshed it on Carson. "Oh, sorry," gray hair said as he started to walk around him.

"Do you work here?" Carson asked, then he said, "I can't feel my left arm and my chest is really hurting right here." He pointed at the area above his heart.

Gray hair's brows furrowed. He put his cup down and grabbed Carson's arm as he swung his head around, then shouted, "James, here! Take this man into the tent and get a monitor on him." A young man ran over and put his arm around Carson's waist. "He's having chest pains," the older man said, then grabbed his coffee and headed toward the clinic building.

"Come with me, I'll take care of you," the young doctor said with a heavy Spanish accent. He walked with Carson passed the extensive line of triage patients and guided him into the tent. He located a bed, eased him down, and then said, "I'll just go get the portable EKG."

Carson grabbed his arm and said, "It's not my heart, the old guy misunderstood, it's my leg that needs attention."

The young doctor froze and asked, "What? You aren't having a heart attack?"

"No. It's my leg." Carson pointed to the dirty bandage. "I had a bad fall and it's really hurting." He laid back and said, "I need stitches, some antibiotics, and pain medicine."

The young doctor frowned and said, "If that's all, then you need to get into the triage line. There are others who need this bed more than you, señor."

"Well, I'm already here now, aren't I?" Carson stretched out, grinned and said, "That old gray-haired man, whom I assume is your superior, did tell you to take care of me."

The young man's face reddened and he said, "He thought you were having chest pains, otherwise he would have told you to get in line with the others."

"Well, it was his mistake, so let's not embarrass him, okay? I'm here, so why don't you simply treat me and I'll be on my way, then you can have your bed back." Carson grinned and said as he crossed his hands behind his head.

The doctor rubbed his face, glanced around the crowded tent filled with people moaning in various stages of pain and said, "You Americans, always jumping the line and wanting first class service, even at a time like this." He shrugged and said, "I took an oath, so I will treat you, but no pain pills. We are in short supply, so you can do this on your own."

Carson grinned broader and said, "Whatever, let's get this done. I have someone I need to find." The doctor stalked off to get his equipment and Carson laughed. He eased up onto one elbow and surveyed the area around his cot. He spotted a young nurse dispensing pills to patients not far from him. Her hair was up in a ponytail, much like Winter wore, but dark tendrils fell around her flushed face and neck. After she handed an old woman a bottle of water, she pulled a pill bottle from her pocket and shook out a couple of tiny white pills into the woman's hand. The young nurse raised up and glanced around the tent and her eyes filled with tears. She looked back at the old lady and smiled as she absently shoved the pill bottle into her uniform pocket. Carson leaned forward and called to her in a voice he forced into a horse whisper, "Nurse, could I please have a little water? My mouth is so dry." She nodded and headed his way. *No problem. His own little walking pill dispenser. Easy peasy.*

***

Winter stepped from the forest onto a road. *An actual road.* Hard packed dirt, but a road nonetheless. Riley sank onto a rock beside the road and took a drink from her water bottle. Aiden placed a hand on Riley's shoulder and asked, "Are you okay?" Riley nodded, grinned up at him.

"Takes more than a sore ankle to stop me, Aiden," Riley said. Her face was pale and her mop of red hair was plastered to her scalp and face. She kept scratching at the red welts on her leg, but she could still manage a smile and a wink.

Winter's admiration for this woman just kept growing. She made eye contact with her and read pain in Riley's green eyes. "I can check out the house while you two rest," Winter said.

Aiden turned and approached her and said, "Let me." He took the doggie pack off and slipped a leash around Pete's neck. "Sorry, boy, but it's for your own safety," he said as he handed the leash to Winter. He leaned close and whispered, "Could you stay with Riley and hang on to Pete for me. I'm not sure who lives this far off the grid, but chances are that they might know me and, well, most folks on the island are friendly and helpful, but not everyone. Remember how I got Pete? I was being mugged in front of a bar."

Winter opened her mouth to argue, but a glance toward the shanty and the stacks of trash and old appliances scattered in the yard of the isolated area made her snap it shut. She nodded and walked Pete over by Riley who put her hand on the dog's head and said, "You look fresh as a daisy, boy. You had the best seat in the house, didn't you?" Winter rolled her eyes but smiled down at them. She turned and watched Aiden crossing the road.

"Yell if you need help," she called to his back. He didn't turn around but nodded and kept going. Winter paced up and down the road for a few minutes with Pete hopping along by her side. An engine sputtered, and then started, so she returned to Riley and they both watched as an ancient truck eased out of what looked like a tangle of weeds. Closer inspection revealed a driveway below the mass of greenery. The rusted blue pickup truck pulled up in front of them and Aiden jumped out of the passenger side.

"You folks need a lift to town?" the driver asked with a toothless grin. His face was a mass of wrinkled brown skin and his watery brown eyes swept from Winter, to Riley, and then to the dog. "Mutt needs to ride in back," he said. The old man was so tiny he could barely see over the steering wheel. Winter eyed the dusty truck and raised her eyebrows.

"Mr. Rodriquez has been kind enough to offer us a ride," Aiden said as he stepped between Winter and the driver, then reached out to help Riley up. He led her around to the passenger door and held her arm as she climbed into the cab.

Riley scooted up on the seat and turned to the old man and said, "Why thank you, Mr. Rodriquez. That's mighty neighborly of you."

Aiden headed to the back of the truck and Winter followed him. He lifted Pete into the back bed and then turned to Winter and said, "You can ride with Riley in the cab and I'll get back here with Pete."

Winter leaned in as she whispered to Aiden, "Like Pete would mess up his pristine truck."

Aiden frowned and put his finger to his lips, then whispered back with a face void of emotion, "This old baby is his pride and joy."

Winter chuckled and whispered, "Okay, I appreciate the ride, but you ride up front with Riley. The good Samaritan may need a little help navigating the road. Those eyes of his looked a little questionable. I'll ride in the back with Pete."

Aiden hesitated, glanced toward the cab and nodded as he whispered back, "Good point. He said his neighbor got through to town this morning, so the road must be clear, but there still might be some debris he won't spot. Okay, but hang on to Pete for me, please."

Winter frowned and said, "I grew up in Texas. I think I can manage a ride in the back of a pickup truck." After climbing onto the truck and scooting to the front by the cab, she grabbed Pete's leash and pulled him to her side. He whimpered as the truck started off and bumped along the dirt road. She held onto the side panel and tried to keep them steady, but she kept sliding toward the back, and the truck was missing the back gate. She scooted against the side panel and pulled Pete tight as she said, "It's okay, boy. Tonight, we get a bath, a clean bed to sleep in, and some real food. We can handle this ride." The dog looked up at her and licked her leg. "It won't be long now," she said as she looked at the jungle behind them. "I can't believe this nightmare is almost over," she said as she pulled him into her lap and hugged his wiry body close.

Chapter 20

Carson sat up on the cot and said, "Thanks, Doc," as he examined his freshly bandaged leg. "You did a respectable job with the stitches. I don't think it will leave much of a scar. Just enough for the ladies to appreciate my South American adventure." He grinned at him.

The young doctor frowned and handed Carson a small paper packet and said, "Here are your antibiotics. Take two now and two before you go to bed. The instructions are written on the packet." He pointed toward the tent opening and said, "Now, please leave so we can use this cot."

"Sure thing," Carson said. He took two of the pills and downed them with the bottle of water the obliging nurse gave him. He stood and started moving toward the door but stopped as soon as the doctor had moved on to the next patient. Carson pulled out his stolen pain pills, courtesy of the cute nurse's pocket, shook out one, and swallowed it. He had taken one before the doctor had returned to stich him up and the oxycodone was working its magic, but he didn't want pain slowing him down, and he could handle the extra dose. He was feeling good after the first pill, but, well, no harm in feeling even better. *Gotta love that oxy*, he thought. Pain free, he no longer needed his makeshift crutch, but it was a good excuse to carry a nice heavy club.

A curvy nurse moved past him and he turned to appreciate the view as she went by. Her backside moved as if two hard melons were trapped under her white pants. *Nice.* The grin left his face and he slipped into the shadows against the side of the tent. The attractive nurse was bending over a redheaded woman. Carson eased closer. *Yep.* It was that old bitch who was with Winter and the drunk. Bright red hair and that hick accent. The nurse handed her a cane.

Her words floated over to Carson. "I don't need this, honey. What I need is something to stop this blasted itching," the redhead said. Carson swiveled his head around but didn't see the familiar dark ponytail anywhere in the crowd, or the mocha skinned drunkard. Carson jerked his head back toward the redhead and edged even closer as he listened. She said, "Seriously, there are other folks who could use this cane and I'm not going far." The nurse said something that he couldn't make out, but the redhead's twangy voice carried as she said, "All right, sweetie. I'll take it. But, my friends are waiting for me with a nice room just over at the Ocean View Hotel. Now where is that cream and prescription you promised? This itching is just about to drive me crazy." The nurse handed her a bottle of water then left, presumably to get her medication. The redhead sipped from the bottle and shifted on the cot as she turned toward Carson. He averted his face and slipped out of the tent.

Carson moved past the line of patients waiting for beds and headed toward the street. When he was almost to Molly, the horse an open-air jeep skidded to a stop on the street in front of the clinic. The driver and passenger jumped out and eased a body on a stretcher from the back of the jeep. Carson stared at the body lying on the stretcher. It was an old man with a head injury. He gasped and mumbled, "No way," then slipped behind a large palm tree.

As he heard the taller young man caution the other one to be careful, a frail voice shouted from the stretcher, "That's Molly! That's my Molly!"

"Shhhhh, Dad. Settle down. We're at the clinic," the older one said as he hefted the front of the cot a little higher and examined the crowd gathered in front of the tent. He nodded at the young man carrying the foot of the stretcher and they headed toward the triage line.

"But, Molly," the old man called.

Carson moved around the tree as the trio approached the tent. He watched as the tall young man at the front of the stretcher spoke to the attendant. The white coated guard stepped back and waved for them to enter the tent. The old man was still trying to rise from the cot and Carson could see his mouth moving. The old geezer leaned forward on one elbow and pointed a skinny brown finger in Carson's direction and shouted something. Carson couldn't be sure with the distance between them, but it sounded like, "It's him, it's him!" His son placed a hand on the geezer's shoulder and eased him back down before they disappeared behind the tent flaps.

Carson decided it was time to go, so he headed for the street on the other side of the clinic. He moved in the opposite direction of the horse and jeep as he slipped across the parking lot. When he could no longer see the tent, and they could no longer see him, he stopped and checked his surroundings. He was pleased to see he was at a street that ran toward the ocean. Carson stepped onto the pavement and looked toward the sea at the end of the block. A high-rise hotel stood just before the beach. It was painted a tacky 80's coral pink and looked undamaged. A sign above the front entrance said, "Ocean View Hotel."

Carson grinned and headed down the street with his walking stick by his side. He paused a moment, flexed his arm, then bounced up and down on his injured leg. "Incredible," he said aloud. *No pain.* His body felt almost normal, actually, better than normal. Carson whistled a tune and wondered if Winter would be surprised to see him, or if she had somehow sensed he was still alive. Either way, he couldn't wait to see her face when he found her. He laughed aloud. It was going to be a delicious reunion.

***

Winter pulled the wash cloth from her face and shifted her position, then winced and opened her eyes. She used her hands to push at the water's surface and move her legs back and forth in a scissor motion. The bath still felt wonderful, but steam no longer rose from the now tepid water, and the white bubbly surface had turned into a greyish translucent consistency. Bruises covering much of her body showed through the murky water and she felt her muscles tightening up again, but she was alive, and relatively injury free. A blister on her sore big toe and only a few bruises was reason for celebration after the ordeal they had survived.

Both Riley and Aiden had gone to the clinic for treatment as soon as they had checked into the hotel. She offered to accompany them, but they had both refused her offer. Riley had scoffed at the suggestion and Aiden said it would be much too crowded with people who needed medical help.

Pete was secured in Aiden's room on the ground floor, and her friends were being taken care of, so there was no reason for her to feel guilty about her luxurious soaking bath, but she did. Winter grinned, the guilt she felt was tiny compared to the satisfaction of the much-needed bath.

She stretched and thought, *I wonder if Aiden is back in his room yet, or if I need to take Pete out for a walk.* She really should call his room and check. Winter sighed and used her good toe to flip the chrome lever to drain the tub as she absently thought, *Maybe they have a spa that's still doing pedicures.* Her lips curved into a half smile. She was in the middle of an earthquake damaged island and still contemplating getting her toenails painted. Something inside her was truly shifting.

Winter used the sides of the sleek soaking tub to push herself up. "Ow," she mumbled as her calves and thighs protested. She stood dripping and said, "Damn." Her towels were on the other side of the hotel bathroom. Resting right where she had left them -- on the marble counter by sink. Yards away across the expansive white tile floor.

She eased a leg out of the deep tub and tiptoed, as if that would help with the puddles she was leaving, until she reached the towels, then took them with her to the walk-in shower. A quick shower and then she washed her hair, before she wrapped one towel around her wet body and twisted her hair up into the other one.

Winter looked at the wet path she left around the bathroom. A trail of water drops instead of bread crumbs. At least she hadn't slipped on the glistening wet tiles. *That would be rich.* Make it through the treacherous jungle, up and down hillside terrain, navigate swamps with crocodiles, only to break her neck on a bathroom floor.

She chuckled and moved to the vanity where she used a dry wash cloth and swiped at the steam covered mirror. She let her wet hair down and shook her dark curls free. After towel drying both her hair and body, Winter slipped into the thick, white robe with the hotel's name embroidered in gold across the back and padded barefoot into the suite. Funny how life could change from intense struggle to luxurious ease within the span of moments. A chill ran up her spine, but she shook it off. *Don't borrow trouble*, she thought.

When they checked into the hotel the only rooms available were the luxury suite and a tiny single on the ground floor. Winter was sharing the two-bedroom suite on the third floor with Riley and Aiden and Pete took the ground floor single. They were lucky the previous occupants managed to get a seat on the outbound ferry just that morning. The seats on the ferry were being given to medical necessities and any remaining were sold by lottery tickets. Winter's group was prepared to camp out in the hotel lobby and beg for bathroom privileges, so the room openings were an unexpected joy.

It felt good to be alone. Riley was wonderful and Aiden was certainly growing on her, but she needed her space to recharge and think about the past few days. *So much had happened.* It was going to take a while for her to process it all. Winter laughed aloud as she remembered Riley's words when she had offered to go with her to the clinic, "I am perfectly fine and don't need hand holding. Besides, until I get some relief from this itching, I don't want to be around anyone. I'm too grumpy!"

As Winter headed for her bedroom to dress, she spotted a note that had been slipped under the hotel room door. She picked it up and smiled as she read it. It was from Aiden. *He must already be back from the clinic.* It said he didn't want to disturb her, but had left a surprise outside her door, and it was her favorite red wine. *How thoughtful*. A glass of her favorite wine after a hot bath could made the horror of what they had all just endured melt away a bit. *How did he know her favorite wine and where on earth did he find it? Wow! He must have asked Riley*. She blushed and tucked the note into her robe pocket and placed her eye on the peephole. The hallway was empty. She unlocked the door, but before she could pull it open, it was shoved inward and knocked her backwards. "Ooooph," she muttered as she hit the soft carpeting.

Winter jerked her head up with an angry retort on her lips, but her eyes widened and her throat constricted. "No," she managed to whisper, then, "you're dead!" she screamed as she scooted backwards across the carpeting on her bottom. Carson moved into the suite and closed and locked the door. A large white bandage encased his right thigh. Her eyes rose higher; he held a stick in one hand and a wicked looking hunting knife in the other. He stood in front of her as his eyes roved over her body, then his lips slowly curled into a thin smile and he said, "Winter."

The ice that formed in her belly as she heard her name coming from deep in his throat immobilized her. She was an ice statue. Frozen in time. She could not move, although her brain was screaming for her to run. Even as he edged forward, and used the stick to part her robe until both of her legs were exposed from her thighs down, the only movement she could manage was a few deep panting breaths. Her body felt as if it didn't belong to her mind. He flicked the knife in her direction and said, "Take it off. I want to see you," as he pointed toward her robe.

The ice broke and a roar echoed in her ears. Memories flooded her brain. *All those years*. In a flash, the feelings of confusion, anger, humiliation and fear raced through her. Her face grew hot and her eyes narrowed as pure rage washed over her. *No more fear*. Her eyes narrowed and she looked up at Carson as she realized she was not afraid of the knife or the bully who wielded it.

She placed her hands on either side of her body and dug her bare heels into the carpet. Carson's face registered acknowledgement of the shift in her body language and he backed up a step, but it was too late. She surged up and butted her head against his chest as she used all her pent-up anger for strength. She heard a moan escape his lips as the breath was forced out of his lungs and he fell backwards. They both went down and she landed on top of him, but she jumped up and kicked his bandaged thigh, then ran across the room.

Winter stopped and her eyes searched the room. *No escape. Third floor. No balcony.* Carson was directly in front of the only door to the hallway. He struggled up and stood swaying as he held onto his makeshift cane. His face was contorted and red with rage. A rust colored stain was showing through the thigh bandage, so she knew his weak spot, but the element of surprise was now gone. There was also the branch and that big hunting knife to contend with. She couldn't get past him without getting stabbed or knocked down. *Where?*

Three other doors. Two were to the bedrooms and one was to the bathroom. There were house phones in the bedrooms but no locks on the doors. She looked toward the open bathroom door. It was the only one with a lock. The door was flimsy, but it could buy her valuable time. He was as close to the bathroom as she was, but injured, so it was a good option. *The only option.* He followed her gaze, shook his head and turned in that direction.

Winter sprinted toward the open door, but as her feet hit the tile, she felt Carson's stick slam into her back. She went down hard on the wet tile, then slid across the floor and banged into the base of the tub. The blow stunned her, but when she felt his hand on her ankle, she began kicking wildly. Carson's grip loosened, and then released. She scooted blindly across the floor on her stomach, then twisted and sat up. Her vision cleared and she tugged her robe back into place as she balled her hands into fists and screamed, "Not this time, *you bastard!*"

Carson blinked and jerked his head back as if she had slapped him. He stared down at her as he gripped the knife so hard his knuckles turned white. Fighting back this hard was new for Winter. In the past, she had learned to go limp and curl into a fetal position when he attacked. *Not this time and never again.* Her chest swelled and her muscles tensed. He would have to kill her, because death was more attractive than giving up her new-found freedom.

As she glared at him something shifted in Carson. What was it she saw in his eyes and painted across his handsome features*? Hatred? Admiration? Maybe even a little fear?* Winter chose fear as his emotion and pushed herself up from the bathroom floor without breaking eye contact. Carson held his position in front of the door, but he tossed the knife aside. She grinned, but the smile froze on her lips when he pulled a gun from his belt and he said, "You can make this less painful."

Winter sighed and said, "No, I really can't, and I won't." She eased a foot toward the door but he shifted also. Her exit was completely blocked. The gun rose and he pointed it toward her chest. "I am not yours. I belong only to me," she said as she felt blindly behind her on the bathroom vanity, but all that was on the counter was a hairbrush and a towel. She gripped the brush in one hand and towel in the other. *Some weapons.* She wished suddenly that she used a curling iron and envisioned it waiting with its hot surface to scar that pretty face of his before she went down from his bullets. Instead she could give him a snap with a hand towel and brush his hair out of place. *Now that would really show him.* Since she could feel the vanity against her bottom and there was nowhere to go, she threw the hairbrush at him and it bounced off his chest.

Carson laughed and then took aim at her heart as he said, "You, Winter, have a lot of spirit." The smile faded as his eyes narrowed and he said, "Pity."

Winter's chin went up and she said, "I'm not afraid of you." She glared at him and gripped the counter behind her as she stood as straight and tall as she could manage in bare feet. She closed her eyes and concentrated on taking even breaths.

A loud crack and her eyes flew open to see Carson crumpled on the floor. Winter's gazed at Carson lying on the floor with his blood pooling around him. She slowly turned her head toward the bathroom door. A familiar voice said, "Y'all okay, sweetie?" Riley was standing in the doorway holding a cane still dripping with Carson's blood. Winter stared at the cane as Riley said, "Good thing that nurse at the clinic insisted I take this for my ankle. Told 'em I didn't need it, but I guess I did after all." She grinned, swung the cane through the air like a bat, then said, "Champion batter on my high school baseball team three years running."

Winter looked at the unconscious Carson sprawled on the floor, then up at her friend and laughed. She moved over and hugged the redhead as she whispered, "Riley, I've never met anyone quite like you, but I'm so glad you came into my life!"

"I'm just glad they gave us two room keys." The redhead said with a giggle.

Chapter 21

Winter put the last brush stroke on the watercolor and stood back to examine the painting with a critical eye.

"Wow! Makes me feel as if I am there!" Aiden's voice came from over her shoulder.

"You think?" she asked as she turned to him. He was still damp from his shower and had a towel tied tightly around his waist. She turned back toward her work. "I don't think I fully captured the jungle on the left and doesn't the ocean look a little too blue?"

"It's perfect. You know you're never satisfied with your own work," Aiden said as Pete hopped from behind him into the room. The dog spotted Patch sleeping on her cat bed next to the easel and plopped down in front of her. He sat patiently for a moment then coughed his hoarse bark at the cat. Patch stretched and turned her back on him.

Winter laughed and turned to Aiden as she glanced at her watch. "I know, I know. Okay, I'll jump in the shower and I can be ready in thirty minutes."

"You better scoot. Uber will be here within the hour and I know how your 'thirty minutes' can stretch."

She gave him a peck on his cheek and thought, *Smooth, he must have just shaved*. Aloud she said, "You smell nice." She gave him a deep kiss, then a little shove and said, "You're right. No time." She turned back to the painting and sighed. "I needed a little painting therapy before we got started." She turned and joined him as they walked from her studio up the stairs to their master bedroom.

As she walked through the bedroom she pulled her paint spattered t-shirt and shorts off and tossed them into the hamper. Winter grabbed an outfit hanging on the closet door. She spent hours putting it together the night before. She mumbled, "You can do this." The conservative suit was not her taste and reminded her a little too much of something Carson would have picked out, but she hoped it would help the jury to take her seriously. "Almost there," she said aloud as she hung the suit on the bathroom door.

"What?" Aiden called from the hallway. He was dressed, but barefoot.

"Nothing," Winter said as she raised an eyebrow and gazed at his bare feet, then added, "I hope you are planning on wearing shoes. That look may work on the island, but not in a San Francisco courtroom."

"Ha, ha, very funny," Aiden said. He headed into the closet to collect his shoes. When he came back out he checked his phone for the time, then looked up at her as he pointed to the digital numbers.

"Right, I get it, okay," she said, then headed into the bathroom. She stepped over to the shower as she turned the dial as hot as her skin would allow. "One day, that's all. Maybe just an hour," she mumbled as she stepped into the steamy shower and let the hot water roll down her back. Winter leaned into the streaming water, turned her head up and closed her eyes as she felt her shoulders loosen. As she squirted shampoo into her hair and scrubbed her scalp she mumbled, "Almost over, almost over."

The Uber ride to the airport was filled with a heavy silence. Winter looked through the car window at the city skyline and sighed. She felt Aiden grip her hand and she turned to him and smiled, but no words passed between them. The plane ride from San Diego to San Francisco was uneventful, but Winter felt it was much too quick. As they left the secure area of the San Francisco airport, two police officers stepped forward and introduced themselves and flashed their badges. No need for them to hold up a sign. Everyone knew who she was by now. They led the couple to an unmarked police car and placed them into the back seat. The ride through the city was uncharacteristically brief, and soon Winter found herself on the familiar bench in front of the courthouse clock waiting to be called.

This time was different, though. *Well, I'm different*, she thought. She was not the same person as before she met Carson, but also not the woman who first sat on this bench sweating and terrified of him. She liked this new Winter. Wiser, she hoped, and ready for new experiences and adventures, much like the early Winter, but more cautious and less reckless.

Aiden was sitting by her side and would reach out periodically and squeeze her hand. It was such a gentle squeeze. He had no idea how foreign that was to her and how precious. So much change in the past few months since the earthquake. It was almost too much to process. Winter sat a little straighter on the hard bench. It helped to have someone by her side, but even if Aiden wasn't there, she was ready for this. She turned her head toward the courtroom door.

Winter was not only ready, she wanted this. Not for revenge, although at first revenge had been her focus, but now, she simply wanted closure. Winter wanted this aspect of her life to be put away, not erased, but designated to the past where it belonged. She wanted to live in the 'right now.' As one of her favorite quotes said, *"Never be defined by your past; It was just a lesson, not a life sentence."* She didn't know to whom she should attribute the quote. It was one of those little gems she had noticed on social media that fit perfectly with her thoughts.

Winter pulled herself from her musings and turned back to Aiden. "You look nice." She touched his lapel. "I've never seen you in a suit."

"Don't get used to it. I practically had to dust the mothballs off this thing."

"I won't. I like your beachy look best." She ran her finger down the sleeve of his jacket and said, "I have to say this does look nice."

"Ms. Winter Pappas?" the guard called from the open courtroom door.

Winter turned and said, "Here." *No hesitation. My voice sounds strong.* She smiled and stood as she thought, *I am strong and I can do this!*

Winter followed the officer into the courtroom and could sense Aiden enter the room behind her, but her eyes were glued on the witness stand. As she moved down the aisle toward it, she felt her step quicken, but then slowed down. There was no need to appear too eager. She held her head high and walked as if she was on a beach, barefooted and enjoying the view. The corners of her mouth turned up as she imagined the lapping of the waves.

After she took her seat, and was sworn in, she turned toward the defendant's table. *There he is.* Winter kept her eyes on Carson and refused to blink as he glared at her. There was a whisper of a scar on his once flawless forehead. Although he had attempted to cover it with a shock of hair, it peeked out like a small beacon of their last meeting. *Way to go Riley.*

Carson was different. Gone was the façade of innocent sadness as he scowled at her. The charming man, full of slick praise dripping from his lying lips, was nowhere to be found. His alter ego, the one only a few had seen, the one Winter believed was the true Carson, was in full view. She had shattered his outer shell and the devil was free to dance for all to see. Carson's expensive mouth piece placed a warning hand on his arm, but he shook it off. He was in full anger mode. Something Winter had seen many times, but how glorious that the world could view it with her.

She turned away and scanned the crowded courtroom. No one ignored Carson David Alexander, III, but she just did. She knew it would fan the flames of his anger and this time, his anger was exactly what she wanted. A sudden thought rocked her to the core. It wasn't Carson who was so different, it was her perception of Carson.

Was that really all it took? To no longer give a damn about him? Winter scanned the crowded room and sighed as she spotted who her eyes sought.

Aiden was seated about three rows back from the front of the courtroom. He smiled and nodded at her. She smiled back. At his side was a familiar redhead who grinned broadly as she gave Winter a big open-handed wave. Riley mouthed the words, "I made it!" She nodded toward the man sitting next to her. He was a large man stuffed into an ill-fitting suit. He looked nervous and kept his eyes mostly on Riley who mouthed, "Elbert," then shrugged. Winter smothered a giggle. The row behind them held four of her siblings. The rest of her family could not make the trip from their various states, but they had sent loving words of encouragement. She had her family back, both her genetic family, and her new-found family. It was comforting to have so much support. She appreciated each of them, but felt lighter when she realized she could do this with or without them. Carson had systematically torn her life down, piece by piece, and here she was building it back up again. Only this time she was stronger. This time, no matter what the verdict was, or what the future brought her way, she was going to be okay.

Winter frowned at an empty seat on the other side of Aiden and a vision flashed in her mind of Becky sitting there. No one had heard from Becky since their conversation on the day Winter flew to South America. *We will probably never find her. Poor, naïve Becky,* Winter thought. A glance back at Carson. She was sure he was the only one who knew what happened to her, and he wasn't talking.

Her focus returned to the courtroom as the prosecutor stood and said, "Good morning, Ms. Pappas. Can you please state your full name for the court?" he asked.

"Winter Julia Pappas," Winter said.

"Pappas is your maiden name. You returned to it after your divorce, but were you previously married to the defendant, Carson David Alexander, III?" he asked.

"Yes," she replied.

Winter took a deep breath and continued to answer his questions. She noticed that this time she felt no dampness under her arms or the back of her neck. Her shoulders were relaxed and her hands lay unfolded in her lap. Then she heard the words she had been rehearsing in her head for days. The prosecutor asked, "Ms. Pappas, could you please tell us in your own words what occurred on the night of March 25, 2016?"

She cleared her throat and looked directly at the prosecutor and said, "Yes, sir. We, uh Carson and I, attended a charity function at the Marriott Union Square hotel. My husband, uh, my husband at that time, Carson Alexander, III, was the keynote speaker and I was there to support him. I thought it had gone well, but when we got back to our apartment I found that he was furious with me. You see, I had left the event for a moment to go to the ladies' room and I didn't get back before the opening remarks of his speech. He thought I had done it on purpose to disrespect him."

"How did you know he was angry?" the prosecutor asked.

"Well, my first clue was when he punched me in the stomach." A gasp from the courtroom caused her to pause. She kept her eyes on the prosecutor and when the room quieted, she continued with, "I fell to the ground and he switched to kicking me in the stomach and chest, so I curled into a fetal position to protect my ribs. That made him angrier, so he kicked me in the forehead," she said.

The courtroom went silent. Not even a murmur or rustle rose from the crowded room. Winter could hear her own breathing as she sat waiting for the next question. She cleared her throat and thought, *Am I in a courtroom or a church,* but she kept her eyes on the prosecutor as he asked, "Was this an unusual occurrence?"

"The beating, no, but kicking me in the head, yes, definitely. When Carson beat me, he was always careful not to leave visible bruises," she said.

"Do you need a moment, Ms. Pappas?" the prosecutor asked.

"No, I'm fine," Winter said in an even voice. She continued to focus only on his brown eyes. Her chest tightened as she noticed his eyes had softened with pity. She didn't look away, but could feel the entire courtroom staring at her. She did not want to see Aiden, Riley, or her family's faces turned toward her. If she saw pity there as well, or worse, disappointment, she wouldn't be able to maintain her current composure.

"Then, please, continue," he said.

I am a rock, Winter thought. *I have no feeling.* She could return to emotions later, but right now, she had to block them out. She took a deep breath and said, "I think at that point I blacked out, but when I came to, uh, when I was fully aware again, I could hear shouting. It was as if from a distance at first, but then I realized my husband was fighting with his partner, Marty West. Marty shouted something and pointed in my direction when Carson hit him in the face. Marty wasn't a big man and he went down fast. It was then that Carson stomped on his neck and I heard something snap." A roar from the courtroom made Winter pause again. She took a breath, nodded at the prosecutor, then continued. "I must have made a noise, or said something, because Carson looked in my direction. I closed my eyes and stayed quiet. When I opened them again, Carson was dragging Marty to the balcony. When he came back, he stood over me and I heard him on his cell phone telling the police that Marty had just attacked me. Carson told them that when he discovered what Marty had done, they fought, and Marty fell from the balcony."

"Ms. Pappas, why didn't you tell the police the truth when they first questioned you at the hospital? The initial police report says you corroborated his story," the prosecutor said.

"Well, I was in and out of consciousness until I woke up in the hospital with Carson by my side. The detectives were there also and asked me what happened. Carson squeezed my hand under the covers very, very hard. I was already hurting and I didn't want to hurt more, so I said what I knew he wanted me to say. I repeated what he had said on the phone when I was lying on the floor. After a couple of days, when I was a little stronger, he left me alone for a moment. I called the nurse and asked her to get a message to the police that I wanted to talk to them alone. She made that happen and I was able to tell them the truth," Winter said. She felt her shoulders slump when the memory washed over her. The hollow feeling of helplessness was edging in and threatened her newfound strength. She sat straighter and her chin went up. *Not again. Never again.*

"Ms. Pappas, did you fear for your life?" the prosecutor asked.

"Oh, yes, I did, but not anymore. He can no longer have that part of me." She turned and looked directly at Carson. "I am no longer his to control with fear or manipulation," Winter replied and then she said, "I will tell the truth. The absolute truth."

Carson jumped up and his chair fell to the floor behind him as he shouted, "You bitch! You will always belong to me! You are mine to live or die!" His attorney grasped at his arm and the security officer rushed over and forced him back into his chair. The judge pounded the gavel and called for order. The courtroom erupted with a roar of voices all talking at once. Winter turned toward Aiden and when their eyes locked, she did not see pity, only pride. She sighed and leaned back against her chair. Her work was done. *I am free.*

***

Winter sealed the crate on the last painting. "Done!" she said.

"How does it feel?" Aiden stood in the doorway of her studio.

She grinned at him and asked, "Do you mean finishing the last painting for my show or getting the news that Carson will never be a free man again?"

"Both," he said.

"Damn good!" she said as she crossed the room and gave him a kiss on the cheek. She stood back and placed her hands on his shoulders and said, "Thank you."

"For what?" he asked as his brows went together and he moved forward and wrapped his arms around her.

"For being you," she whispered and then kissed him full on the mouth. He returned the kiss as he pulled her close.

"Want to go upstairs?" he whispered against her ear.

"Mmmmmm…sounds nice, but what I really want is to get a run in before dinner. Rain check?"

Aiden laughed and said, "I'm going to hold you to that." He pulled back and gazed at the painting crates that filled the entire wall by the door.

The studio was full of light with east facing floor to ceiling windows and multiple skylights. They were lucky to find a house right on the beach. It was old and in poor repair when they bought it, but a little sweat equity took care of that. Idyllic and rare, but it was still crowded Southern California and that made Winter a little crazy sometimes.

"Want to take some time off and head back to South America after your show is done?" Aiden asked.

Winter smiled. She knew how much he craved the isolation of his jungle house at times. In truth, so did she, so she said, "That sounds nice. I want to see Phyllis while we're there. I still can't believe she survived the fall over the cliff. Her son, Jose, said she was doing well and will soon be back to teaching yoga. Maybe we can get Riley and Elbert to join us for a week or two." She shook her head and looked at Aiden as she said, "I can't believe she took him back, but I want to support her in her decision."

"I can understand why she took him back," he said as he started walking toward the door that connected the studio to their house. "You could tell she still loved him even when she was bad mouthing him when on our trek through the jungle."

"I know, I felt it too. I hate to admit it, but I can see how much he adores her, also. I think it might have been that fear of growing old syndrome that got to him." Winter sighed and said, "Still, what an ass he was!"

"It can happen," Aiden replied.

She poked her finger in his shoulder as she said, "See that it doesn't happen to you, mister."

He turned to her and said, "Never! You are more than enough woman for me." He laughed and added, "Besides, I know you pack a mean punch." He stretched his back and said, "If you wait for me to change, I'll go with you for that run."

"Good answer," she said. She moved over to put away her packing supplies and said, "Sure, I would enjoy your company, but don't expect me to slow my pace for you."

"Ha, ha. I'll take that pace and raise you an ice cream cone from the Sugar Shack," he said as he moved toward the door. He turned and asked, "Should we take Pete?"

"I just took him out for a walk and we can take him again when we get back," she said as she reached down to scratch the dogs scruffy head before adding, "When we run he can't keep up on the sand and he gets frustrated."

"Sounds good. The little guy does well with just three legs, but you're right, sand is a little hard for him," Aiden said, then turned and sprinted up the stairs.

Winter moved to the back of the house and stared out at the sandy beach and the Pacific Ocean beyond. *It is so beautiful.* She opened the sliding glass door and moved out onto the deck. A cool breeze moved over her and the smell of salt air tickled at her nostrils.

She leaned on the railing and watched two seagulls fight over a shell fish. Her thoughts turned to the men in her life. *Past and present.* She couldn't help but compare Carson and Aiden. When she met Carson, he seemed perfect: handsome, charming, and polite, but he was the opposite of all those things. When she met Aiden, he seemed like the last person she wanted to be with, handsome, yes, but she thought he was a rude, drunken loser. Reality: he was gentle, kind, and eaten up with grief. Instead of an abusive husband he had been caretaker for his wife through a horrendous illness. "Funny how things turn out," she mumbled.

Winter bent to retie her running shoe and then stretched her legs as she prepared for the run on the beach. Aiden came through the door, locked it, and pocketed the key. "Ready?" he asked.

Winter smiled and said, "Absolutely. I've never been readier."

Aiden arched an eyebrow and Winter noticed the little crinkles at the edge of his eyes were just a little deeper than when she first met him. It endeared him even more to her. She had a vision of Aiden with silver hair and a wave of peace washed over her.

"You are one funny lady," Aiden said as he sprinted down the stairs to the beach and turned and ran in place, "but, that's not going to help you when I leave you behind for the ice cream."

Winter laughed and followed him down the steps, but then passed him as she called back over her shoulder, "Winner picks where we go for dinner!" Aiden caught her and they pounded down the beach in unison just as the sun began its descent toward the horizon.

The End